the
vain girl

CINDY WILLIAMS NEWSOME

ISBN: 978-1-7369383-2-4

Publishing imprint *Walking in Mercy Press*

The views expressed or implied in this work do not necessarily reflect those of Walking in Mercy Press.

Dedication

For Ivy, Miranda, Brandon Jr., Caleb, Chris,
Chrystian, Nyasia, Aaron, Jream
My Legacy of Faith Scripture to You,
John 15:9 "As the Father loved Me, I also have loved
you, abide in My love."

Acknowledgments

Thank you, God, for the air I breathe and for giving me creativity to write and bring to fruition a second edition of my sophomoric work. I humbly accept your gracious gifts.

To my husband, Willie, I love you.

For my dear daughters, grandchildren, great grandson, son-in-law, and godson, whom I dedicate this book to, I thank God for the gift of loving you all.

Heartfelt gratefulness to fellow author, Tempie Williams, for writing the Foreword to *The Vain Girl*. Also, for her always encouraging, uplifting emails and, a surprise telephone call from England. You are so special, my sister of another mother, love you, girl.

To my publishing coordinator, Sharon Kizziah-Holmes at Paperback Press, thank you for making the process of bringing the work to print as seamless as possible. It is a pleasure working with you.

Pastor Emmanuel Bada and Associate Pastor Lavinia Bada for spiritual covering as the under shepherds of Rock of Ages Christian Fellowship Church.

Model on book cover, Destiny Jackson. Thank you, my beautiful grandniece. Love you! Model photographed by Patricia Abbott © 2011.

Foreword

I am honored to write the Foreword for Cindy Williams Newsome's highly anticipated second work, a novel, *The Vain Girl*. Her first book, *Hobbstown: The Forgotten Legacy of a Unique African American Community*, is a creative non-fiction, award-winning, historical work. *The Vain Girl* will introduce readers to Ms. Newsome's great ability to create and develop believable, interesting characters, bringing about an intriguing love story with a spiritual foundation. It is as well a saga of an American family with personal conflicts and spiritual soul searching.

Ms. Newsome's writing style reads as though chiseled by a skillful sculptor, producing characters with honesty and beauty. She has masterfully developed exciting plots with a heroine and secondary characters that readers will love and loathe, as well as identify with. The characters grapple with universal issues that can bring a closer walk with God. Readers will love the drama leading the main characters to victorious testimonies. It is a brilliant page turner, an exhilarating journey.

Many thanks to you, my friend across the pond, for the privilege of penning the Foreword to *The Vain Girl*. It has given me the distinct pleasure of reading and enjoying a wonderfully written love story. I wish you much success!

Tempie Delois Williams
Author of *Feelings*
ISBN 1-4241-0706-7
Crawley, West Sussex,
United Kingdom

Chapter 1

SEVENTEEN-YEAR-OLD MARLOE VAIN WEIGHED HER WORDS as if she were the post holding up two legal scales. Her mother, Rosette, was increasingly unpredictable as to what conversation might throw her into swift anger or initiate a solitary pity-party. That knowledge, coupled with Marloe's own guilt for the unspeakable sin she committed made her even more cautious to approach her. Hope abounded, since upon Marloe's early arrival home from Kinsey, North Carolina that day, Rosette smiled brightly at her. The scale could very well tip in her favor since it appeared her Mother's Day was favorable thus far.

I'll take my chances. Taking a deep breath, Marloe tried not to sound overly excited. "M-Mother, can I visit Jorene for a little while to catch up on things before it gets too late?" Her eyes hit the floor; she needed to hide the buoyancy racing through her body like wildfire. Confident that she momentarily smothered the blaze, she raised her head to look at Rosette, quietly awaiting her response. Rosette glanced at her, continuing to silently sort soiled clothing. *Anger, pity, anger, pity,* Marloe could almost hear the feelings churning in her mother's head. *Which would it be?*

"Not a thing has changed in two weeks Marloe. You

didn't stay away long enough for anyone to miss you." Rosette smiled, but a tell-tale frown creased her forehead.

A smile is a good sign, but that frown?

"Well, since you were so determined to cut your vacation short with Kate," Rosette gave her a stern look, "come right back after you've seen Jorene so we can get these clothes washed up and put away. Don't stay long, you understand?"

"Yes Mother. I won't be long. Thank you."

~ ~ ~ ~

As she ran the familiar trail and crossed the intersection that would take her to Lawson James' home, Marloe's guilt dissolved into heady exhilaration. Her arms felt as if she could sprout wings and soar like an eagle to her destination. *Oh, how I've missed him!* She decided to forgo knocking at the front door of the huge two-story house. *I'll surprise him.* She giggled at the thought. It was Saturday evening and Lawson often played solitaire in the tree house, their special spot. Running through the backyard, she cupped her forehead from the gleaming sun with one hand and looked up at the enormous red oak that held the oversized tree house. *He's there.* She smiled as she imagined how elated he would be at her week-early homecoming back to Potters Edge, New Jersey. She envisioned the expression of love on his face; the rush to tenderly gather her in his arms once again.

Silently, barely able to control the laughter bubbling like a river in her tummy, she climbed the ten-step wooden ladder leading to the entrance. Soon, she heard muffled voices, concluding that Lawson's brother Ashton was with him. Mounting the last step, she heard the unmistakable lilting laughter of a female. Suspicion sliced through her body like a knife. She shrugged the feeling off, probably one of Ashton's friends.

"Lawson, please tell me you love me now, not just when we make love." The words pierced Marloe's heart like a dagger. Disbelief held her captive at the same moment Lawson's eyes met hers at the tree house entrance. He lay beside the girl. Their scantily clad bodies glistened in the summer heat. Marloe struggled to keep her balance on the ladder as her hands shook out of control and her thoughts went haywire. Blood thundered in her head; her world tumultuously turned upside down as she remembered that night…the night she broke her promise to God.

~ ~ ~ ~

It was June 28, 1966, the night before she would leave Potter's Edge for Kinsey, to spend time with her grandmother, Annie Kate, as she did each summer. There in the tree house that night she and Lawson pledged undying love to each other forever. He held her close, so tightly that their hearts seemed to entwine as one. So secure was his embrace, physically and mentally, that Marloe could have died a sweet death from the sensation of his caress. Dizzy from his kisses to her lips, neck, and down the small of her back, she squirmed out of his arms. "Lawson, don't. You know we can't; not until we're married."

"'Marloe, baby, l love you, girl, and you love me. It's driving me crazy. You're the only one for me. Anyway, we're getting married after you graduate next year. I promise we'll be together forever, baby. Why should we wait?'"

As he continued to plant butterfly kisses here and there and whisper words of love in her ear, her reasoning became clouded. The force of her affection for him overwhelmed her, filling her with all of the unbridled passion that comes with first love. *Of all the girls in the world he loves me. We're getting married. Mrs. Lawson James! Dear God, I*

3

love him so much.

"'Please, Marloe. Please, baby. Let me love you. I'll love you forever, you and only you.'"

This time she felt lost. Lawson's sugarcoated promises of endless love and marriage broke her shaky barriers of celibacy down. So much so that she took a sabbatical from her family prophecy, the oracle that came with being a Vain girl. According to family oral history, Grandma Juniper Vain became pregnant as a teen. A prophet cursed her and, true to the curse, she lived a life of horrific pain and strife. She was always financially stressed, sickly, and unwise in every endeavor she put her hands to. The oracle further pronounced that, following Juniper, Vain women descendants by blood must remain virgins until marriage or suffer the same gruesome fate.

Having broken the vow, feeling raw with guilt, Marloe prayed with the hope that God would forgive her. She left for the summer, anxious, but subconsciously convinced that all would be well with her betrothed, Lawson. How would she get through three weeks without Lawson, and how could she hide her guilt from dear God-fearing Granny Kate? She consoled herself that the intensity of she and Lawson's love for each other mollified the severity of the act, the consequences. We're getting married soon. Lawson promised, I trust him, and God is a forgiving God. Still, each day thereafter she begged God's forgiveness for her trespass.

~ ~ ~ ~

But she now realized that trusting Lawson was an unfathomable mistake. She scurried down the ladder, nearly tripping in her haste to retreat from this daytime nightmare. Paralyzed with the realization that Lawson used her, blinded by tears and wretched self-hatred, she mindlessly ran through the street. In the warm summer heat, she trembled as if she were in the midst of a bad winter storm. Suddenly, Lawson was beside her. Breathing heavily, he reached for her hand.

"Don't you touch me," she screamed. "Don't ever touch me!"

"Mar, baby, listen to me. It meant nothing. I just missed you so much. I love you girl. You're the only one I'll ever love. We'll still get married; that hasn't changed."

A new awareness engulfed her as she gazed at Lawson. She had been such a fool, stricken by what she believed to be true love. She shook her head in bewilderment at how he had effortlessly captured her heart and then just as swiftly severed it into a million little pieces. *What is he saying, everything has changed? I've disrespected the family pledge and the seriousness of what I've done in the eyes of God will haunt me forever. I've broken the "Trust," revived the anathema. How can I ever face father, mother, Granny Kate? They trusted me.* The punishment that Juniper suffered vicariously reached out in her thoughts from the grave.

In that moment she hated Lawson. She spat her words at him. "You said forever; that there would never be anyone else, that together we could win any battle, even a promise to God. I broke my family vow to God for you because I thought you loved me. I believed you. Never let my name cross your lips again, ever! I'm dead to you."

Ignoring the injured look in his eyes, she turned and ran away from him, A train had run over her heart and left the remainder of her existence on the sidelines staring in agonizing incredulity. She covered her ears to block the sound of Lawson calling her name over and over until it became a distant echo. When she finally reached Jorene's house, she staggered inside the unlocked living room door like a Saturday night drunk.

"Child, what's the matter? Come. Come in," Jorene's mother, Bettye, reached out for Marloe at the door.

"We didn't know you were back from North Carolina already." Taking Marloe's hand, Bettye guided her to a chair. "Jorene's upstairs. Rene!"

Marloe heard the alarm in Ms. Bettye's voice. She tried to speak, but the huge knot in her throat threatened to choke her. She sank to the floor, absolving into a heap of tears. The world no longer made sense. Ms. Bettye bent down beside Marloe; her face etched with concern. Fighting with every fiber of her being to speak, Marloe reached for Ms. Bettye's hand. She vaguely recognized the mechanical sound of her own voice. "P-Please tell Rene…to call…my brother Wesley to come for me."

"Rene, come down here now!" Ms. Bettye shouted louder this time towards the stairwell. Marloe saw the distress in the elder woman's eyes but could not assure her there was no cause for worry. She wanted death to swallow her up and take away the heartbreaking pain of the wound satiating her soul. As cobwebs floated in her head, she heard a faint knock on the door.

"Come in."

Marloe wondered why Jorene sounded so far away. Where is she? She had no idea that Jorene had earlier rushed downstairs to find her curled up on the floor and she had not left Marloe's side.

Ms. Bettye paced the floor, ringing her hands in prayer. Wesley Vain entered the room. Marloe lifted her head from the pernicious gray cloud to see his bewildered gaze; the blood drain from his face, leaving it pale with confusion. *Wesley will help me; he will make this awful hurt go away.*

Chapter 2

THAT WAS HER LIFE AS THE LITTLE SISTER OF
Eubanks and Wesley Vain. They had always taken
care of "Lil' Mar." She was an unexpected child
who came along when her brothers were ten and nine
years-old, respectively. The Vain's were a deeply religious
family with a clandestine virgin pact dating back many
generations. Although her father, Bailey Vain, did not
wholeheartedly believe in the myth, the majority of the
Vain's did. And with the possibility that his third child
might be a girl doubt began to plague him. He secretly
prayed for another boy.

Marloe Alice Vain debut into the world on January 10,
1948. Bailey anxiously readied himself for the challenges
that raising a daughter might bring. Instead, Marloe became
the apple of his eye. She was a good girl, assiduously
taught by the elder Vain women to remain virtuous, to
downplay her striking countenance. Granny Kate especially
instilled modesty into Marloe's thinking, "the Lord hates a
proud look, vanity. Remember that beauty is fleeting,
always remain humble."

In grammar school Marloe obediently wore her semi-
curly, ash-brown hair in one thick braid that hung to her
waist. When she started high school, she had it cut to her

shoulders for ease in donning a tightly wrapped bun. Her face was void of cosmetics since that was considered 'adorning the body.' Nevertheless, no amount of obscurity masked her stunning beauty. As well, she inherited the Vain trademarked creamy bronzed complexion. Long, soot-colored eyelashes embellished almond-shaped ebony eyes. She appeared wiry, tall, and slender like her mother.

~ ~ ~ ~

Wesley kneeled down to lift Marloe from the floor. Her vision, blurred by the cobwebs still running amuck, traveled to another dimension. Lawson was before her, gleaming from the sweat of his deception. He stretched out his hand, calling her name. A female shrouded in mystery stood beside him, laughing triumphantly. Marloe cowered from his reach.

"Marloe, it's me, Wesley. Come on baby girl." He gently picked her up in his arms.

Somewhere inside the sinister fog that was now her world, Marloe heard Jorene's voice tremble with concern. "What are you going to do Wesley?"

"I'll take her home. She'll be alright."

"I'll come over tomorrow to check on her."

"Okay Jorene, Ms. Bettye, thanks for everything." Wesley carried Marloe to the car, gently laying her in the back seat, he quickly drove away.

~ ~ ~ ~

Weeping softly during the ten-minute drive home, Marloe languished in a death-wish. The betrayal had left an indelible mark, filling her with unbearable shame. The sting of what breaking the family tradition actually meant now hit her like a ton of bricks. It was a treasured family lineage, one that had been stringently carried out by the

Vain women for generations. It was of little consequence that the majority had married by age 16. They had all upheld the family standard after Juniper, remaining virgins until jumping the broom or walking down the aisle to wed.

With optimistic anxiety Marloe's family gradually loosened their grip on her every move when she turned 16. She had proven to them that there would be no act of impropriety on her part. The truth was that she had not been interested in anyone of the opposite sex until Lawson came into her life. Even then she fully intended to remain chaste until they married.

Chapter 3

Everything about Potter's Edge came alive when the James family moved to the sleepy little town in northern New Jersey in 1964. Jonas and Dolly Ann James were professional ballroom dancers from Harlem. They once danced with ensembles that began with the Harlem Renaissance in the 1920s. The couple took Potter's Edge by storm, bringing with them a worldly class and charm. They purchased a roomy house on Larchmont Avenue, a wealthy Black area, not far from the business district. Soon, they opened a small dance studio and a supper club in one wing of the home. At that time, their sons, Lawson, and Ashton were 17 and 15, respectively.

Marloe observed schoolgirls falling over backwards to be in Lawson's presence. He was the new "guy to get," tall and *Ebony Magazine* handsome. Walking the halls at Potter's Edge High she was too shy to even return his smile. "Let the man come to you," was what she had always heard from her family. So, she coyly avoided him, going about her school days quietly studious.

However, Jorene Clinton, her best friend since elementary school, had other ideas. "Marloe, I swear," she laughed as the two walked their daily trek home from school. "You ignore Lawson like he has the plague. Girl, can't you see he likes you?"

"Says who?" Marloe's heart fluttered at the thought. "Why would he be interested in me with so many girls running after him?"

"Marloe Alice Vain, why are you so hard on yourself. You're gorgeous and smart, everybody can see it except you."

"Rene, you know all about my family. I just want to make them proud, that's all."

Jorene scrunched her nose as if she smelled something rotten. "Mar, you're 16 for goodness sakes. Don't you want guys to flirt with you? I know I do. I love it when Dugey gives me that look," she giggled. "And there's nothing wrong with a little kissing. I know how far to go."

"Yeah, and if Ms. Bettye knew all that you wouldn't go far at all," Marloe laughed.

"Well, I know how to keep a secret and so do you," Jorene squealed with laughter. Suddenly, Jorene increased her stride as if to prevent a passerby from hearing their conversation. "Marloe, let's go to "Teen Night" at the supper club this Friday. I've been dying to see what it's like since they opened it. C'mon Mar, please say you'll go. I won't go without you. Everybody says it's so much fun, food and dancing. Stay over at my house Friday night; then we can stay a little pass curfew. Dugey will get us a ride to my house."

"Oh Rene, I don't know."

"Mar, please say yes for me, your best friend in the whole world."

Marloe giggled in spite of feeling caught between a rock and a hard place. "Okay, okay, I'll go." She always found it difficult to say no to Jorene. "But I know Father won't let me sleep over, sorry Rene. I'll ask one of my brothers to pick us up by curfew."

Jorene looked crestfallen. "You are just pitifully honest," she said, shaking her head. Marloe smiled as they linked arms. Their conspicuous laughter ripped through the hazy September day as they meandered their way to Marloe's residence on Spruce Street, a mile from Larchmont Avenue.

"See you tomorrow morning Mar."

"Okay Rene, see you tomorrow." She watched her friend turn the corner to continue the mile long walk to her home across the railroad tracks.

~ ~ ~ ~

Bailey was solemn that Friday night when he pulled his car in front of the James' home. Worry lines creased his forehead as he cut the engine. Marloe sat quietly in the front seat dutifully awaiting the speech that was sure to come. Jorene remained equally compliant in the back seat. *Father behaves as if I'm going away on a trip, never to return.* But she too found herself more than a little nervous about "Teen Night" at the James' establishment.

"Thanks for bringing us Father. Remind Wesley to pick us up at eleven." *As if he would forget that.* At times, the protection she received from the men in her family amused her; she definitely felt loved. However, on occasion she thought she might suffocate under the weight of family scrutiny.

"Alright baby girl," Bailey turned to look at her. "You and Jorene look for Wesley at eleven o'clock. Behave yourselves like young ladies and have a fun time."

Marloe was shocked. *That was it? No long-winded speech about what to do if things weren't going right? No rhetoric on calling should I want to come home early?* She certainly was not going to sit around and wait for Bailey to rethink the situation.

Trying to keep the glee from her voice she quietly said, "thank you Father." She quickly pecked Bailey on the cheek and exited the car before he could open his door to come around and open the door for her and Jorene. Not one to be outdone Jorene was right on Marloe's heels. They walked towards the door leading to the entrance of the supper club. Turning to wave to Bailey as he gently pulled the vehicle away from the curb onto the street.

"Heeee...girl, we're gonna have some fun," Jorene shouted. Her eyes lit up like two burning candles. It warmed Marloe's heart to see Jorene so happy, although by now Marloe's nerves had gotten the better of her. She timidly followed Jorene through the door leading into the establishment.

"Hello ladies," Lawson greeted them warmly, ushering them to a table. He hurriedly pulled a chair out for Marloe and another for Jorene. The place was everything and more than Marloe expected. It was beautifully decorated, exuding an atmosphere of modern grandeur. Thick red velvet drapes hung the length of window to floor on two panes. Eight round tables, each accompanied by ten chairs covered in white floral laced fabric with place settings sported the same deep red color as the drapes. Lighted candles centered on each table cast a cozy ambiance throughout the space. Silverware sparkled as if each piece donned a private sun. Soft red lighting bathed the dance floor situated in the center of the room. Popular music flowed from a jukebox in one corner of the room.

Although mesmerized with the surroundings, Marloe felt Lawson's lingering gaze as she took her seat. "Thank you," she modestly bent her head.

"Can I take your order?"

"Yes, thank you," Jorene smiled widely at Lawson. Marloe swore she saw all 32 of her gleaming white teeth. "I'd like a burger, fries, and Coke please."

"I'll have a burger and Coke," Marloe added. "Thank you." She could feel the heat of angst rush to her face. Later, she hid her disappointment when Ashton brought their order instead of Lawson. They paid the $1.75 for their food and soon the eight tables were nearly filled to capacity with young people. *Oh, no, here comes trouble.* Mabel Adams sat down at their table along with a few other students. She knew the others only by sight, but everyone knew Mabel because she was loud and arrogant.

"Lawson is my man," she quipped, cutting her eyes at Marloe.

I will not let Mabel get under my skin. Besides, perhaps she's right. There is nothing between me and Lawson. Mabel was attractive, fair-skinned; short and thick, with a face full of freckles matching her fiery red hair. With bodacious firmness she had long boasted that she and Lawson were an item, although they were never together at school.

"Don't my man look fine in his Zoot suit?" Mabel ribbed the table as she pointed to Lawson. Again, she cast an under-eyed glance at Marloe.

"Well, since when did he get to be your man?" came Jorene's clipped response.

"Hump, don't worry about when, just remember he is," Mabel shot back.

Marloe picked at her burger, the earlier buoyancy of the evening losing its savor. She tried to abate her fluttering heart when she glimpsed Lawson making his way to another table with an order.

"Marloe, wanna go to the girls' room?" Jorene said to Marloe, ignoring Mabel's remark.

"Sure." *Thank God. She must have read my mind.* Grateful to escape Mabel's unruly tongue, Marloe rose from the table. On the way to the restroom, they passed Lawson. He leaned down close to Marloe's face, whispering in her ear. "You look beautiful tonight, but then you always do."

Marloe's heart went to her throat. She managed a weak "thank you" and bolted into the bathroom behind Jorene.

"Rene," she was both thrilled and petrified. "Did you hear what Lawson said to me? Oh gracious. What do I say Rene, what do I do?" She was babbling but could not control her tongue.

Jorene rolled her eyes toward the sky, shaking her head. A playful smile of empathy crossed her face as she stared at Marloe. "Mar, just follow his lead. You'll see what I'm talking about after that first kiss girl," she teased.

By the time Wesley picked them up that night Marloe's head danced in the clouds. Lawson had asked her out to the movies, a first date. She trembled at the thought of her family's reaction. *I've been obedient, a good girl. They can't deny me.*

~ ~ ~ ~

Although that first date was fraught with a family on the brink of imploding, to Marloe's relief, Bailey kept the lid on. She gritted her teeth as he questioned Lawson about his family background, things that she was sure he already knew. His taxi business afforded him the opportunity to know about everyone in and around Potter's Edge. Marloe had not a shred of doubt that Bailey had learned everything possible about Lawson and his family beforehand. Wesley and Eubie sullenly shadowed their father's probing, menacing to Lawson, she was sure. One of her brothers would escort she and Lawson to and from the theatre. With veiled embarrassment, Marloe observed Lawson's grimace from the malignant clench of Bailey's handshake. His message behind it explicit.

The two fell deeply in love. In school, he carried her books; there were not enough hours in the day for their intense conversations about life, paths to take in fulfilling their dreams. There were long walks in the park, feverish kisses that neither wanted to end. Lawson earned an athletic scholarship to play football at Morehouse College in Atlanta, Georgia following graduation that year.

"What am I going to do without you when you leave for college? I hate to think about it," Marloe lamented one evening lying encircled in Lawson's arms. It was springtime, April, and rather cool in the tree house. Lawson tightened his grip, pulling her closer.

"Quit school and come with me to Atlanta Marloe. Marry me," he whispered in her ear. "I'll take care of you. I can't live without you Mar."

Her heart melted with the intensity of love she felt for him. Early in the relationship she shared her family heirloom with Lawson, the virgin history. How it was that she would curse herself and any children she bore would also become victims should she fail. The threat of Satan's evil was the thing that kept her grounded to the belief like a root to a tree. The thought of it made her shiver in the deepest chambers of her heart. Although Lawson claimed to respect her wishes, he consistently attempted to change her mind. In his quest to transport her mind, body, and soul into his world, he sometimes pulled her hair out of the restraining chignon. Curly brown locks cascaded down her back as he gently ran his fingers through her hair. It never failed to ignite a fire between them that went out with the same regret. For her, vow over passion; for him, frustration, and disappointment.

"Marloe," Lawson moaned in her ear. "You are so beautiful. You have my love forever. Be mine, my love."

Consequently, her mind reeled with indecision during a momentary lapse of judgment. But then she imagined the horrific pain she would cause her family and herself. Quitting high school to marry was out of the question. Marloe's charge was to set the family education standard higher. The virgin until marriage criteria was a given; she had lived with that understanding all of her life. With college added to the mandate, Marloe happily won acceptance to Spellman College. She definitely wanted a successful career, and college was her best avenue to achieve it. Secretly she resented that her brothers were not held to the same standard. After graduating high school, Wesley and Eubie went to work full-time with Bailey at the family business. However, for Marloe, upon marrying Lawson after her high school graduation, they were expected to reside in Atlanta until both obtained degrees. Following their graduations, they promised to return to Potter's Edge to live. *But what if we like Atlanta and want to remain there? My family would be devastated, Father would be heartbroken. I love them all dearly, but...so many decisions, Lord, please help me.*

Chapter 4

"MARLOE, MARLOE," ROSETTE'S GENTLE whisper in her ear brought Marloe back from the cliff of insanity. She shivered with shame under the bed covers at the expression on her mother's face. It was a look that brought 17 years of proving that she would not be like her mother to a bitter end. Although shrouded in words of comfort, Marloe caught the glimmer of secret pleasure in Rosette's eyes at her unexpected fall from grace.

She never understood the tongue-wagging throughout the years about her mother from her father's family. "'Rosette is uppity now, but you can't turn a goat into a lamb,'" they would say.

While the comments aroused her interest, Marloe did not pry. She loved her mother very much, and deep within her heart, she knew Rosette loved her too. But in this moment Marloe admitted what she had felt from her mother most of her life, an obscure envy. It was smothered in kisses to the cheek and bright smiles for Marloe in front of others. But behind closed doors Rosette was often distant and critical.

"'Stand up straight Marloe. Stop slouching. Just because you're pretty doesn't mean the world will fall at your feet. You better learn to square your shoulders and stand up on your own. Bailey and the boys won't always be around to take care of you.'"

After delivering such disapproval Rosette would walk away, leaving Marloe confused, with her self-esteem lower than the floor she stood upon.

~ ~ ~ ~

Rosette stared at her daughter, mortified that she felt a sense of satisfaction in her distress. If the gibberish that flowed from Marloe's lips while in her dreamy state of mind were true, her princess Vain reign had indeed ended. Soon Rosette's thoughts became lost in what brought her to this loathsome feeling of miserable joy.

It was a crushing blow when Rosette found herself pregnant with her third child in 1948. With her two boys in grade school, she had patiently bided her time to leave Bailey. She had reached the end of endurance. The stinging insults from his relatives had taken their toll, and through it all Bailey behaved as if he were deaf and blind. She was well aware of her undesirable lineage as a Dunney, a family with an objectionable reputation. It was a quagmire that, to a degree she felt they deserved. However, even during that regrettable time, Rosette hated what she did with a passion, it sickened her, but felt she had no other choice.

She barely remembered her father, Carter Dunney. He disappeared when Rosette was five years old, her twin sisters, Jessie, and Justa, were age seven. Desperate for work, but with no viable employment skills, her mother, Vessie, took a job as a short order cook at the 'Shack.'

The 'Shack' was the local 'watering hole' in Calgon, New Jersey, the town where the Dunney's lived. As Rosette grew into maturity, the whispers from strangers as her family walked downtown Calgon aroused her suspicions. The peers she thought were friends ran away from her like rapid heartbeats, leaving Rosette depressed and lonely. Soon, she understood the deleterious nature of her mother's 'second job.'

The Dunney home was a tiny dilapidated two-bedroom apartment in an unfavorable area of Calgon. How well Rosette recalled her mother's financial woes as she attempted to keep food on the table and clothes on their backs. The twins dropped out of school at age 16 to work and assist Vessie with finances needed to run the home. Their family apparently blackballed when seeking employment at nearby factories, out of desperation the twins joined their mother at the 'Shack,' cleaning and performing "odd jobs."

Rosette vowed to graduate high school, secretly harboring a desire to become a nurse. Believing everyone would find her aspirations amusing, including her family, she kept them hidden. After all she was a Dunney, expectations were extremely low.

Vessie's sudden illness seemed to evolve overnight; she quickly took a turn for the worse. The smell of death was rampant in the little apartment as she coughed up blood as black as midnight. Cancer ravaged her body. Her labored breathing resonated throughout the tight quarters. Rosette watched her mother suffer many nights while her sisters partied their nights away. One particular evening she cried her heart out as she witnessed Vessie squeezing the pillow on her bed so tightly that her knuckles turned white.

"Mama, where's your medicine bottle?" she asked, gently stroking Vessie's matted hair, trying to comfort her. Holding the ever-present tattered washcloths that lay on the bed, she tenderly wiped the perspiration from her mother's haggard face.

Vessie lifted her head from the pillow, inhaling deeply as she struggled for air. "I-It's alright baby. I should be getting a little money soon. Stump called today and said he's putting me something in the mail. Then you can get my medicine." Her head fell back on the pillow, she closed her eyes.

"You need medicine now Mama. I can't sit here and see you suffer and do nothing." *Why can't Stump just give the money to one of the twins?* But then she sadly answered her own question. *If he gives money to Justa or Jessie, it will never make it here.* Rosette wanted to explode with the anger she felt. At that moment, she hated her sisters. She had not a dime to her name, but as she observed her mother's labored breathing the 'Shack' whispered her name. For that reason, she willed her heart to stone and went there; martyring her body for medicine to ease her mother's suffering.

Vessie died one month later. It was 1935. Just as there had been no medical insurance, neither was there any burial insurance. Mercifully, Stump Rollins, the owner of the 'Shack' paid for Vessie's funeral expenses. Rosette graduated high school, and soon after eagerly left Calgon. She had earlier applied to a job ad in the newspaper for a live-in domestic, and to her astonishment she was hired. Clutching her diploma close, with $25 dollars to her name, she counted the days for her departure from Calgon.

On that glorious morning, she boarded the bus bound for Potter's Edge, New Jersey, 150 miles north, to the home of Stephen and Barbara Feinstein. She was 18 years old. Overjoyed to obtain decent work and pay, she delved into the job with her whole heart and soul.

Soon, she registered for nursing school. Being busy helped her focus less on her former life. She prayed that the distance she placed between herself, her sisters, and Calgon might somehow relieve her from her past, rid her of the demons that nibbled at her self-worth. To her delight, her live-in job at the Feinstein home was a delightful blessing. She cooked and cleaned, and it seemed to sooth her entire being. As she completed chores, washing laundry and dishes, scouring bathrooms in the gargantuan house, she almost felt clean again. Still, she could not shake the sinister shadow that consistently lurked at her heels. The feeling that someday she would encounter someone from her past and the skeletons would come tumbling out. She felt confident that it would not be her sisters. She had cut all ties with them, did not attempt to write, or call them, carefully keeping her whereabouts secret. As far as she knew, the twins remained engaged in that life as if it gave them oxygen to breathe, the life she desperately wanted to forget. She resented them to the very marrow of her bones for 'good-timing' their money away while Vessie lay dying. No, she did not want to see the twins; she wanted to be as far removed as possible from anything that smacked of her previous life.

~ ~ ~ ~

Rosette swiftly shut the refrigerator door when she heard Bailey Vain's deep bellowing voice. It was grocery shopping day. He was early.

"Well, Miss Rosette, how are you today?"

"I'm fine," Rosette looked away. She opened the pantry door for no good reason, turning her back to him.

"I'm a little early so take your time. I need to talk to Mr. Feinstein anyway, business matters," he said. He knocked on the drawing room door and quickly disappeared into the abode with Mr. Feinstein.

Rosette had decided she did not care for Bailey Vain. He appeared bigheaded and too inquisitive for her liking. She imagined he was in his 30s to her 19 years of age. His attitude of authority within the Feinstein home incensed her. She knew the story well. He had been their chauffer for many years before he opened a taxi business. Every few weeks he faithfully visited Mr. and Mrs. Feinstein and escorted Rosette grocery shopping for their household. But with all of his flamboyance, Rosette secretly admitted he was the most handsome man she had ever laid eyes on. Always impeccably dressed in a dark suit of navy or black, tall, broad shouldered, and 'down-south' chocolate. His skin looked kissed-by-the-sun, and as smooth as freshly poured cream. His hair was a muddy brown, thick, wavy, and when he smiled, pearly white teeth gleamed as even as the kernels on a corn cob. Although he irritated Rosette, she found that beneath his booming voice there was kindness. At her request, he often swung by the 'five-and-ten' store so she could pick up personal belongings for herself at a cheaper price. Nevertheless, his incessant bragging made her simmer like a tea kettle.

She gave the already gleaming counter tops another once over with the dish cloth while Bailey conversed with Mr. Feinstein. Their muffled voices were melodious, a cheerful back and forth conversing. Soon, Bailey came out, entering the kitchen. Rosette didn't give him time to speak.

"I'm ready," she quipped, plucking her heavy coat off the hook behind the kitchen door. It was early November, but winter snow blanketed the yard. Bailey exited the house, striding quickly to his taxi parked in the driveway. Before she could open the front passenger door, Bailey beat her to it. Swinging the door open, he waited for her to step in. She was silent as she settled herself in the seat, praying that he was not in a talkative mood. Lately she wrestled with dreams of Vessie. They touched her with such believability that upon awakening her mother's familiar 'Jean Natè' scent seemed to linger in the air.

The anguish of not being able to visit Vessie's grave was unbearable. She longed to array it with fresh flowers, especially during holidays. No, today she only wanted to contemplate on the soft remembrances of her mother. Her deep mother love because that was the one thing she was sure of, that Vessie loved her. Presently, she was in no mood to hear Bailey rattle on about his wealth. She wanted to stay in that warm place with thoughts of sweet Vessie. But Bailey soon interrupted her plans of quiet meditation.

"Stephen and Barbara are wonderful people Rosette. Mr. Feinstein guided me to some of the best stock funds on the market, funds with longevity. You see, I didn't know a thing about the stock market, basically feared it after the 1929 crash. But I trusted Stephen. If it wasn't for him sharing his knowledge with me, I wouldn't have been able to open my taxi service. So, I'm grateful because I got my finances in order."

Oh, here we go again. Rosette fidgeted in her seat and stared straight ahead. "That's nice," was all she could think to say. *Just be quiet and take me to the store.*

"Where are you from Rosette? I've never heard you mention family. Are your folks from around here? I might know them from my travels, I just about know everybody in this area."

Her heart pounded out of control as she clamored to reclaim her rehearsed response to such questions. *Nosy man, what business is it of yours anyway?* And then the same lie that she told Stephen and Barbara Feinstein dripped from her lips like warm maple syrup from a jar.

"I have no living family; they died in a fire down south. Alabama, two years ago; I was the only survivor." It wasn't an all-out lie since Vessie was born and raised in Alabama. But beyond that, it was total fabrication. Rosette had never traveled any further than Calgon and Potter's Edge.

"Can you take me to Corky's?" she scrambled to change the subject. "I need to pick up a few things for myself? I-I mean after I make grocery if you have the extra time?"

"Sure. I'll take you to Corky's. No problem."

She hated the way her heart tugged when Bailey smiled at her. She wanted further reason to dislike him. And, to her chagrin, as time went by, she found herself looking forward to grocery shopping day.

The thing she had willingly brought from Calgon was staunch emotional survival skills. She determined to remain as cold as ice. But Bailey chipped away at her hardened spirit like a pick to an icy freezer. A slow thaw began, and somewhere down the road she reached a comfort level with him that she had never known or expected with any man. He didn't seem to want anything from her except friendship and she desperately needed a friend. The hard chunks of ice that surrounded her heart dissolved to a thin glaze. Transparent enough for them to laugh together and to find that, despite their age difference, they shared a love for many of the same things.

They both loved sports, especially baseball. Bailey took her to some of the local Negro League baseball games. They laughed gaily as they wolfed down hot dogs and Coke. The two were also cleanliness competitors. While Bailey kept himself and his limo in meticulous condition, Rosette was equally methodical about the Feinstein home. It was everything she dreamed of as a child, and she made it sparkle. She too held great affection for her employers. Rather than a housekeeper, the Feinstein's treated her like a member of the family.

Nevertheless, Rosette was afraid to become too close with anyone, taking great care to guard her conversations with them. She was terrified that the lie she told them might come back to haunt her. She stayed to herself most of the time. They seemed to take her silence for shyness, and she did not try to convince them otherwise.

One Saturday evening Rosette and Bailey sat in the Feinstein's parlor eating ice cream, another shared affection. "I know I got some years on you Rosette, but you have an old soul that I adore. I'd be honored if you would marry me. I'm in love with you baby girl. You can quit school and work, just be my pretty little wife. I'll take care of you for the rest of your life. Will you marry me, Rosette?"

After the initial shock of his words sank in, shame overwhelmed her so deeply she was momentarily at a loss for words. "Oh Bailey, you don't want to marry me. I'm not good enough for you. I don't deserve marriage."

"Rosette, beautiful baby girl, what do you mean you don't deserve marriage? I know you've been broken hearted, but I can make you happy. We'll have a good life together, I promise. I'm a Vain man, and when we vow marriage, it's forever."

It was amazing that she fell in love with Bailey after initially disliking so many things about him. But the irritants that she previously loathed were now the very things that endeared him to her. She learned that he was not being braggadocios when speaking of being newly affluent. Instead, she now understood that he was in awe of his success. Her thoughts turned to his humble beginnings.

Chapter 5

BAILEY, JR. WAS THE ONLY SON OF FRUIT FARMER, Bailey Vain, Sr. and his wife, Annie Kate. A year older than his only sibling, Zola, he, and his father worked their North Carolina fruit farm for their livelihood. The two drove a battered pick-up truck monthly to deliver fresh fruit up north to long-time customers who owned small businesses. Then out of left field, Bailey Sr. died of a massive heart attack, leaving 19-year-old Bailey, Jr. man of the house. Grief stricken and duty-bound, Bailey struggled to continue the fruit deliveries, the heart of their survival. He remembered what his father always told him. "'In tough times, keep putting one foot in front of the other and pray. Cry while you're walking, but never stop walking and praying.'"

It was hard to find a reliable person to travel with him to deliver the fruit northward in a timely manner, as well as to help with the farming. Things started to go awry; they lost money at an alarming rate. It was a gut-wrenching decision, but the family decided to sell the farm before possibly facing foreclosure. With some of the proceeds, Bailey purchased a small ranch-style home for the family in rural Kinsey, North Carolina. They lived modestly on Bailey Sr.'s life insurance and the remaining funds from the sale.

One of their faithful northern customers was Stephen Feinstein, who owned a deli and fruit stand in Potter's Edge, New Jersey. A year after the death of his father, with the promise of a chauffeuring job with Mr. Feinstein, young Bailey decided to relocate to New Jersey. A few years later, Zola married her childhood sweetheart. Pining for her brother, the couple moved to New Jersey as well. Bailey pleaded with his mother to come north to live with him. Annie Kate declined, bent on remaining in North Carolina so she could properly care for Bailey Sr.'s grave. Neither was she fond of the northeast's frigid winters. Disappointed, Bailey soothed his guilty conscience by mailing cash to Annie Kate each month. He was also comforted that two of her sisters lived within close proximity to her in Kinsey.

No, Rosette thought. *Bailey wasn't puffed up; he was simply happy that he could make others comfortable.* Over time she learned that was something he loved to do. So, with the Feinstein's as witnesses, 20-year-old Rosette married 31-year-old Bailey at a Justice of the Peace. True to his word, he showered her with beautiful gifts; a full-length mink coat, exquisite diamonds, exotic perfumes, and the finest apparel that money could buy. Impromptu stops at department stores to purchase gifts for his lovely bride after taxiing his customers became the norm. Rosette felt like Cinderella at a never-ending ball.

The ecstatic couple settled into an oversized English Tudor on Spruce Street in Potter's Edge, a wealthy, predominantly black area. Like an obedient child, Rosette eagerly fell into the rhythm of her new life. She turned their home into a warm oasis of colorful motif window dressings with beautiful antique furniture to enhance the shiny white marble and hardwood floors. Determined to push thoughts of her deception to the deepest recesses of her mind, she did everything in her power to please Bailey. They appeared the idyllic couple.

Although Bailey's sister did not live in the immediate area, he assured Rosette that they would all become her new family.

"'You're the kind of woman my sister will welcome because you're young and innocent.'" He sounded so proud. Rosette tucked her head in shame. The Bible verse: 'what is done in the dark will come to the light,' increasingly plagued her. She knew she had to come clean to Bailey.

"Bailey, I need to tell you some things about my past," she attempted to explain one evening as she prepared supper. Although she had settled into her life with guilty ease, the deception ate at her like a canker worm. The façade took its toll; it was taxing to remember the lies she had told him about her earlier life. Many nights her sleep was broken with dreams of exposure. At times, her sisters haunted her in dreams, exaggerated laughter on their painted lips, or she experienced falling back into the black abyss of the 'Shack.' She bemoaned the fact that Bailey believed her to be something that she was not.

He was a godly man, a deacon at Eternal Baptist Church, admired in and out of Potter's Edge. Although she quaked inwardly at the possible outcome, because he was a man of God, she determined to tell the truth. *Perhaps he will forgive me. After all he once said that a Vain marriage vow was forever.* She had to reveal the truth for the sake of her sanity, knowing it could very well end her fairy-tale marriage.

"You're too young to have a past baby girl," Bailey nestled her close from behind, running his hands through her charcoal hair that licked her shoulders as she stood at the stove. He pulled her away from the stove and turned her to face him as he continued speaking.

"Every woman I've gotten involved with closer to my age, my family had problems with them. But this time I fixed them good, didn't say a word about you. I knew you were the one. The Lord sent you to me, my beautiful, sweet Rosette."

She shivered in his arms, overcome with remorse. He kissed her forehead, and suddenly looked thoughtful.

"Rosette, I need to see Sweetnin' tomorrow. She's traveling to North Carolina next week to see Mother. I wanted to put something in her hand for the trip and give her a little money for Mother. It's about time you met my sister and her family anyway."

The depth of love that Bailey showed for his family always touched her. There was such affection in his voice when speaking of them, especially his mom, Annie Kate. *He is a good man*, the anxiety in her stomach began to subside. Again, she thrust the desire to tell him down into the darkest part of her being. *Let the past stay in the past.*

"We can start out early in the morning," Bailey playfully ruffled her hair. "It's not a long drive, just a few hours."

"Alright Bailey, that's fine." That night she fell into a restless slumber.

~ ~ ~ ~

They headed south on the highway early the next morning. Bailey was talkative, full of energy. But soon, Rosette began to yawn, and the soothing hum of the rolling car rocked her to sleep. Upon awakening she looked out of the passenger window and involuntarily jumped in disbelief. *I'm dreaming!* She blinked her eyes, intent on abating the dream. But to her despair, the 'Shack' was now in clear view. She would know that brown-stained, raggedy looking door that led to its entrance anywhere. As she desperately tried to hide her shock her body trembled in dismay. She turned to look at Bailey. Her face must have registered what she felt because the two large furrows in his forehead grew deeper with concern.

"You must have had a bad dream baby girl. Are you alright? Just another ten minutes or so and we'll be at Sweetnin's house."

"Your sister lives here in Calgon?" She fought to keep the hysteria out of her voice. She knew she had not done a good job by the inquisitive look in Bailey's eyes.

"Well, yes. Rosette, I told you they lived outside of Potter's Edge. Sweetnin' has lived here for at least ten years; her and her husband, Jasper Lewis, and their three boys. They lived outside of Potter's Edge first, but the kids started coming. Jasper got a better job in Calgon and so did my sister. So, they eventually bought a house here. Sweetnin's given name is Zola, but everybody calls her Sweetnin'."

He then unraveled the complicated anathema involving the women of his family. "My father's great, great, grandmother, Juniper, supposedly was cursed in the church. She got pregnant and wasn't married, although she married the child's father, Kelsey Vain, before the child was born. The prophet that put the hex on her pronounced that with each child she bore her pain would be so unbearable she would cry out for death.

Her first born would die as an infant, any other children would live a life filled with doom. Juniper would die a horrific death. Supposedly, future generations of blood Vain women would meet a similar fate if they broke the chain of virginity before marriage.

"My mother never knew Juniper but was told that events happened almost to the letter as predicted. That's why I don't talk much about my family's history. They would have you believe that if we were to have a daughter that she would be a victim of their belief. I don't buy it; it's more like superstition, ungodly."

Rosette wanted to disappear. She could feel herself slipping away to some dark corner of the earth reminiscent of her brief time at the 'Shack.' It was all she could do to keep from flinging herself out of the car into oncoming traffic. *Why didn't I tell him,* she cursed herself to the bone. By the time Bailey eased the car into the driveway of his sister's home her legs felt as if they were immersed in buckets of ice. She was afraid to look up and try as she might she could not cease shaking. An attack of vertigo had her head spinning like a wheel gone wild.

How had this happened? How could I have been so unaware to not know Bailey had relatives in Calgon? Maybe he thought he told me, but he didn't. Surely, I would have remembered. After all of her efforts to distance herself from her past, fate had dealt her an immeasurable blow. One that she knew she was powerless to fight. When Bailey opened the car door for her to step out, she felt faint. Her throat tasted as dry as sun parched paper. She willed herself not to fall apart.

Bailey frowned at her. "Rosie baby, are you okay? You look sick. C'mon in the house and let's see if Sweetnin's got some aspirin."

~ ~ ~ ~

"Hey Bailey," the big hipped pretty brown woman smiled broadly and hugged her brother affectionately. Eyes the same sandy shade as Bailey's raked over Rosette in one fell swoop. She peered into her face as if she were looking for something that was not readily visible to the eye. Rosette's heart thundered in her chest. Then the woman backed up to the door and clutched her hands to her bosom.

"My Lord, you're one of Vessie Dunney's daughters." The words rolled off her tongue as if they had an unpalatable stench. Rosette stood glued to the top step of the front door entrance. She prayed the earth would open and suck her in. When she dared look at the woman, her eyes were two wicked flames of fire. All the devils in hell seemed to be harbored in her throat, exploding with a vengeance through her lips.

"Yes Ma'am, you're one of them Dunney girls," she screamed, as if trying to convince herself and everyone in the house that came to the door curiously gazing.

Bailey looked dumbfounded. He eyed his sister, inhaling deeply before speaking. "Sweetnin,' what are you talking about?"

Rosette saw the confusion in his soft brown eyes. If she had not been so submerged in her own self-pity, she would have reached out to comfort him. She was *thinking, thinking, thinking*, where had she seen the woman called Sweetnin'? *How does she know me?* Then she inwardly berated herself for asking such a ridiculous question. Calgon was not a large city, and fed off negative gossip, half-truths spun out of control.

And then it hit her, the arrogant way the woman cocked her head and pursed her lips in disgust. She had been a dressing room attendant at Beck's Department Store in downtown Calgon. The only Black employee, so she was hard to miss. Rosette's memories unraveled to a time when she was about 13 years old. She and her sisters had the unexpected pleasure of shopping for school clothing at Beck's that year. Ms. Lewis gave them an icy reception when they were ready to try on garments.

"'I want my store to stay clean,'" she clucked to another attendant, while staring at Vessie in revulsion. Yes, now it all came back, that familiar repugnant glare. But now the aversion was to the ninth power because a Dunney stood on her doorstep, and not just at the retail store. Bile clung to Rosette's throat as she realized the thing that had caused her undoing, a family nickname. She only remembered Zola, or Sweetnin' as Ms. Lewis.

"You can't come in my house," Sweetnin's voice was gritty and peppered with disdain. "Bailey," she screamed at her brother while her body heaved forward from the wailing escaping her mouth. "That whole family of women from mother on down prostituted out of that dump of a bar over on the north side. She's no good Bailey, and you married her! Lord, this will kill Mother. How could you do this? Of all the women you took up with, none was this bad. Oh, help me God, I can't believe it."

Her screams brought a swell of neighbors out of their homes to peer at the Lewis' front porch. Rosette wanted to run, but there was no hiding place. The foul odor of her worse sin permeated the air as though she had never left Calgon.

I'm back where I started. 'You reap what you sow.' But I did it out of love for my mother, no other reason. She wearied at the thought of being dirt poor once again. But even more, her heart broke for the immense pain she had caused her beloved Bailey. Thus far, her young life had been like a roller coaster crisscrossing on an ambiguous path. She sat tightly in the careening car, gripping the sturdy handle with all of her strength, waiting for the outcome. But seeing Bailey so broken she imagined holding her arms up at the highest peak, plummeting out of the zigzagging coaster to float into blessed serenity.

Bailey had believed in her, but now he knew without asking her that she was a sham; a liar not even bright enough to cover her own shady tracks. Tears of shame trickled down her face. Vertigo returned with a vengeance. The house and the many curious faces went round and round, closing in on her. As she tried to catch her breath the earth became airless. *Thank you, God, let me die.* She faintly heard Bailey call her name as she collapsed on the steps.

~ ~ ~ ~

When she opened her eyes again Bailey stood over her weeping uncontrollably. She prayed for God to strike her dead right there rather than see Bailey shed such tears of sorrow. He was such a proud soul; his pitiful countenance filled her with unbearable hurt. And then like a faucet turned off he ceased sobbing, squared his broad shoulders, and picked Rosette up. He carried her to his car, uttering not a word, and the whole world became eerily silent.

Bailey took Rosette home, back to Potter's Edge. But from that day forward he withdrew from her mentally and physically. Sex became a thing of duty; gone was any spontaneous show of affection for her. She was no longer his *baby girl*. As far as the east is from the west, that was the extent of Bailey's passion for Rosette after the trip to Calgon. A marriage that once wantonly flowed with the sweetest love was now as cold as the dead of winter in New Jersey.

Chapter 6

SHORTLY AFTER THE OUTING OF HER INNER MOST secret Rosette learned she was pregnant. With this news, and for the course of her pregnancy, Bailey's extended family teetered on the brink of madness. When Bailey stopped visiting his sister, Rosette knew it was from shame. But that didn't stop Sweetnin' from coming to their home, although she had barred Rosette from entering hers. She was like a recurring coffee stain on teeth that wouldn't go away. No matter how many times Rosette washed her hands of her, or left the home when she arrived, Sweetnin' never failed to return.

"'Lord, help us if it's a girl,' she lamented under her breath as Rosette coolly ignored her. 'Might take the Dunney side and that will be the end of our pure line. We'll be cursed forever. My Aunties would turn over in their graves if they saw how Bailey disgraced the family.'"

This kind of rhetoric was common with Bailey's folk. Not only from Sweetnin,' but with other relatives visiting from the south. When Rosette gave birth to a baby boy, Eubanks, a unified sigh of relief went up from the Vain clan. A year later they simultaneously exhaled with the birth of another boy, Wesley. With a second positive birth outcome, Rosette was given an insult reprieve. However, it was too late to assuage her desire for freedom. Inwardly, she seethed at Bailey. *How long must I pay for sins I committed when I was so very young and confused.* She had dutifully swallowed the perennial whispers and snickers leveled at her to ensure her sons the best life possible. But Bailey's insensitivity to her feelings over the years became more painful than she could bear. He had never said a word in her defense, mutely giving them his approval to verbally abuse her.

Eubie and Wesley were Rosette's refuge; she dreamed of leaving Bailey when they finished grade school. She was ecstatic when the doctor advised that health issues with her second pregnancy would prevent her from conceiving more children. With this news the Vain's rendered Rosette long overdue clemency, as there would be no girl-child for Bailey. Surprisingly, even Sweetnin's outward grumbling waned. And then wham! It was 1948, Rosette found herself pregnant again after many years. She was devastated beyond words, beleaguered with heartbreak. Her plans to leave Bailey were now out of the question.

Throughout the years she had clandestinely tucked away money from her monthly pay in keeping the books for the business. Bailey also provided her with a $200 weekly allowance. She packed much of the money away in a medium-sized brown suitcase covered with a fancy blanket in her private armoire. At last count she had reached over $25,000. The money would be their means for living until she finished her nursing degree and became financially stable on her own. She had promised herself that she would not take a dime from Bailey after she left him, not even for the children. But her plans had boomeranged with the pregnancy. She now lacked the courage to leave.

The doctor advised Rosette that her third pregnancy was life-threatening, with so much scar tissue, hemorrhaging was a great possibility. She had spotted terribly while carrying Wesley. This time she was confined to the bed at the outset of her pregnancy. Somehow, death did not frighten her for she died a slow death daily from inward grief. But to everyone's surprise Rosette breezed through her third pregnancy without so much as nausea. Her good health was fodder for Sweetnin' to once again resurrect the devils that lay temporarily dormant in her vocal cords.

"'She's carrying low,' Rosette heard her remark to other family members. 'The boys were high. God help us, this one's a girl. We're doomed.'"

Rosette watched Bailey slump lower with each reminder of what might occur. When Marloe was born the Vain's wept and wailed to the point that Rosette wished she had died if only to avoid hearing the calamity. They were out of control with their deep-rooted fear and predictions. Sweetnin' led the pack. Annie Kate arrived and stayed for three months to calm the turbulence that hit the family like a tidal wave. With the birth of Marloe, Sweetnin' altogether revoked the earlier reprieve extended to Rosette.

"'Sweetnin' leave it alone,' Kate admonished her daughter. 'We have a girl, and we will deal with it just like the Vain's have always done.'" The family respected Annie Kate, things did settle down to a degree, and Bailey's attitude was truly puzzling. He was extraordinarily gregarious when it came to Marloe. It was easy to see he loved his little girl with his heart-of-hearts.

Rosette looked on in discreet envy as Bailey showered Marloe with beautiful dolls, and crinolines to wear under exquisite satin and chiffon dresses, just as he had once pampered her. And as the years went by it became obvious that Marloe would jump over her ten times to get to Bailey. Twice dethroned, Rosette turned all the more inward, clamming up like a shell.

By the time Marloe reached five-years of age her resplendent beauty and sweet spirit were apparent. After hearing, 'Can anything good come from a Dunney?' for so long, Rosette waited for the shoe to drop on the other foot.

But not one of their children gave them a moment's trouble. Marloe was a precocious child. She listened to the wisdom of Granny Kate and did not seem to mind the ever-present watchful eye of her father and brothers. During her mid-teens, the overprotective posture of her family relaxed, as it appeared the 'Dunney blood' had not prevailed.

Sweetnin' persistently extended the olive branch to Rosette by the time Marloe turned 16. But Rosette, hardened from the bitterness of Sweetnin's past slander, avoided her at every turn. The love she once felt for Bailey had dried up like a river in a desert, just as his seemed to have ended that wretched day in Calgon. She was miserable, trapped in a loveless marriage. Some days her thoughts wandered to the trunk in her armoire, she had continued to stuff it with cash. It gave her comfort to know she would not be penniless if the marriage ended.

A thousand times she brandished herself for allowing Bailey to persuade her to give up her nursing ambitions. She had one year of nursing school under her belt when they married. Smitten with her gloriously happy life, to please Bailey she had placed her nursing dreams on hold. Life became too hectic to return as she raised her three children and helped out with the family taxi business.

Working from home, Rosette managed the financial records of the business, which gave her a sense of self-worth. She fantasized that performing her job well might help to ease Bailey's ill feelings toward her, but it had not worked. The business thrived in every way and, while he paid her an abundant salary, he treated her as though she were just another employee.

He was careful not to share his business aspirations with her. Rosette knew that if she left Bailey then she lacked the means to live in the lifestyle that she and her children were accustomed. Shadows of her impoverished childhood haunted her in dreams. The fear of being destitute once again kept her rooted to Bailey's side like a weary shadow.

Marloe was nearing adulthood, yet Rosette remained too fearful to leave Bailey now that she herself had grown older. She lived her days in pretense, abhorring herself for the hint of jealousy she felt towards Marloe. *I love my daughter so much. How can I feel this way?*

Marloe's soft whimpering brought Rosette back to the present. The look in Marloe's eyes mirrored the agonizing pain that seemed to have been Rosette's forever. Mother love triumphed in her heart, she succumbed to the overpowering devotion she felt for her daughter. Suddenly, it was as if all of the agony she experienced in life came crashing down, attempting to project itself onto Marloe. Rosette became a mother lioness protecting her cub. She knew Marloe needed her now more than ever, a mother's special touch and love. *No time for a pity party.* She cuddled her daughter in her arms and rocked her as they both sobbed. "My baby, oh my sweet Marloe. It's going to be alright. I know the Lord will help you get through it."

~ ~ ~ ~

Although Marloe heard her mother's prayers, her mind was shattered, she could only moan and sink deeper into Rosette's bosom. *How can I tell mother what happened?* But deep within she knew she must. Her mother had just shared her most private secrets with her. *Mother will understand. She'll help me.* How she wished she could remain eternally sheltered in the newfound comfort of her mother's embrace.

Chapter 7

BAILEY PACED THE KITCHEN FLOOR FOR THE umpteenth time. The temptation to knock on Marloe's bedroom door was overwhelming. But soft weeping, with the subdued rise and fall of their voices stopped him in his tracks just as many times. He wasn't a total fool, although he knew he had acted like one for a very long time. Oh, how he had loved pretty, big-eyed Rosette, from the moment they met. She was shy and inward, slow to smile with a lost-puppy countenance. Her fragility drew him in like a magnet. He had never felt such a need to protect a woman as he did her.

The decade of years between them only added to his desire to shield her, especially when he learned her family perished in a raging house fire. Nothing could have prepared him for the realization that Rosette had deceived him with such ease and cunning. That revelation crushed him to the core; for he had truly believed she was God sent. So great was his humiliation that he became insipid, his once monolithic ego unexpectedly deflated like a blown-out tire.

He thought to divorce her, but his would have been the first in a family that reveled in the fact that there had never been as much as a marriage separation. It was a sin against

God. The Vain's believed that as long as a person had a living spouse, even if they divorced, in the eyes of God they were still married. So, he kept Rosette and treated her as if he had done her a tremendous favor. He abated his love for her by keeping her mentally and physically at a distance. Sex was performed out of his physical need, and he saw to it that it was never elicited from a show of affection from him. It was her wifely duty and she submitted.

As the years passed, to his distress, with the birth of each child his heart grew softer towards her. He had wanted to remain unforgiving, to hold on to the conviction that she had disgraced him and played him like a deck of cards. There was some kind of depraved comfort in not allowing her back into the deepest part of his being. It was not that he didn't trust her. Rosette never strayed far from home and had few friends. How well he remembered the visceral attacks on her character by family members that numbed his very soul. But the need for personal revenge overpowered the need to protect her. They had the nerve to do what he could not do; to verbally punish her.

However, something unfathomable happened in his heart when Marloe was born. She took him back to the soft cherished love that he buried from Rosette. The child was like a little angel. He never had to tell her to do something twice. She had learned the Vain women's way from Granny Kate, her great aunts, as well as Sweetnin,' and seemed to hold fast to her lineage. With each passing year he breathed a little easier and admittedly had lowered his guard where she was concerned. He had gotten comfortable, too comfortable. He groaned with melancholy as he sat down at the kitchen table. Placing his hands to his head he prayed, "Lord, please help my little girl."

The kitchen door opened; Wesley walked in with Eubie at his heels. Bailey saw the deep worry in their eyes as they studied his face for an indication of Marloe's condition. He stood up from the table.

"How is she?" Eubie asked. His jaw jutted in anger.

After bringing Marloe home, Wesley called Eubie to tell him about Marloe. Wesley had gone back to the station to close up, and both men arrived on Spruce Street at the same time.

"I-I didn't talk to her yet," Bailey stammered in his inability to right his world again. He felt as if his very heart bled, and at any moment the blood would spill from his mouth onto the kitchen's shiny white marble floor. His sons stared at him and, in that instant, although not a word was said, a pact was made. It was as sound as the spoken promise Bailey had made to remain with Rosette.

~ ~ ~ ~

Tears streamed down Rosette's face as she quietly entered the kitchen. Bailey's instinct was to take her in his arms and comfort her. Instead, he stood stoic, a pillar of granite, watching, waiting for her words. Wesley rushed to pull a chair out from the table for her to sit down. Bailey wished there were some way to escape the calamity that he knew her words would bring. She wearily pulled a tissue from the pocket of her robe, wiping her eyes, she squeezed them tightly before speaking.

"It's over," she said. "Marloe is not a virgin anymore." The words came crashing down around Bailey's head like thunder. They hit his ears with all the force of a lightning bolt. *Marloe is not a virgin anymore!* The sound resonated off the walls of the room like a sad song stuck on one lyric. He did not want her to continue, yet his curiosity forbade him to stop her from speaking.

"Before she finally fell asleep, she told me bits and pieces." Rosette looked up at Bailey. "It happened once, before she left for Kinsey. She was all wrapped up in

Lawson's promise that they would marry next year after her graduation. Well, she surprised him when she came home early today and caught him in the act with another girl in the James' tree house."

The blood that had previously attempted to burst from Bailey's throat was now curdled like vomit in his stomach. It took him back to the day he learned of Rosette's deceit, the way he felt, destroyed beyond belief. He sat back down, bent his head in his hands and waited for tears; tears that had not fallen since that time. They would have been a welcome relief to ease his excruciating sorrow. But tears did not come, only the painful knowledge that his daughter was sorely wounded. And for that there must be retribution.

Rosette stood up sadly shifting her eyes downward. "I'm going to bed," her voice was a near whisper. Bailey could see she looked tired; exhausted. Her eyelids drooped and her thin shoulders sagged as she turned to leave the kitchen. Those old feelings of love pulled at Bailey's heartstrings. She still had his heart and soul as much as he denied it. Hearing the bedroom door close behind her he turned to his sons. The force of rage emanating from the three men was like a wild thing in the room waiting to unleash. Bailey knew they waited for his direction.

"Mess him up," he hissed.

~ ~ ~ ~

Marloe went through the next month in a fog. The light had left her world, each day she found herself existing in midnight black. Annie Kate arrived to lend her support, and although Marloe wanted her there, it somehow amplified her sin. In Marloe's eyes, Granny Kate epitomized what it meant to live a saintly life. Up with the birds each morning, she was on her face before God for at least an hour. Then she broke open her worn, note-filled Bible and read for another hour. As she whipped up a hearty breakfast for the family, her favorite hymn, "Nearer My God to Thee," flowed from her lungs like a soft morning breeze. Sausage and fat back bacon, grits, eggs, topped with her famous homemade buttermilk biscuits, sliced, oozing with butter and maple syrup.

As Marloe lay in bed listening to the familiar sounds of Granny Kate in the kitchen, she turned to face the wall. Feigning sleep, she prayed Granny would leave the plate on the folding tray by her bed as she sometimes did. Her night had been colored with fitful dreams of Lawson. It began with breathtaking reciprocal love, only for the dream to end with the heartbreaking realization that she had been nothing more than a conquest.

Lawson never loved me. She trembled under the covers, drawing them closer as the prophesy fate flooded her mind; the consequences of those that followed in Juniper's footsteps. She could recite those words with more accuracy than a Bible verse. *You will lose a firstborn and be cursed with childbirth pains so insurmountable you will cry out for death. Your children will be the tail and not the head. That which their heart and soul desires will always elude them. And your death will be horrendous. This is the curse of the Vain women who do not wed as virgins.*

"Marloe baby, I brought you some breakfast," Granny Kate bustled into the room. "You've been eating like a squirrel. C'mon now. I made your favorites, buttermilk biscuits and grits." Had it been a few months earlier Marloe would have run a country mile for such a meal from Granny Kate. But now the thought of food turned her stomach. Slowly, she sat up and turned towards her grandmother. *She won't leave until I at least try to eat.* Annie Kate's smile was laced with anxiety as she sat the plate on the tray. She then eased down on the bed to sit beside Marloe, smoothing disheveled locks escaping Marloe's bun.

Marloe picked at her food, wishing she knew how to express the deep hurt within her heart to Annie Kate. But she remained quiet and so did Annie Kate. Somehow, the silence did not separate them, but brought them closer together. Kate hummed softly, and for her grandmother's sake, Marloe managed to down a spoonful of grits. She almost gagged, the grits stuck to her dry tongue and throat like paste. Keeping a straight face, she downed some milk.

"What do I do now Granny Kate? My life is cursed." Water welled in Marloe's eyes. She felt the sense of becoming unraveled once again, knowing her indiscretion had wounded her family to the bone.

Granny flinched; tears sprang to her eyes. "Well baby," she said softly, as she patted the cover over Marloe's legs.

"God has a way of fixing everything for good if you ask Him and believe. Prayer changes things. We've been fasting and praying for mercy for this whole situation, and God is merciful."

Willing herself not to cry, Marloe trembled with regret. Her grandmother looked bone-tired this morning. She did not want to cause her more concern. The deep circles under Granny Kate's eyes were evidence of sleepless nights. Guilt pierced Marloe's heart for causing such turmoil in the family. How she longed to curl up on the bed and die; ridding every one of the grief she had caused. *I believed Lawson when he said we would be together forever, that we would marry next year; that together we could bear anything. What an utter fool I have been. I thought I was outsmarting God.*

~ ~ ~ ~

Jorene chattered as if she would never have the opportunity to speak again. She had come to the Vain house to check on Marloe. It was Saturday afternoon.

Marloe lay in bed feeling lethargic, still unable to function in totality.

"Marloe it's hot out, get up girl, let's go to the Ice Stop. You know how you love vanilla malts. C'mon, you got to get out of the house. We need to shop for clothes, school starts in a few weeks."

Jorene always had a lot to say, but Marloe knew it was what she did not say that screamed from the four walls. *She thinks I'm going to ask about Mabel, but it wasn't her. It was someone else. Anyway, it doesn't matter who the girl was, it can't be undone.* The window fan in the room blew in fresh air, yet the space remained tight, stiff, waiting for the words that might give it relief. Marloe observed her friend closely. It was her eyes that held the secret as her voice rose and fell in false gaiety. She looked everywhere except directly into Marloe's eyes. Suddenly, Jorene bolted from the bed and went to the large mirror attached to Marloe's dresser drawer.

"Where's the lipstick you bought the last time we went shopping at Fishers?" Jorene asked. Her eyes dived downward towards the drawers.

"In the middle drawer," Marloe answered, looking at Jorene curiously.

Jorene pulled the drawer out and picked up four lipsticks. She shook her head. "Honestly, Marloe. I don't know why you buy make-up and don't wear it. A little lipstick and rouge never hurt anyone."

Jorene's avoidance heightened Marloe's inquisitiveness. She knew her friend about as well as she knew herself. "So, what does my not wearing lipstick have to do with you being so nervous you can't look me straight in the eye? Tell me Rene, it can't hurt any worse than it already does."

Even as she voiced those words, her stomach quaked with fear at the thought of hearing Lawson's name. The pain smoldered within her like a dying ember; hurtful words thrown on it threatened to ignite it into a fiery flame.

Still, she obstinately stared Jorene in the face until their eyes met. Jorene grew quiet for the first time since entering Marloe's bedroom. She reticently sat down on the bed.

"Tell me Rene. Don't let me walk around a worse fool than I already am. No secrets between us, remember? We're best friends, forever."

Jorene stared at Marloe. "Oh goodness Mar," she practically whispered. "I promised Mr. Bailey I wouldn't say anything about it to you. You know your father can get mean, especially when it comes to you."

"How will he know you told me anything? I'm certainly not going to tell him."

Jorene's eyes filled with tears; Marloe readied herself for more agony.

"Well, that night after everything happened, Lawson came to my house." Jorene's voice trembled. "He was beside himself, upset that he couldn't talk to you. Mama screamed at him to find out if he hurt you in some way, you know, physically. Lawson said he didn't, that he would never lay a hand on a woman. He said he went to your house first to try to talk to you and your parents. He wanted to apologize for everything; to stand up like a man. Well, he said Mr. Bailey cursed him high and low. Said if he ever came near you again, h-he would not live to tell it."

Marloe dropped her head.

Jorene grew quiet. "I'm sorry Mar, but you wanted to know."

"I do. But it's not easy."

"I know girl. We don't have to talk about it anymore. It's alright."

Marloe heard the relief in Jorene's voice. "No Rene. Please, go on, finish telling me." She hated that she felt an ounce of pity for Lawson. But she could not deny the shadow of fear that came over her after Jorene's story. She knew the men in her family were capable of making Lawson pay dearly.

"Well," water glistened in Jorene's eyes. "Stories are rampant that your brothers beat Lawson really bad and threw him on the James' front porch. At first people said Lawson was dead because he hadn't been seen after that night. But it came out that Mr. and Mrs. James sent him to family in the area where he's going to college in Georgia."

She hesitated briefly, biting her bottom lip, as if contemplating her next words carefully. "They're afraid Mr. Bailey might find out where Lawson is and finish the job. Mama saw Ms. James in the grocery store a few weeks ago, said she looked wild in the face; like death was at her heels. The Supper Club is closed."

Marloe squeezed her eyes shut as she considered all that Jorene said. She didn't doubt the beating at all; but for someone to think her father was capable of murder, never. *Father is a deacon at the church.* Oh, she had seen his wrath, a voice that could boom so loud it would make the most herculean of men fall to their knees. But that was a rarity, most of the time he was quite genial.

"Rene, they were upset, but they would never go that far. That I know for sure."

Someone knocked softly on Marloe's door. "Come in," she called, gingerly swinging her legs off the bed to the floor. *It's time to get up and pull myself together. How selfish of me to wallow in self-pity while my family bears the brunt of unfounded gossip.*

However unspoken, Marloe felt her brothers were trapped within the web of the curse as tightly as she. Wesley had seriously dated a woman named Lana for many years. Their sudden split came as a shock to the family. They adored Lana but suspected she had grown weary waiting for Wesley to propose and finally broke it off. Marloe understood Wesley's dilemma for it paralleled hers; he was petrified of the possibility of raising a daughter. Although never voiced, she was convinced there was no other reasonable explanation. Easy-going, smart, and financially stable, Wesley was a knight-in-shining-armor for any woman.

Her brother Eubanks had his own story as well. Married to work, he claimed to be too busy to develop a significant relationship with anyone. And true to his word, if not at the taxi station he was sure to be found at his fishery. Nevertheless, Marloe saw no prudent reasoning for his lack of social life since he had a full staff at his store. She suspected that she and her brothers shared the same debilitating adversary, a silent demonic threat. If she were to somehow conquer its merciless grip on her life, she might also free her siblings from their subliminal fears.

Granny Kate stuck her head in the door. "Girls, come on in the kitchen and have some lunch. Got coconut cake too," she smiled widely.

"Okay Granny. I'm getting dressed. We'll be out shortly. I love you."

"I love you too baby." The sudden lilt in her grandmother's voice warmed her heart.

Marloe deftly pulled her hair loose from the tie, spiraling tresses spilled to her waist. She couldn't hold back a giggle as she looked at Jorene's astonished expression. Moving closer to her dresser, she peered at her image in the mirror. Her skin looked sallow from her recent weight loss. She had been a good size eight, but now her nightgown hung on her a few sizes too large. *Thank goodness Mother is a stickler for hanging on to old clothing.* She had never let them forget her meager childhood.

"'These are good dresses,' she would often remind Marloe. 'Some you've only wore one time. When I was your age I prayed for pretty clothes, but we were about the poorest family around.'"

Jorene continued staring at Marloe in uncertainty. "What are you doing?" she asked.

"You said you wanted to go to the Ice Stop, so, I'm getting ready."

Marloe saw relief flood Jorene's big brown eyes. It was then that she noticed how pretty Jorene looked. *I should be ashamed, only thinking of myself.* Jorene's jet-black, pageboy coif gleamed like the sun against her caramel skin. Dressed in an olive-colored shirtwaist dress with yellow flower appliqués, it was slimming to her abundantly built frame. "I love your dress Jorene. And your hair looks so pretty and shiny."

"Thanks Mar. I washed it this morning and mama pressed it for me. Want me to pin your hair back up for you?"

"No, I'm wearing it down," Marloe spoke softly. She again eyed her reflection in the mirror. *What is the point in looking like 'little miss innocent'? Hair up, hair down, there's nothing pure about me anymore.* The realization that she would never be the same was a harsh awakening. Her heart grew cold with the desire for revenge, a feeling she had never before experienced. The sky-blue shift dress was one of her favorites. Marloe pulled it from the trunk and slipped it on. Last year it fit too snugly on her hips, so Rosette stored it away. But now it clung to her lean figure just right.

After putting on white bobbysocks she stepped into snow white Keds. Bending down to tie her shoes, the lipsticks lying on the dresser caught her eye. Her heart pounded in her chest with excitement. She picked the tubes up and turned to face Jorene. "Which one should I wear?"

"Ooh, the pearl pink," Jorene squealed. "Here, let me put it on you." She took the lipstick from Marloe's hand. "Sit down," she patted the chair at the dressing table.

Marloe felt nervous, but she also felt a prickle of defiance. She sat down, letting Jorene take charge. With swift, meticulous strokes, Jorene applied the color to Marloe's lips.

"Wow, that color looks so pretty on you. I knew it would," Jorene exclaimed. Not waiting for Marloe's response, she whipped out her rouge compact from her pocketbook on the bed. "Let's put some color to your cheeks, you're a little pale."

Well, I've gone this far, why stop now.

Jorene skillfully applied the blush to Marloe's face, and quickly stepped back. Marloe turned to face the mirror. The reflection of a stranger gazed back at her. She stood, moving closer to the mirror, amazed at the spectacular metamorphosis. Still, her new appearance did little to remedy the gaping hole in her heart that consumed her every waking moment. Determined to shake off gloomy thoughts, she picked up her purse and smoothed her dress with one hand. She breathed in deeply before speaking.

"I'm ready Rene. Let's go. I need a vanilla milkshake."

And I need to give my family their lives back.

"Yeah, girl, you're so skinny, you need a few."

As she walked on eggshells into the dining area of the house, Marloe braced herself for her family's reaction to her transformation. Sweetnin' sat at the table engrossed in an oversized slice of Granny Kate's coconut cake with pineapple filling. Marloe had never been fond of her Aunt Sweetnin.' What Sweetnin' called advice, Marloe viewed as put downs. There was also no love lost between her mother and Sweetnin.' Yet, as Marloe grew in knowledge, she understood that Sweetnin' too was a victim of family circumstances. Lost in the misery of the heirloom, Sweetnin' could not find her way out. With that realization, Marloe suffered a tolerance to her aunt's overbearing nosiness and accusatory tongue.

Nevertheless, there they sat today, her mother and aunt, two adversaries dining with her father while Granny Kate poured them coffee. Bailey jumped to his feet when Marloe and Jorene entered the room. The others seemed to follow in slow motion; all intently staring at Marloe as if they watched a horror show on television. *Well, isn't this what they wanted, for me to get back to life?*

In brighter days, the crazy expressions on their faces would have brought her to her knees with laughter. Their eyes bugged out like frogs, their mouths hung open, gazing holes of astonishment. Granny Kate's hands shook; She suddenly appeared incapable of placing the coffee pot back on the warmer. Marloe rushed to her side, gently taking her by the arm, helping her release the shaking pot into its place.

"Granny Kate, are you okay? Please Granny, sit down." Marloe placed her arm around Granny, guiding her to a chair. "You work too much around here." Marloe commented. She tenderly hugged Granny close before helping her sit down. As she did so she felt her grandmother's body tremble. Her gaze softened as she reared her fatigued body back into the seat. Bailey, at a loss for words, remained riveted to the spot. Marloe glanced at her mother; the initial shock on her face was now replaced with a look of pride.

The preceding clear alarm that Sweetnin' showed rapidly transformed into heated vexation. Her voice dripped with malice as she locked eyes with Marloe. "Marloe Alice Vain, where do you think you're going all painted up like a street walker? You're a Vain girl, go wash your face and do something with your hair, put it back up. You look like a little tramp! Didn't you learn your lesson with everything that's happened to you?"

Suddenly there was mutiny in the Vain camp. Marloe defiantly tossed her hair back from her face. She glared steely eyed at Sweetnin.' She had held her temper in check for years where Sweetnin' was concerned, the forthcoming outburst was imminent.

"Oh yes auntie, I know I'm a Vain girl, you would never let me forget that. To be normal for one day like everyone else is just too much to ask of you. Nothing I've ever done has ever been good enough for you. Well, listen to me Sweetnin,' I'm not changing anything today, not my face, not my hair, nothing! And if I should choose to walk around as naked as the day I was born, you can't do a thing about it!"

The room went stone-cold silent. Bailey had surfaced from his state of shock at Marloe's appearance only to have the wind knocked out of him again by her out-of-character outburst. He stared at daughter and sister; his face etched in disbelief.

"Marloe don't talk to your aunt like that," he growled. "You were raised to respect your elders."

Marloe knew Bailey was conflicted, but she refused to give an inch. She had reached the last knot on the rope. Something had snapped and sweet little Marloe Vain went temporarily incognito.

"Father, I've always been respectful, you know that. But I've had it with her downing me all the time for no reason. Not to mention how badly she's treated mother. I've never understood that. Why do you let her do it? Even as a child I remember her accusing, always smearing Mother's name in front of her as if she weren't even in the room."

"No little girl!" Sweetnin' shouted. "I didn't have to do it; she smeared her own name!"

"Don't you start with me Sweetnin'" Rosette's voice was uncharacteristically blunt, bold. "You're a liar. You know darn well you rubbed my name in the dirt whenever you had the chance. I should have slapped you silly a long time ago, God alone kept me still. But you better shut your mouth today if you know what's good for you. You leave Marloe alone, that's my daughter. As much as you hate it, she's a Dunney too, and a good one at that."

Marloe's heart swelled with admiration for her mother. Finally, Rosette had put Sweetnin' in her rightful place, out of their family business. Bailey sat down as if he carried the weight of the earth on his shoulders, voiceless and confused. Marloe momentarily thought to comfort him, to allay the fear she knew he felt. But good girl Marloe remained on hiatus, her fury not yet dissipated. *He deserves to stew in the pot for a while; he should have gotten Aunt Sweetnin' straight years ago.*

"We're all going straight to hell!" Sweetnin' shouted. She stood with her immense body bent forward and her palms flat to the table, balancing her frame. "I mean it; the whole family is hell-bound."

~ ~ ~ ~

Rosette wasn't surprised that a little make-up had transformed her daughter into the beautiful creature that stood before them. Contrary to what Sweetnin' declared, Marloe looked anything but risqué. But she also understood that Marloe was in a fragile state of mind. Bailey's crestfallen countenance conjured up memories of him leaning over her sobbing uncontrollably in Calgon. She swiftly shut the door of her heart at the unexpected ache of sadness for him that came over her. *Bailey doesn't need any emotional support from me. He's certainly made that clear over the last 27 years.*

She glanced at Annie Kate sitting in her chair, rocking, and softly praying. Sweetnin' mumbled to that other world she knew so well. Marloe had stirred a simmering pot just by letting her hair down and putting on a little lipstick. *What do they expect; she's 17 years old?*

Rosette chose her words carefully. "Marloe baby, you let your hair down?" She hated that her voice shook.

"Yes Mother, I need a change. I'm tired of the bun."

"You look lovely." She decided not to beleaguer the conversation as she eyed Annie Kate whose cheeks were on fire. Like a wounded puppy, Sweetnin' finally took her seat at the table. Her eyes watered profusely as she cupped her face in her hands. Bailey sat stone-faced; his eyes glued to the floor. *No, this discussion has to end, everyone is too emotional.*

"I just need some fresh air," Marloe stated. She hugged Rosette close. "Thanks mother, Rene and I decided to go to the Ice Stop. We're taking the bus, be back soon."

~ ~ ~ ~

To heck with the Vain's. Rosette cleared the table after the girls left while everyone else in the room remained comatose. *Them and their crazy curse talk.* She shook her head in exasperation. Both she and Bailey were active members of their church. Rosette was well versed in the Bible. Each Sunday she smiled obediently sitting in a familiar pew next to Deacon Bailey Vain while he shook hands and holy-hugged people as if he were a saint. The hypocrisy turning her stomach.

She read from Vessie's tattered Bible each night, interpreting scripture for herself. The Bible was her only beloved keepsake from her mother. To preserve it, she had it covered in soft black leather. From her studies she concluded that every man paid for his own trespasses. Unfortunately, she stood a better chance at unearthing the secrets of how the pyramids were built, verses convincing the Vain's of her belief. *And Bailey once told me that he didn't believe in the curse? Well, they may be hopeless, but Marloe isn't. I will not let her ruin her life over some ridiculous superstition. It's time to put a stop to it. How can someone curse what God has blessed?*

Chapter 8

MARLOE WAS DUMBFOUNDED BY THE ATTENTION she and Jorene encountered as they climbed onto the local bus headed for the "Ice Stop." Second glances from the opposite sex were taken with the humility ingrained in her all of her life. But today proved more than glances; these were outright stares. Guys offering their seats to them when there were empty seats available. Following the bus ride, traffic came to a halt as they strolled down Potter's Edge Main Street.

"Girl, they're carrying on about you, you're so beautiful Marloe, can't you see it?" Jorene asked. "Mar, you have power, and you don't even realize it. Men will fall at your feet if you let them and give you anything you ask for. If I had that kind of power Dugey and I would already be engaged. Um, I'm telling you he would be like a little lap dog all the time." She threw her head back laughing gaily.

Marloe shrugged her shoulders. "Rene, I really don't care about the attention. I-I'm flattered, you know, but it doesn't really mean anything. Besides, whatever you're suggesting I have, wasn't enough for Law…him."

Jorene dropped her head as they entered the Ice Stop. Marloe knew she had hit a nerve of truth. The sweltering heat had brought a crowd of people looking to cool off with an ice cream treat. The two girls took their place in line to order. Finally, they made it to the front. Mr. Nickson, the owner, stood behind the ice-cream counter. He broke into a toothless grin when he saw them. His leathered brown face seemed to fold into a thousand wrinkles.

"Yeah, you're the Vain girl ain't you? Bailey Vain's daughter? Child, I almost didn't recognize you."

Marloe lowered her head; heat rose to her cheeks. "Hello Mr. Nickson. Yes Sir, it's me, Marloe."

"My goodness, you sure have grown into a lovely young lady." He nodded his head at Jorene. "Nice to see you Jorene, looking pretty like Bettye."

Good. Jorene loves flattery. Relieved that the focus shifted to Jorene, Marloe concentrated on her order. Although her appetite wasn't great, the beads of perspiration on her face from the heat made her thirsty. A vanilla shake would hit the spot.

"Hi Mr. Nickson." Jorene beamed at the elderly man like he had handed her a million dollars. "Thank you."

They ordered milkshakes and sat down at an empty table. Each time Marloe lifted her eyes they were met with smiles from the opposite sex. An unexpected thrill coursed through her body. She never thought of her physical appearance as being *powerful*. Suddenly, the thought awakened a convincing confidence. *Never will I let a man steal my heart and soul again.* And the new transformation began.

Chapter 9

MARLOE GRADUATED HIGH SCHOOL WITH HONORS, winning A full math scholarship to Rutgers, Douglass College. Her initial plans to attend Spellman College were scrapped since that would have placed her in Lawson's direct path. After earning a master's degree in finance in 1974 she moved in with Wesley, joining the family business. Bailey bought her a shiny new powder-blue Cadillac as a graduation present. The Vain siblings took the business to a new level. They updated the name from "Vain's Taxi Service" to "Vain's Taxi and Limousine Services." Operating with a staff of eight drivers, two dispatchers, and a secretary, they chauffeured weddings, proms, any occasion that called for transportation services. Semi-retired, Bailey frequented the station regularly to ensure it continued to run with precision. As 'Head of Financial Operations' Marloe took over the record-keeping from her mother.

This gave Rosette time to further transform their residence into a shining beacon of perfection with the fruits of her labor. The home was magnificently decorated with oversized sweeping chandeliers adorning each room. Rosette spent a significant amount of time designing and sewing drapes for window treatments throughout the spacious home. The floors were gleaming cherry hardwood, except for the bathrooms and kitchen, which boasted pearly white Italian tile flooring. She felt a semblance of peace that after revealing the murky secrets of her past to Marloe they now enjoyed a close mother/daughter relationship. Marloe now understood the reasons for her mother's erratic temperament, her deepest heartache. Their talks became curative, forging a bond of kindred spirits, as both fought to abate ghosts of the past.

~ ~ ~ ~

A month after the devastating incident in 1968, Jorene had given Marloe a letter from Lawson. She placed the letter unopened under her mattress and there it stayed. *What could he have to say to me that could take away the pain or disgrace of that time?* It did not come as a surprise when Lawson was drafted to the National Football League (NFL); that was his ultimate dream. A lofty goal that once included her. In her efforts to sear him from her thoughts, she avoided the hometown newspaper touting its local star, and any media that might mention him. Coincidentally, as well as by her design, their paths had not crossed since that day. If she had reason to venture to the Larchmont Avenue side of town, she drove miles out of her way to avoid the tree house.

Slowly, she embraced the power of her beauty, spending excessive sums of money on wardrobe and hair care. She purchased chic clothing that clung to her small shapely frame like a glove. The stately up do of yesteryear was long gone, replaced by naturally flowing auburn curls that danced around her face to the middle of her back.

And although financially independent, she dated to accumulate more beautiful "things." It was both an addiction and a nemesis. Still, no matter how many diamond necklaces, gold watches, or expensive perfumes she amassed, they did not fully ease the lonely ache within her heart. In her quest for recompense, she accepted gifts from unsuspecting suitors who fell passionately in love with her. She would then severe the relationship after obtaining substantial valuables. Although consciously convinced it was too late, she vowed to treat her body as a living sacrifice to God. The idea of passing that evil vexation to children further strengthened her obeisance to sexual abstinence. Her indiscretion had traveled throughout the family like a runaway train. She was the Vain girl who broke the vow after Juniper and thus to them she had revived the curse. *If only I had been strong enough to bear that sin on my own; I could have at least spared my family from the shame. But no, I had to almost lose my mind, tell Mother, who thought it was her duty to inform Father. But the deeper issue is that God knew what I had done.*

~ ~ ~ ~

"Marloe did you hear the terrible news?" Jorene sounded near hysteria on the telephone line. She had married Douglas (Dugey) Scott the summer of high school graduation and gave birth to two daughters in rapid succession.

Marloe's heart froze with fear. She clutched the receiver tightly. Bailey's heart attack a year earlier in1975 had done a number on her nerves. She had yet to fully recover. Her father had always been the rock of the family. Seeing him weakened and near death truly shook her world. The panic in Jorene's voice brought those dark memories roaring back in an unwelcome flash.

"No, I haven't heard anything Rene," her heart raced as she waited for the news. "What is it?"

"Mr. and Mrs. James were killed in a terrible car accident this evening. I can't believe it, both of them gone," Jorene sobbed.

Marloe's body went limp with unbelief. She sat down at the kitchen table, stunned, trembling. "Rene, no, it can't be?" she moaned. Her hands shook, tears filled her eyes. As Jorene filled her in on the details, she remembered Dolly and Jonas James. They had always treated her with kindness, even after her nasty breakup with Lawson. But Marloe distanced herself from them, too much baggage, too many ill memories.

She had run into Dolly a few months earlier at a department store. They greeted each other warmly, attempting small talk, but it was an awkward meeting. Marloe felt relieved when their brief encounter ended. The short conversation was exhausting; she had caged her words to avoid hearing Lawson's name.

~ ~ ~ ~

It was cold and overcast as though it might pour down raining that January morning. Jorene drove, and Marloe sat in the front passenger seat. They were on their way to the funeral. Marloe nervously fussed with her hair. *This is going to be so uncomfortable, but I did care deeply for Mr. and Mrs. James.* Grateful that Jorene was not in a talkative mood, she concentrated on alleviating her nervous stomach with deep breathing. They approached the church. A large procession of people stood in line waiting to enter the church sanctuary. Marloe was not surprised at the vast outpouring since the James' were well-known and extremely charitable.

They joined the crowd standing in the frosty weather, the group slowly gaining entrance to the church. When Marloe saw the two hearses parked in a designated area the reality of her fondness for Dolly and Jonas hit her hard. She squeezed Jorene's hand. Two chauffeur-driven automobiles sat in front of the church. Bailey requested the limousines be provided to the James' family, free of charge. It was his attempt at making amends for the heavy transgression they committed against Lawson. Wesley had sworn Marloe to secrecy years later; admitting that he and Eubie had indeed beat the daylights out of Lawson in 1968.

Her heart turned over twice when one of the limo doors opened. Ashton stepped out, followed by Lawson. He was as handsome as ever, immaculate in a dark blue suit. Marloe convinced herself that the softening of her heart was due to the unfortunate circumstances. To lose both mother and father at the same time was unfathomable. *I could have buried my father if it wasn't for the blessings of God. Thank you, Lord.*

Jorene eyed her with concern. "You, okay?"

"I'm fine."

~ ~ ~ ~

"I'm so sorry for your loss," Marloe spoke softly to Lawson and Ashton in the receiving line after the service. She felt Lawson's eyes sweep all of her as they shook hands; his grip firm, inviting. He flashed a familiar smile.

"Marloe, Rene, thank you both so much for coming."

"I was very fond of your parents." Marloe replied. *Don't be nervous. Look at the way he's looking at you. Remember, you have the power.*

"They loved you very much Marloe. Will I see you at the repast?" his eyes begged for a 'yes.'

She momentarily waivered with indecision, knowing Jorene would like nothing better. "No, I'm sorry, I have a prior engagement." She could have kicked herself for offering an explanation. *I don't owe him anything. I should have just said 'no.'*

She was amazed that the intense attraction she believed might overwhelm her at seeing Lawson did not happen. Nevertheless, a moment of sad nostalgia overcame her. *Sentimental reasons, that's all.* She was no longer a fresh-faced naïve little girl. Life's journey was teaching her how to handle men in what people called a 'man's world.'

Lawson's gaze penetrated her thoughts. "I'll be in town for a while. I'd love to talk," he said, cupping her hand in both of his.

"Perhaps," she gracefully removed her hand. "It was nice seeing you both. Take care." She turned, walking away with Jorene by her side. Suddenly, she felt a tingle of empowerment rush through her veins.

"Rene, can you believe that? He came on to me after all this time. What nerve."

"Will you see him Mar? He was so happy to see you."

Marloe laughed wryly. "Please Rene, why would I spend time with Lawson James? It's best we leave those old memories under my mattress, right beside the letter you gave me from him that I never opened."

A slight smile played across Jorene's lips; she shrugged her shoulders. "You should have opened that letter a long time ago, just for the sake of hearing his side."

"His side?" Marloe was incensed. "Rene, you can't be serious. There was only one side, my broken heart, remember? I never want to feel that pain again. Reading an apology from Lawson at that time could have made me weak in vowing to never see him again. And reading it now will only open old wounds that took years to heal."

Jorene cast her eyes downward. "You should know that Lawson may be staying in Potter's Edge for some time. They have to settle the family's estate and, from what he told Dugey, he's got some kind of injury."

Oh, for the love of joy. Marloe's mind was already working on avoidance plans. "Hey, it's a free country." But deep within she knew that to be totally liberated in her spirit she must deal with her past. The thought of being alone with Lawson James again was unnerving.

Chapter 10

"**Y**OU NEED ME TO RUN YOUR BATH BAILEY?" Rosette asked. It was nearing bedtime and Bailey sat in the recliner in the bedroom reading his Bible.

Why does she have to look so gorgeous? Age had only enhanced her delicate features. She still had that baby doll face, although her big, beautiful eyes had lost some of their sparkle. He knew he was responsible for the unhappiness that hung over their marriage like an endless cloud. Her hair, now peppered with gray, fell just past her ears in a neat straight cut. As he stared at her his heart tugged in that old familiar way when he had openly loved her to his soul.

When he suffered a heart attack earlier that year, Rosette waited on him hand and foot, attending to his every need. *I couldn't have made it without her. She's always been a good woman; good-hearted, but broken-hearted mostly because of me.*

She had pleaded with him to forgive her for lying about her past. Letting him know that during her mother's illness she felt forced to do what she did for a short time to help her mother because of her sisters' abandonment. Her countless tears scorched his being with indecision. But his pride was mortally wounded, her sin unpardonable. At that time, she sought to leave him, asking him for funds to keep her on her feet until she found work.

"You will not leave me, and I will not give you a dime," came Bailey's stormy retort. "There will be no divorce." *I knew she wouldn't leave me when she found out she was pregnant. She came up hard and stayed for the financial sake of the children.*

Their marriage soldiered on like that of a 'cold war' for years, and then the unthinkable happened. He awoke one morning to excruciating pain racing up his left arm to his shoulder. He torturously pulled himself up to a sitting position on the bed. His chest throbbed; he was in agony, gasping for air. Breath left him as he fell back on a sleeping Rosette. Thick gray smog surrounded him. *I'm dying.* Yet, he could hear Rosette's tearful voice through the mysterious haze turning darker every second. Someone stroked his head, gently kissing his face.

"Bailey don't leave me. Please don't leave me, I love you," he heard Rosette's voice fading into the darkness.

Rosette, my beautiful baby doll. And now I'm going to die without her knowing how much I love her. Immersed in fog, the image of Bailey Sr. hovered above him, dressed in familiar blue overalls and a straw hat. His smile confirmed to Bailey Jr. that he was truly in the passageway of no return. Suddenly his world went black. Subsequently, as swiftly as the lights of life shut off, they miraculously turned on again. Bailey lay in a hospital bed, awake, shivering from the coldness of the room. Grateful to God to be back among the living. The massive heart attack had done its damage, but with triple bypass surgery, physical therapy, and a change in diet, his prognosis was quite positive.

~ ~ ~ ~

In the bedroom now, Rosette leaned over Bailey, and he could smell the soft rose scent of her perfume. Yes, he had given her the finer things in life. She had wanted for nothing that money could not buy. But then Rosette had not asked for much. In fact, over the years she showed extreme frugality. She bought clothing on sale for the children as they were growing up although he gave her carte blanche to purchase the best. Instead of hiring a professional decorator, she custom-designed beautiful apparel for the house, creating her own patterns.

Bailey knew that Rosette's throwing herself into housework helped her cope. He remembered similar behavior when she worked for the Feinstein's. And now, he deeply regretted his inability to show her how much he cared. He was in his sixties, read his Bible every day, and still did not know how to forgive. When he thought of how badly he had treated the *love of his life*, he was besieged with shame.

"Bailey," Rosette softly placed her hand under his good arm. "Come. Let me help you to the bathroom." She guided him from the chair as he pushed himself upward.

She could have let me die that day and been a rich widow. But instead, she helped nurse me back to health. How selfish of me to ask her to give up something she loved so much.

During his illness he realized nursing was Rosette's true calling. She was responsible about his health to a fault, setting up a schedule for medication times, and implementing a new menu to ensure he ate properly. His eyes moistened as he thought of all the love his family had shown him. Marloe had moved back home into the guest suite to help Rosette with his care. Although he and Rosette tried to talk her out of it, Marloe would not hear it. Under the care of Rosette, Marloe, and his mother, Bailey improved tremendously, but by no means was he out of the woods.

"Thank you, Rosette." He watched as she scurried ahead to the master bath, running water in the tub. Slowly, he made his way to the bathroom. Rosette left, quietly shutting the door behind her.

"I'll be right in the bedroom. Call me if you need me," she said.

Stay with me, he pleaded in his thoughts. *I need you near me.* He wanted to hold her tightly, kiss the worry from her face, her eyes. But for all of his desire to embrace her, pride kept him obstinate, elusive. He would be the first to admit that Rosette exonerated herself long ago for simply remaining with him, her purposeful killjoy. Pigheaded for so long, he asked God to cut through the hardness of his heart to ask for her forgiveness. He also feared that upon his improved health Rosette might again return to her quest to leave him. At age 13, Wesley had innocently told him of her earlier plans to exit.

"'Father, why can't you come with us?' the child unwittingly inquired. 'Mother said we're moving to a smaller house in another town to save money and you have to stay here to run the business.'"

Bailey was stunned. He periodically checked with the two local banks to find out if Rosette kept private bank accounts listed under Dunney or Vain. There were never any such accounts. With that, he realized she had to be storing cash because she never spent much money. However, when she became pregnant with Marloe, she was inconsolable. And so was he, although for a different reason.

Anguish filled him now as he thought of how she had given him three wonderful children, and he had been thankless. *Even when I resorted to evil when Marloe got hurt, Rosette kept a level head. But I'm learning something about forgiveness*, he thought, looking at his balding head in the bathroom mirror. His conscience had pierced him to the marrow and made him examine his own mortality when he heard about Jonas and Dolly James' untimely deaths. Although it was too little too late when he ordered the limos for the James family for the funeral service, he felt he had to do something.

He had long understood that he put his daughter on a pedestal, and she had fallen off. Instead of recognizing that it was she who had given up her virginity, he chose to blame Lawson for everything. It was easier that way, but even then, he knew his thinking was not spiritual.

And how he needed Rosette's forgiveness for allowing Sweetnin' and other family members to trample on her feelings without as much as a word in her defense. He had to find a way to break the icy glacier that their marriage had become over the last 30 years. He eased his body down into the steamy water. The temperature was perfect, and he expected no less from his precious wife, Rosette.

~ ~ ~ ~

While Bailey took his bath, Rosette's thoughts ventured back to the day he fell ill. His heart attack had seared the hatred right out of her, making it apparent that she still cherished the ground he walked upon. As he lay on the bed near death's door, she ached with the awareness that he might never know how much she truly adored him. She frantically called 911. Suddenly Bailey's struggled breathing became silent. Attempting to find a pulse, she seized his wrist, finding a slight rhythm. She had to act quickly. *Love heals, that's what the Bible says.*

"'Bailey, please don't leave me. I love you,' she whispered in his ear. 'Hang on Bailey, help is coming. I love you; I love you.'" As she stroked his thinning hair; salty tears fell on his face. She prayed that God would let him live. *And the Lord did spare him.*

She had rarely left his side during his hospital stay, leaving the facility only when one of their children relieved her. These were short respite intervals to refresh herself or grab a bite to eat. Upon Bailey's release from the hospital, he was sullen and aloof at home. Annie Kate arrived, taking charge of household chores along with Marloe, while Rosette cared for Bailey. She supported him in basic functions he could no longer perform without assistance, such as clothing and feeding himself.

"'Aw, poor dear, you'll feel better soon Bailey,'" she sought to cheer him one day, guiding a fork full of food to his mouth.

"'Don't pity me Rosette,' he barked. 'I can't take pity.'" His attitude stopped her dead in her tracks. Remembering the sting of past rebuffs, she remained dutiful, but again emotionally removed herself from him. As if Bailey carried the watering can himself, visions of the bounty in her trunk began to take root once again. *I would never leave him while he's sick, but if he doesn't want me around...well I'll be prepared just in case.*

~ ~ ~ ~

A loud thump from the bathroom awakened her from her daydream. *My goodness, did he fall?* She crept to the door to listen for footsteps, any sign to let her know he was alright. Suddenly the door opened so quickly she had no time to move away. "I-I heard a loud noise, I was about to knock to make sure you were okay," she stammered.

He stood still in the door opening, his face softened as he looked at her. "Oh, I tried to open my shaving kit and dropped it on the floor."

"Bailey you should have called me. I could have…." She stopped in mid-sentence knowing he despised having to rely on others for much of his needs.

"I was able to bend and pick the kit up Rosette. I wanted to see if I could handle it by myself. Like you said, it is getting better. Next time, I'll be able to shave. I'm fine baby girl. I'm fine. You go ahead and get some rest now."

Baby girl? Her heart soared. It had been ions since Bailey had called her by his pet-name for her. She smiled but said nothing. Bailey's spirits went up and down during his recovery, perhaps this was just a passing occurrence. However, his words gave her a remnant of hope.

Chapter 11

MARLOE LIFTED HER MATTRESS AND PULLED OUT the yellowed envelope as she had done many times. She thought to tear it into pieces many times, pretend it never existed, but something within always held her back. Seeing Lawson again opened scars of yesteryear that left her heart doing a precarious slow bleed. *He's done well for himself; he certainly exudes the confidence of a celebrity.* Quickly, before losing her nerve, she sliced the envelope open with a silver nail file and pulled out the folded sheet of paper. With trembling hands, she unfolded the letter and lay across her bed to read it.

Dearest Marloe, My Love,

By the time you read this letter I will have left for college. I tried my best to see you, but your family forbade it. Believe me, I do understand their reasons. I am so ashamed for the way I hurt you. If I have lost you forever, I want you to know that you still have my undying love forever. My prayer is that you would give me the honor of speaking with you again. I can't imagine my life without you. It was a foolish thing I did, but I can assure you that it would never happen again. Marloe baby, you mean the

world to me. Please call me so we can talk this thing through. My number at school is 555-234-1100.
I pray you will call me.
Eternally Yours, with all of my love,
Lawson

"I can't imagine my life without you," she read the words aloud. *Well, you seem to have managed just fine.* In retrospect, the betrayal was a blessing in disguise. It revealed Lawson as the charlatan that he was, ultimately saving her from more heartache had she married him.

So now he wants to talk, huh? Perhaps I should take him up on his offer, after all I possess my own power with men. She picked up the phone to dial the James' residence. Just as quickly she slammed it down. *If he really wants to see me, he'll try again. And when he does, I'll be ready.* She was confident in her ability to play any game he might try and to also guard her heart at the same time.

~ ~ ~ ~

Dang, I need something stronger than wine tonight! Lawson was in the basement of his parents' home rummaging through the tiny bar. *Nothing there.* Dolly and Jonas always kept a modest amount of wine for guests, not being partakers themselves. It was after eleven p.m. and Lawson could not sleep for the staggering reflections swirling in his head. The black hole where he now lived since the death of his parents consumed him.

Why God? His mother, Dolly, had been the sweetest person on earth; a true guiding light for he and Ashton. And, despite his Father's shameful womanizing, Jonas had mentored them into men of caliber. Nonetheless, with each covert indiscretion, Lawson witnessed his mother's growing disparity. However, with the family move to Potter's Edge his parents appeared to be a happily married couple. Ruefully aware that he carried the same promiscuous proclivity as his father, Lawson struggled to keep those feelings secret.

After losing Marloe, along with the near loss of his life courtesy of the Vain brothers, he had left Potter's Edge for college. The sudden plenitude of young women at nearby Spellman College held his interest for a season. However, beautiful, irreplaceable Marloe never left his heart.

She never responded to my letter. I asked for her forgiveness, literally poured my heart out to her. What else does she want me to do? A thousand times he thought to contact her when he came to Potter's Edge on school break. He longed to see her, to tell her how much he still loved her. But fear of her family and remembering her unwavering rejection immobilized him just as many times.

He would never forget the lethal sight and sound of Bailey Vain that night eight years ago as he stood at the Vain's front door. His eyes glistened like black ice; his words cut into Lawson's psyche like the tumultuous thrust of a jagged saw. "'If you so much as take a breath near Marloe again, I'll kill you,'" Bailey snarled. Although Lawson loved Marloe to the depths of his soul, he conceded. He could literally feel the clear and present threat to his demise.

~ ~ ~ ~

He opened the refrigerator door to find a lone bottle of red wine. Grabbing a glass from the rack, he poured it, quickly downing the drink. The heat of the soft liquid warmed his throat and chest. He felt his body begin to unwind and lowered himself onto the nearby loveseat. Thoughts of Marloe plagued him. *She is even more beautiful than I remember. I wonder if she still believes in that curse nonsense.* She had warned him of her family's heritage when they began dating and made no apologies for her parents' stoic religious beliefs. Even so, as much as he had cherished her, he was unable to control the demon that aroused his heart to wander in other territory.

But today was like a dream come true. The moment he laid eyes on her, heard her sweet husky laugh, he knew the attraction remained. He would love nothing more than to wrap his arms around her exquisite body, to hold close the hauntingly beautiful woman she had become. The pristine bun of high school days now undone. Her sand-colored locks free falling to waist-length in enchantingly wicked spirals. The same midnight eyes that never failed to pull him into her world as a teen remained as captivating as ever.

Life as a professional football player had afforded Lawson the opportunity to travel, to enjoy the finer things in life. While he appreciated his fans and his affinity for the people of Potter's Edge was truly genuine, for the moment he sought solace. He needed time to absorb the fact that life would never be the same for him. His grief was too tender for small talk, autograph signing.

Marloe, I need Marloe. Perhaps their conversation of that day could lead to a second chance to rekindle the bond of love they once shared. *We're adults now. I can face the Vain's. If they wanted me dead, they would have finished the job that night. Bailey even provided limousines for our family today. He must be getting soft in his old age or feeling guilty.*

He glanced at the clock. It was after eleven, too late to call. *I'll call her tomorrow at the taxi service. She still cares for me; I can feel it...a love like ours lasts forever. Otherwise, as fine as she is, she would be married by now.* Satisfied with his intended plans, and exhausted beyond measure, he drifted off to sleep on the loveseat.

~ ~ ~ ~

Marloe prepared breakfast the following morning for her parents as she often did before leaving for work. It was her way of giving her mother a break since she ran on auto pilot daily caring for Bailey and tending the home. Annie Kate had gone back south now that Bailey was doing better. *I'll make pancakes, father's favorite.* He had grudgingly given in to the less sugary marmalade preserves verses pancakes oozing with the thick brown Karo Syrup he loved. But when Marloe opened the cupboard there was no pancake mix. *Darn. Well, they both love grits. I'll make eggs and toast to go along with it. No more fried fat back for father,* she smiled at the thought.

Bailey loved pork, but grievously gave it up. To the family's delight, he eventually ceased complaining about his new diet which consisted of much less fat and more vegetables and fruits. He looked quite healthy having dropped thirty pounds from his once 260-pound frame. Marloe glanced at the clock; it was seven-fifteen. Time was getting away; she would need to leave within the next hour. Her brothers were meeting with clients in New York City that day and not expected to return until evening shift. Marloe always arrived early to the station to get a jump on the day. She was thankful that Margaret, the secretary, was an early bird too.

Marloe knocked softly on her parents' bedroom door to let them know breakfast was ready. *I'll sit with them for a few minutes.* Although Bailey's heart attack seemed to have brought her parents closer, they eventually drifted back into the familiar non-loquacious couple that Marloe knew well. Strangely enough, while growing up she believed that was just the way married couples behaved. But after her mother divulged her earlier life and, knowing how unbendable her father was, she understood their distant interaction with each other.

R-I-N-G, the blaring telephone interrupted her thoughts. "I'll get it," she yelled to her parents. She heard them stirring about in their bedroom. "Hello," Marloe picked up the phone in the kitchen.

"Good morning, Marloe. I'm very sorry, but I can't come in today," Anna Jane spoke softly on the other end. "My son Karl is sick; I've been up all night with him. I need to get him to the doctor today."

Marloe's body tensed. Anna Jane was their full-time dispatcher. Today was Friday and, Carol, the part-time dispatcher wouldn't be in until Saturday. With that, her plans to devote her day to reviewing the books went out the window. She would need to don her dispatching cap today.

"Oh Anna, I'm sorry to hear that. We'll be okay for today and if you need to take off tomorrow, don't worry. Carol will be in. I hope your son feels better soon. Thanks for calling."

Don't tell me this is going to be a "Murphy's Law" day. It had all started with no pancake batter. She went to her parents' bedroom door, tapping lightly. "Anna Jane called out, so I'll need to get down to the station right away. Enjoy your breakfast. Call you later. Love you much."

~ ~ ~ ~

We might need another part-time dispatcher. Marloe pondered the thought while picking up the dispatch line for the fourth time within as many minutes. As a teen she had loved that job. But today, with pressing financial responsibilities screaming her name in unison, the ringing phone felt like a thorn in her side. *Oh well*, she smiled wryly. *If we had no fares to dispatch, we would be out of business.*

From an early age Bailey had Marloe's hands in many areas of the business. She helped with the books and on numerous occasions crisscrossed New Jersey and New York with her brothers as they chauffeured fares. The ride into Harlem was especially exhilarating. The streets were alive with flourishing Black businesses, charged with an atmosphere of warm enchantment.

"Margaret, can you please bring me a cup of coffee? It smells wonderful." *Thank God for Margaret.* A six-year clerk with Vain's, Margaret was as dependable as a Rolex watch. She also made a mean cup of coffee. Her history with the Vain's was in stark contrast to Anna Jane's who, although she was an excellent dispatcher, had a well-documented tardiness record.

Despite the fact that Anna Jane was an eight-year employee, Bailey came close to firing her more than a few times due to absenteeism. Marloe had taken her to task on the same issue and thankfully she did improve. *I hope she's not lying today; she sure sounded upset.* Carol, the part-time dispatcher was another steady-as-a-rock employee. *She'll be in tomorrow and I can get back to auditing the books. Lord, thank you.*

Upon Bailey's semi-retirement, Wesley became President and Eubie Vice President. The company also employed eight drivers. As well, Eubie maintained his thriving fish market on Mulberry Street in Newark.

It was nine-thirty in the morning. A flock of customers entered, and Marloe deftly patched through to the drivers for drop off and pickup timelines. She looked up from the dispatcher's desk situated in the center of the room. Her eyes lingered on the distinguished looking gentleman entering the station. He was average height, flawlessly dressed in a full-length brown tweed overcoat and matching hat.

"Good morning," he said, as he hurried towards Marloe at the desk. She waited for the perpetual second glance as he stood before her. But to her surprise it did not occur. *Oh, he's trying to be cool. Um, we shall see.*

"Good morning," she smiled at him.

"I need a car as quickly as possible to 56 Baker Avenue."

Brown & Dunson law firm. She knew it well. His aloof behavior became a test. Gambling on the power of her external appeal, she did her count down, waiting for his facade to disintegrate into thin air. *It always does, one, two, three, nothing.* She pulled an annoying strand of hair back from her face with one hand.

"I can have a car here in ten minutes. Would you like coffee while you wait for the car?"

"No thank you. I don't drink coffee," he bluntly replied. He turned away and strode to the seating area. *Well, isn't he the anti-social one?* She noticed his hands were ring-free. *Good.* She did not date married men. What might he add to her burgeoning trunk of trinkets? *Probably a lawyer, um, if so, he can afford me.* Believing her beauty was her greatest tangible representation of herself, she vigorously protected it.

While a day at the spa may have been a temporary escape from reality for other women, it was Marloe's weapon of choice. She weekly paid for the works, sauna, facial, full body massage, including manicure and pedicure. The ultra-care was a boon to extend her right of passage, beauty. *"Beauty is fleeting," I must take care of myself for as long as possible. When my looks fade, I'll be old, alone.*

It comforted her to know that she would have all of her dainty treasures from her journey to reminisce in her golden years. Each souvenir told the story of a heart she had broken as commonplace as the nightly appearance of the moon. She believed the 'curse' gave her the right to persist in this behavior given her bleak future.

The beeping phone brought her back to the job. "Come in three," she addressed the driver. "Okay, see you in five." She decided to advise *Mr. Aloof* that his car would arrive within a few minutes. It would also give her the chance to display her 'total package.' She strolled to the seating area.

Let's see how distant you are now. He looked up as she approached. Standing in front of him, she felt confident that his demeanor would soften as he took in her comeliness. "Sir, your car will be here in five minutes."

He smiled slightly.

Well, that's more like it; wondered how long it would take for you to come around.

"Excuse me Miss," he sounded agitated. "Five minutes ago, you told me a car would be here in ten minutes. I believed you the first time."

Her face flamed. He was clearly annoyed. Thus far, her day had truly unfolded like *Murphy's Law*. Everything that could go wrong had done just that, beginning with the absent pancake batter. Her confidence fizzled to a stammer. "I-I only wanted to assure you that a car is on the way, that's all." She felt foolish. Their eyes locked.

Suddenly she felt an unexplainable shift in her reasoning. It was a jolt to the protective walls she had built around her heart. A copious, underlying energy came alive with this gaze that caught her by surprise. It overshadowed the icy barricade that dwelled around her soul for survival. *This is not happening. I always have the upper hand. After all, I have the 'power.'*

"Yes, I know you were," he sounded less gruff. "I'm sorry, I apologize. I'm having a rough morning. The train from the City was delayed, and now I'm late for a meeting with my client."

She saw his cab pull into the station. "There's your car sir. Enjoy the rest of your day." Her plan was to flippantly turn and walk away, but he extended his hand to her.

"I'm Syril Barrett. Nice to have met you, Miss?"

"Marloe Vain, same here," she tried to sound nonchalant as their hands clasped in a handshake. A delicious flame raced through her body. Numb with the inability to keep her feelings under control she somehow managed a fake smile. "Enjoy the rest of your day." She quickly pulled her hand away.

"You do the same." He turned and walked out of the door.

Marloe's stomach quivered as she sat down. The man was a complete stranger. Yet their physical contact had brought a magnetic pull to her heart that made her quake with vulnerability. She inhaled deeply, cupping her head in her hands. *Calm down, this is a trick of the enemy. You know how to handle it.* She exhaled slowly calming herself down and getting back to work. *If we ever chance to meet again, I'll be prepared.*

~ ~ ~ ~

"Vain's," Marloe chirped into the telephone. She glanced at the clock. *One o'clock, where has the day gone? I'm going to be backed up with paperwork tomorrow* but *closing the books for year-end tomorrow is a must.*

"Hello Marloe," Lawson's deep sexy voice reached out to her over the line. She was standing, but swiftly sat down to gather her thoughts. A thousand times she had rehearsed her reaction should he call. She would be indifferent, self-assured. *Be cool. It's been eight years and you have not only survived, but you have also thrived.*

"Hello Lawson, I'm surprised to hear from you."

"Marloe, it was so good to see you yesterday. I hope I'm not imposing by calling you at work?"

Get ready girl, you know he's slick. "It's okay. I can chat for a few minutes. It does feel strange speaking with you after all these years?" The silence was so lengthy on his end for a moment she thought he hung up.

"And they have been the most miserable years of my life. Marloe, please listen to me. After I wrote you and you didn't respond back, I was devastated. I was young and, I admit, your family scared the hell out of me. But I have never gotten over you, and that's the truth. I'd love to take you to dinner to talk, to clear the air between us. You were the best thing that ever happened in my life."

As much as she tried to fight them, ancient memories began to creep into her mind. She determined to return them to that chamber deep within her heart where she kept them under lock and key. *I can handle it.* After all, for those men who professed undying love for her, she had become a connoisseur at discarding them like yesterday's newspaper. However sinful, it gave her intense gratification that every man she dated paid for Lawson's transgression against her. It was her private revenge. *You won't fool me this time Lawson James. Just try it, and I will tear your heart out and serve it to you on a golden platter.*

"Okay, so where shall we talk?" she asked.

"How about Sparks, tomorrow night at eight?"

She smiled coyly. Sparks was a cozy little jazz club three blocks away from Vain's Limo Service. *Eight o'clock Friday night, which will give me time to swing home, change clothes and blow his mind when I walk into Sparks. Oh, this is going to be big fun.* "Alright, I'll see you there tomorrow at eight."

~ ~ ~ ~

Jorene's joviality did not surprise Marloe when she divulged her plans to meet with Lawson. "Oh, that's great Mar," she exclaimed as the two chatted on the telephone. Marloe knew that somewhere in Jorene's sweet little head she held fast to a fantasy that she and Lawson would one day reunite.

"Whatever you say Jorene, but please believe me, it's no big deal."

"But you love each other Mar, love like that never dies," Jorene persisted. "You two will marry one day Mar; things have a way of working out."

Yes, they do, but sometimes not the way we think they will. "Go ahead and dream girl. I gotta go Rene. I just wanted you to know that I decided to take Mr. James up on his offer, just for old time's sake. I'll talk to you tomorrow sweetie."

"Okay, call me girl. I want to know every detail from beginning to end."

"Bye Jorene."

~ ~ ~ ~

Marloe was obsessed with a desire to astound Lawson with the woman she had become; the woman he had so callously demeaned. She chose her outfit carefully from her closet, a black curve-loving silk sheath. It hugged her body in every place that mattered. A pearl necklace with matching earrings and bracelet, a 25th birthday present from her brothers, complimented the round-necked dress. She smiled, pondering her brothers' good taste; the oval-shaped pearls dazzled. After putting on the jewelry she retouched her make-up one last time.

Examining her reflection in the mirror, she held her head back, shaking her mane until it fell just right below her waist. She slipped her feet into black leather pumps, pulled on her full-length brown mink coat, and grabbed her purse. Another quick glance in the mirror assured her that she was still traffic-stopping gorgeous.

She stepped into Sparks acceptably late. She spotted Lawson standing at the bar. Immediately, she felt irritated that he had not waited for her in the entrance area. She quickly shoved the annoyance away. *You have not seen this man in eight years, nothing he does should bother you.*

She thought to walk into the bar, but intuition held her there in the lobby to witness his interaction with a woman sitting on a stool. The two laughed merrily, and as he threw his head back in gaiety, Lawson spotted Marloe in the foyer. *Same old Lawson. Women follow him like bees to honey, he loves it.* He walked towards Marloe with a grin; his eyes drinking in her presence.

"Hey Marloe, how are you? I was getting a little worried that you may have changed your mind." He leaned his lanky frame down and pecked her softly on the cheek. "It's so good to see you again," he took her hands in his. "You look more beautiful than ever."

She ignored his reference to her being late. *Just like him to think I would beat him here, still arrogant.* "Hello Lawson. I'm fine, thank you. Time has been kind to you as well." She tried to sound unmoved as butterflies flitted every which way in her belly like they had no place to land.

"I had a really busy day." *It's not an out-and-out lie since work is hectic right now.* But she had left the job early wanting to arrive looking breathtakingly fabulous. She knew the tactless foe she faced in Lawson, and she was determined that before the night was over, she would beset his mind with desire for her.

To quietly lure him in and then toss him to the wind like a fluttering leaf would be the greatest revenge. Her body shivered with the sweetness of the thought. *But you're a Christian,* her inner conscience whispered. *Let God take care of it.* God would fight her every battle. That is what Marloe heard all of her life, but she had skillfully learned to compress that idea over the years. Her church family would never suspect that obedient, charming little Marloe Vain had a ravenous dark side. Deep within her core there laid a malady of bitterness that craved retribution. *Yes, my brothers tore you up that night, but now it's my chance to settle the score my way.*

"I'm just glad you made it. Come with me love," Lawson took her hand. He led the way to the lounge where soft melodies oozed from the jazz band. It had been some time since she dined at Sparks. A sudden wave of memories enveloped her, taking her back to the James'

Supper Club. *No time for that. You know what you have to do.* She pushed the remembrance away and hardened her heart. As the band played, by the time they finished their dinner of tossed salad, lobster, and Dom Perignon champagne, the lounge was full.

The two caught up on life; his NFL career, her aspirations for Vain Limo Services and beyond, and talk of mutual friends from childhood. The uncustomary glass of champagne chased her anxiety away. Lawson's hazelnut eyes danced as he spoke. *This would be so much easier if he weren't so breathtakingly handsome.* Still, she marveled that she did not feel the intense, almost tangible attraction for him that once captivated her very essence.

A wave of melancholy hit her as the reality of what she once believed to be true love was destined for destruction from the beginning. For when it came to matters of the heart, she understood that Lawson was not trustworthy. *Yes, we've talked about everything, everything except the thing that tore us apart. He said he wants to clear the air, um huh.*

As she smiled at Lawson, his look turned serious. "Marloe, listen. I'll be staying in Potter's Edge for some time, maybe for good."

"What? Oh, Lawson," she laughed lightly. "You can't be serious; you're famous. Potter's Edge will bore you with its quiet lifestyle."

He shook his head, taking her hand. "Mar, my career is over. Injuries have taken me out of the game. I'm washed up professionally." He looked crestfallen; his eyes becoming moist. "If there's any chance in the world that you and I could…"

This was the moment she waited for. She squeezed his hand tightly and gazed into his eyes. The lie, dripping from her lips like the sweetest nectar. *I want you to remember how it feels for someone to look you in the eye and lie, like you did to me.*

"I have to confess that I've thought about you many times, and how it would feel to be with you again."

For a moment she thought tears would spill from his eyes. He gripped her hand tightly. "Marloe baby, you don't know how happy this makes me. Just the thought of us spending time together gives me hope. I never stopped loving you. Wherever I was, you were never far from my thoughts. You're the only one that can save me from..."

She moved in close to his face and planted a soft kiss to his cheek. "Let's dance," she whispered. They walked to the dance floor hand-in-hand. *This is going to be too easy. So, he thinks he can come back here broke-down from his career and pick up where he left off? What nerve? Perhaps his war with the rest of my family is over, but not with me.*

Chapter 12

"ROSETTE, PLEASE COME WITH BAILEY ON Sunday," Sweetnin' pleaded with Rosette on the telephone. Her sister-in-law called to tell them Annie Kate had arrived safely to her house from Kinsey. "Mama wants to see you, we all do, Rosette."

If someone had earlier told Rosette that she and Sweetnin' would engage in such civil conversations of late she would have dismissed them as being a few cards short of a deck. She was in a quandary, ruminating over whether or not to forgo a visit to Calgon, which would also mean squandering another opportunity to visit Vessie's grave. Her one and only memorable visit to Sweetnin's home had been her last.

As coincidence would have it, her sister-in-law had done an about face. Her loathing abruptly crested following her son Hershel's sudden marriage and a baby girl was shortly born. With the birth of a granddaughter Sweetnin' slipped back to the verge of lunacy. But this time the subject of her ire was within her immediate family. *After all these years, she still believes in that curse. She'd rather continue driving herself crazy then trusting in the word of God.*

Rosette's first inclination was to rub Sweetnin's nose in her 'misfortune.' She wanted to badger her in the same despicable manner done to her when Marloe was born. *You got a girl, so what will you do now Sweetnin'? This time it has nothing to do with Dunney blood, huh?* She had ached to throw it in Sweetnin's face after all the malice Sweetnin' spewed her way over the years. But instead, with fervent prayer, that right part within her that wished to abide by the Bible triumphed over her fleshly desires. *God fought this battle.* It had been a lengthy wait, but she had not tarried in vain.

"Alright I'll come," Rosette carefully responded to Sweetnin's request. She had grown to love Annie Kate dearly, and that love in part caused her to accept the invitation. As always, Annie Kate came north to see Sweetnin's family through yet another 'crisis.' But the root of Rosette's decision was to assuage her guilt for failing to visit her mother's grave. She longed to touch the ground where Vessie lay, but shadows of her past kept her away.

Even now it seemed more than she could bear to return to the place where such odious memories abounded. At times they played in her head with yesterday's clarity. Dreams filled with murky images of the twins. Their bony hands reaching for her as she fell screaming from some mysterious mountaintop. Like a swirling tornado, she whirled through a midnight abyss awakening winded and filled with unspeakable fear. *Justa and Jessie, what became of them? I wonder if they think of me as often as I think of them.*

God's word and the passage of time had mellowed her resentment towards her sisters. She now understood they were all victims of desperate circumstances; she had unfairly blamed them for her mistakes. And, in spite of her previous efforts to cut them out of her heart her love for them would last to the grave. As years passed, Rosette vicariously kept them alive in her thoughts. Afraid she might stumble about her early life; she held acquaintances at a distance. As a result, she had not one close confidante.

While the children were growing up, she had submerged herself into their lives. But they were now adults with busy lives of their own, and the loneliness that permeated her being now was difficult. As a deterrent, she focused her energy into converting their home into a beautiful showcase, a resplendent contradiction to her marriage.

At times happy childhood memories overpowered melancholy remembrances. It warmed her heart when she thought of how her sisters sought to shield her from wicked insults hurled at them as youngsters. Both twins inherited Vessie's feisty personality and flung strings of retorts back at whoever dared to antagonize them. They could also be generous. One particularly lean Christmas somehow the twins scraped together a few dollars and gave it to Vessie to buy Rosette a doll.

"'She deserves it,' Rosette heard them speaking to Vessie. 'Rosette is smart and gets good grades. Let her have a good Christmas.'"

Rosette remembered the words that became her mother's mantra when she fell ill. "'Girls, you only have each other, always stick together.'" Her sisters could be deceased for all she knew. She shook her head, attempting to rid herself of that dreadful thought. *Maybe I can find them; perhaps it's not too late. But they may not want to see me. After all, I walked away without so much as a "goodbye."* Rosette was filled with remorse for her actions.

Bailey had recovered enough to drive short distances; but the two-hour drive to Calgon could be challenging for him. *Although he would never admit it, he'll need me along for the trip. Hopefully, he won't mind stopping at Tower Cemetery.* The notion of being in Calgon once again sent a chill down her spine. But the gratification of paying homage to her mother overpowered her fear. She swallowed deeply and wondered why guilt and regret had not yet killed her.

~ ~ ~ ~

Bailey's heart hammered in his chest; he clutched the telephone receiver tightly.

"Alright brother, I found out some information on the twins," Sweetnin' sounded excited on the other end of the line. Bailey was overjoyed that she responded back to him so quickly. When he approached her a week earlier with the idea to search for Rosette's sisters, she quickly advised him that she heard the Dunney twins moved out west many years earlier. Bailey was thankfully aware that the 'Shack' was leveled and replaced with a grocery store.

In addition, Sweetnin' let him know that everyone affiliated with the lowly little tavern had either died or left town. Therefore, leads to the twins' whereabouts appeared a dead end. She had promised to check further, so Bailey felt confident that she had information but was it positive? Sweetnin' was well-known in Calgon from her previous employment at Beck's. She was also happily nosey.

Bailey took a deep breath before speaking, feeling eager and fearful at the same time. "Well, come on sister; tell me what's going on?" He wanted to bombard Sweetnin' with questions that tumbled around in his head all that week. But he knew his sister; to rush her could create a bastion of purposeful delays. She liked feeling important. Still, he had hope. For all the years she offended Rosette, this appeared to be an effort to alter her wrongdoing.

His own shame was enormous for allowing his family to treat Rosette so terribly; he knew his transgression was great. Even after his close brush with death he had held on to stubborn pride. But somewhere during his odyssey to recovery God cured the volcanic unforgiving sting to his ego, healing him both physically and mentally. Rosette's faithfulness in nursing him back to health forbade him to one day die with such a wedge between them. *Surely, hell will be my home if I don't try to set things straight.*

"Good news Bailey," his sister's raspy voice brought him back to their conversation. "My friend Ester still works for Motor Vehicle. She did some checking around and found out the twins lived out west for a time, but later moved back east to Shomson, here in Jersey."

Bailey's heart bounced with joy. *Thank you, Jesus!* However, that achingly methodical part of him needed reassurance that what Sweetnin' said was true. "Shomson, that's just 30 minutes or so west of Calgon. Was she sure Sweetnin'?"

"Bailey, stop worrying. Ester was always a sleuth. Between the two of us on our jobs we knew just about everybody around, and most of their business. Now, you didn't think I would drop it there, did you? I called the station and asked if ya'll travel as far as Shomson? Now, of course I know you do. But see I needed more information, and the station has phone books for all the surrounding areas. I talked to Margaret, disguised my voice a little so she wouldn't know me. She said, "'Yes, of course, what street?'"

Bailey chuckled at his sister's creativity. He was also delighted to hear her laugh, however short-lived it might be. He had come to understand that every good thing that came Sweetnin's way she downplayed. But any problem, no matter how trivial, she embellished it, languished in it. At that moment, they played a game of baseball, Sweetnin' had rounded third base, and as badly as he wanted her to make it home, he did not interrupt.

"I said to Margaret, I'm not sure of the street, but could you tell me if you have a listing for a Justa or Jessie Dunney? I got a number Bailey, a listing for Justa Dunney!"

Bailey's hands shook. He gripped the line tightly, sucking in his breath, exhaling in relief. "Thank you, Lord." He grabbed a paper and pen by his bedside table. "I'm ready, what's the number?"

Sweetnin' called out the telephone number.

"You don't know how much this means to me Sweetnin.' Thank you, sister."

"I'm glad I could help Bailey. And I think I do know what it means to you. H-How much it means to me. I believe the Lord will lead you to them."

Bailey buoyantly hung up, astonished at the optimistic outcome. Still, he hesitated. He never heard Rosette voice any desire to see her family. However, it seemed obvious from the restive dreams breaking her sleep that the need was paramount. He was that captive audience as Rosette tossed and turned through the night, mumbling her mother's name. Undeniably, Bailey knew he had caused Rosette many tears, and much of her sadness came from isolation. She had no blood relatives except her children to love and who loved her dearly. Yet, he could imagine the agony she felt living in the shadows of his family as well as living a loveless marriage with him.

He placed the paper with the number on the dresser, as he did so he caught sight of his reflection in the mirror. The bitter-looking image that stared back at him was stunning in its reality. During his bout of sickness and recovery he seemed to have aged overnight. His curly brown sprinkled-with-salt hair was now a distant memory, replaced by bristly silver strands. His jaws sagged, and he wore a look of smelling something rotten.

I've been a fool. Rosette stood by my side and showed me her love in so many ways. I was so wrong. Perhaps it will ease her loneliness if I can bring her and her sisters together. He decided to call them first without telling Rosette. He didn't want to give her false hope should things turn out negatively.

~ ~ ~ ~

The woman who answered his knock on the door looked slender and drawn, but familiar luminous doe-eyes stared at him in uncertainty as he stood on the doorstep. She looked hardened, but the resemblance to Rosette was striking. Bailey introduced himself and the woman threw both hands over her mouth, gawking at him in disbelief. He extended his hand and felt hers tremble as their hands clasped in a handshake.

"C-Come in." She stretched the door wide and beckoned with her other hand for him to enter the home. "Justa," she yelled towards the hallway as Bailey stepped inside. She quickly shut the door. "Justa, come to the front room," she shouted. "Mr. Vain is here, the gentleman that called." She continued gazing at him in awe.

He now knew that she was Jessie. Suddenly, her eyes swept over the polished room, as if making sure it was suitable for a guest. "Have a seat Mr. Vain. Would you like something to drink sir, water, coffee?"

He could tell she was uncomfortable and attempted to put her at ease. "Thank you. I'll have water, but only if you promise to call me Bailey," he smiled at her warmly.

Jessie smiled back, nodding her head in agreement. She headed for the kitchen just as Justa entered the living room. If he thought Jessie looked worn out, Justa was the picture of failing health. Limp salt and pepper hair hung haphazardly to her shoulders in much the same way her dress hung too big for her thin body. She coughed; a deep gut-wrenching hack that seemed to shake all of her.

Bailey stood, and after their introduction she wearily sat down on the sofa. She eyed him wistfully; her huge eyes empty and filled with a pain that Bailey was sure went beyond the physical. He again took his seat.

Jessie came back with a tray and three goblets filled with water, each topped with a slice of lemon. Bailey took a glass. Jessie placed the tray on the sand-colored wooden coffee table. She then took a seat beside Justa on the sky-blue, plastic covered three-piece sectional sofa.

Gasping for breath, Justa spoke slowly, her eyes penetrating Bailey's. "Is it true you're married to Rosette, our sister?" She went into a jagged cough, covering her mouth with a cloth. Jessie rubbed her shoulders, glancing at Bailey. He would give them both the answers he knew they desperately wanted to hear. Questions about Rosette bounded off their lips as if they ran from a fire. Minutes grew into hours, with Jessie putting together a lunch of tuna sandwiches and tossed salad. As they ate and talked, Bailey felt easy with them. There was an earthiness about the sisters, no airs. They were just two unpretentious women who appeared to have had many hard knocks in life but had somehow met the challenges with courageous resilience.

When he shared that he and Rosette were parents to three children Jessie squealed with pleasure. Justa's eyes grew wide with wonderment. She loudly cleared phlegm from her throat, and suddenly began weeping softly.

"We missed Rosette so much," she halted between tears. "Me and Jessie tried to find her, but it was like she dropped off the face of the earth."

Jessie nodded in agreement as she comforted her sister with a hug. "Rosette was angry when Mama died; angry at us for good reason." Her voice trailed to a whisper. "Bailey, does she really want to see us?" Shame filled her eyes. She hung her head.

The question caused a knot of uncertainty in Bailey's chest. The truth was he did not know for sure how Rosette might react. Neither did he want to lead her sisters down a blind alley. "She wants to see you, even though she may not realize it. She doesn't know about any of this, my visit. I'll talk to her first and then give you a call."

"I sure would love to see Rosie before I leave this earth," Justa's voice filled with melancholy. "I pray that God will grant it."

"Me too," Bailey said, taking his leave from their home.

Chapter 13

I T WAS A BRISK SUNNY AFTERNOON WHEN BAILEY AND
Rosette made it to Calgon that Sunday. Almost looking
away when they reached the locale of the 'Shack,'
Rosette forced herself to look there. *I have to conquer that
fear*. Still, the memory of the shabby nightclub burned into
her brain as though branded like cattle. She breathed a sigh
of relief when they turned the corner of Dalton Street, away
from the area. *Thank you, Lord*. Bailey shot her a look of
concern. Rosette marveled to herself that after so many
years, he still had the power to make her heart turn over
with adoration. Lately, he had shown signs of the Bailey
she first married. But she did not trust that it was for keeps.

"You alright, Rosie?"

"Yes, I'm okay, thank you."

"It won't be long before we make it to Sweetnin's." he
assured her.

Rosette nodded and settled back in her seat. *I know*. Her
stomach turned at the thought. *It will be alright. God will
help me through it.*

The dark circles under Sweetnin's eyes did not surprise
Rosette. It was obvious the woman had taken herself to hell
and back a million times. As she gave Sweetnin' an
obligatory embrace, she asked God to forgive her for her

lack of pity. She hugged Annie Kate tight, wrapping her arms around her mother-in-law, becoming alarmed at Annie Kate's obvious weight loss. Thinning gray hair pulled up in a familiar bun now replaced her once thick, luxurious mane. Within the past six months since they last saw her in New Jersey, it was apparent that Annie Kate's health declined. The look on Bailey's face told her that he too was troubled with Annie Kate's appearance.

Fragility aside, Annie Kate clearly was not yet ready to relinquish her role as family matriarch. She clucked and fawned over everyone as always, especially Bailey, going on about his rapid recovery. Rosette sat quietly on a nearby sofa, fighting the surrealism of being in Sweetnin's abode once again. She inhaled deeply, suppressing her inner demons. *Just a few hours here and we'll be leaving. Bailey promised to take me to the graveyard today. I'll feel better once we're out of here.*

At that moment Bailey engaged in conversation with his mother about her future welfare. "Mother, I want you to sell the house and move in with us. We have plenty of room. I'm not taking no for an answer this time."

In truth, Rosette would welcome Annie Kate into their home. In fact, it had been a running thread of conversation throughout the years, but Kate had always won out. Even with Marloe moving back home into the guest suite they certainly had plenty of room. Rosette observed Annie Kate as she eased her thin body down onto the sofa. She looked drained; her face a sweeping roadmap of the ups and downs of her life.

Sweetnin' was surprisingly reticent on the subject of Annie Kate moving north. She had always pulled Annie Kate in her direction, determined that she spend the majority of her time with her family in Calgon when she visited Jersey. *With the new baby girl, and two of her own children still living at home, I doubt if she has room to spare.*

Through the years Annie Kate gave them her many reasons for remaining in Kinsey. Uppermost was to stay near Bailey Sr.'s grave to provide perpetual loving care. She was also an active church mother, enjoyed tending her garden, and had formed close friendships with neighbors. But this time, to Rosette's astonishment, Annie Kate sat quietly, nodding her head in agreement with Bailey.

"Let's get you moved as soon as possible; we can rent your house out for the time being." Rosette heard the relief in Bailey's voice.

She reflected on how generously Annie Kate had given of herself to her family over the years. Even knowing the stain of Rosette's past, she had always treated her kindly. Never judging, but always looking to God for a solution. *Yes, it's time for us to take care of Annie Kate.*

Rosette's eyes filled with tears as her memories of caring for Vessie during her illness came to mind. *Annie will be alright, she's just older now, tired, that's all. Thank God her financial situation is different than Mama's. We'll make sure she receives good medical care.*

~ ~ ~ ~

The drive to the cemetery was interesting. Bailey had been upbeat all day, happy-go-lucky. On occasion he showed that playful side of himself that Rosette loved; lighthearted teasing, making her laugh. But she could not fully succumb to his recent show of affection because of her troubled spirit. *How can I call myself a true Christian? Wanting forgiveness from Bailey, but I couldn't forgive my own flesh and blood. I'm no better than him.* She glanced at Bailey as he maneuvered the car through the busy streets.

"Ten minutes and we'll be there," he said, glancing at Rosette.

There he goes again looking at that watch. Maybe I should ask him if he needs to get back to Potter's Edge by a certain time. No, I'm sure he would have told me. I'm here and I need to visit Mama. It's been too long. She sat back in her seat and prayed for a peaceful heart.

~ ~ ~ ~

If there was such a thing as a beautiful gravesite, *Tower Cemetery* was certainly one. The lush evergreen lawns were impeccably manicured. Rather than a headstone, each grave housed a flat memorial marker. *We couldn't have wished for a nicer resting place for Mama.* She thought of how costly it must have been for Edgar "Stump" Lester to pay for all of Vessie's end-of life expenses. *Stump loved Mama like a sister.* Vessie endeared herself to him and many 'Shack' patrons with her quick wit and easy smile. She was lovingly loud with a generous heart.

As a child, Rosette did not appreciate her mother's gift of giving. In fact, it enraged her. They barely had enough food to sustain themselves. Yet, she watched with livid anger as Vessie stretched a pot of chicken soup to include a friend in need on more occasions than she could count. Vessie's preparation of soul food dinners at the club: fried chicken, collard greens and cornbread, brought the club extra business. Rosette had heard rumors that Stump would provide Vessie with finances to open her own restaurant, which never materialized. Meanwhile, household bills were due. She had to provide for her children and cook's pay was just not enough. So, Vessie found herself...

~ ~ ~ ~

They entered the cemetery, Rosette turned right with Bailey at her heels. The scene of visiting Vessie's grave had played a thousand times in her head. When she found Vessie's grave marker, she dropped to her knees, overwhelmed with emotion. She had never forgotten the spot. With silent tears she fingered her mother's name on the emblem, Vessaria Mae Dunney, 1900 – 1934. The center of the plaque housed a heavy stone vase for placement of fresh flowers. Bailey bent down with his handkerchief and gently wiped Rosette's tears away. Under one arm he held a beautiful bouquet of red roses.

"Let me pull the vase up," he offered. He then handed Rosette the flowers and she centered them in the container. Bailey helped her to her feet.

Rosette noticed two women walking towards them from the gate. *I wonder who they lost,* she thought sadly. She contemplated on how death left loved ones behind with the weary task of carrying on without them. She had climbed the tallest mountain that day and, thus far, descended unscathed. *I came back to Calgon, and I visited Mama's grave, things I couldn't do for years. Yes, perhaps now I can move forward without so much guilt. Thank you, Father.*

Bailey took her hand gently and guided her a few steps away. The two women were now a stone's throw away. Rosette graciously stepped back a few more feet, believing Bailey nudged her to let the ladies move closer to the gravesite of their loved one,

Bailey's face suddenly lost its color, striking fear in Rosette's heart. *Please Lord: don't let him get sick again, not when we may be working things out.*

"Bailey, don't you feel well. What's wrong?"

"R-Rosette, listen to me," he stammered, taking her hands in his. "I should have told you, but I just didn't know how."

"Tell me what?" Now she was truly concerned. "Bailey, what is it; are you sick?"

"Look behind you Rosette."

She turned quickly to see both women a few feet behind her with their arms linked together. They held their heads down, and one hacked a bottomless cough. The woman with the sickness looked up, tears streamed down her face. Rosette glanced at Bailey still confused, to her relief the color had somewhat returned to his face. Her mind played tricks on her when she again faced the weeping woman. *Am I delusional, it looks like...*Rosette measured her steps as though she were on a tightrope, easing closer to the women. A plethora of ecstasy raced through her body. She was rail thin, but no one had more pronounced eyes than Justa. *Oh my God. Please tell me I'm not dreaming!* Her body trembled, but not from the cool weather.

All doubt left when Jessie looked up. Rosette's world became surreal. The three stared at each other for what seemed an eternity. Justa's choking cough broke the vacuum of time separating them, transporting them back to reality. Soul stirring screams of joy erupted, followed by glorious tears. The three women enveloped each other, holding on for dear life.

"R-Rosie," Jessie cried, as she attempted to wipe away Rosette's tears with a hanky. "Look at you little sister. You're still beautiful. Somehow, I knew you would be alright, but we missed you so much. Love you so much. I'm sorry baby. Please forgive us for the wrong we did when mama was sick. I'll regret it for the rest of my life. Rosie, we tried to find you so many times. After so many years we gave up, thinking we'd never see you again."

The guilt that Rosette felt threatened to disarm her from the reunion that she so yearned for with her sisters. Truly, she had forgiven them, but not herself for judging them so harshly. *What gave me the audacity to pass judgment on them when I was just as guilty? What, because I wasn't out there long?*

"No Jessie," she regained her resolve to forgive. "I'm asking you both to forgive me for being so hardhearted. I was wrong, and I'm sorry. As I grew older, I realized that we were so young when Mama got sick, we had no guidance in a lot of ways."

Justa bent her head. "Dear God, Rosie, it was so painful watching Mama dying. The 'Shack' became our escape. We should have been stronger for you. I have never forgiven myself for being so selfish. It's such a hurtful memory for me."

Rosette stared lovingly at her sisters, basking in the miraculous wonder of seeing them once again. *We're together again devil. That's all that matters.* For the first time in a very long time her heart filled with joy, not grief. She would not let anything rob her of that. The sisters locked arms in a circle, something they did as children.

"I know mama is smiling down from heaven right now," Rosette said.

"That was mama's wish, for us to always stick together," Justa's voice broke.

"And that's what we're going to do for the rest of our lives," Rosette replied.

"It's wonderful, I'm so happy Bailey found us," Jessie spoke gaily. "Oh, my goodness, it was such a shock when he called and said who he was, you know? That he thought it would be good for all of us to mend fences. He seems like a nice man Rosie."

Rosette looked around for Bailey and saw him walking towards the car; her heart fluttered with love. *He left so we could have privacy.* She swallowed the sudden lump in her throat. *Yes, he's stubborn, but he's still a good man. He promised to take care of me, and he has. He's given me everything... except the full return of his love. But he did this for me. He found my sisters.*

"Yes, he is a good man," she said softly. "I'm sure he told you we have children, two sons and a daughter, no grandchildren yet. But enough about me," she laughed. "I'm anxious to hear about your lives."

"I never married," Justa spoke between profuse coughing. "Had some boyfriends, but it just didn't work out for me that way. But Jessie married Morris Lester, Stump's son, remember him?"

"Oh sure, yes, I do," Rosette said. "He was a lot older than any of us as I remember." *And kind of hard to look at too*, Rosette smiled inwardly.

Jessie chimed in. "Yes, he was older, but it seems like we have something in common little sister." She snickered, pointing to Bailey's car.

Rosette laughed. "Well, I guess you told me. Yes, Bailey is quite a few years older than me." They laughed easily and the years of separation rolled away.

"Morris had a head full of big ideas," Jessie continued. "It didn't make any difference to him about any wrong I had done. He decided we should move out west to get a fresh start; said that's where it was 'happening.' He borrowed money from Stump to open a restaurant in Las Vegas. Justa moved with us, and we did well with the business for about ten years."

She dropped her head and took a deep breath. "Then one day Morris had a stroke, right at the restaurant. I found him dead on the kitchen floor. That was a horrible time for us. I couldn't bear to walk in the place anymore, so I sold the restaurant, and we moved back east. Anyhow, Justa and I were never that fond of the West Coast."

Justa's eyes beamed bright with excitement. "God double blessed Jessie because when Stump died, he left the 'Shack' to Morris. When Morris passed, it went to Jessie. Morris was a good man, and he loved Jessie to death."

Jessie quietly nodded her head. "And I loved him. I found a buyer pretty quickly for the restaurant, made a little money on the sale and split it with Justa. Sometime later I bought a twenty-room motel in Shomson. It came with a small house on the property for maintenance workers; that's where Justa and I live. We did all the cleaning and laundry ourselves for years and hired a repair man to come in when we needed it."

Justa coughed deeply, hard, attempting to clear the raspy mucus that sounded glued to her throat when she spoke. "W-Well I don't do much cleaning now because I'm sick and weak, but Jessie hired a few ladies to help out."

So, they had done alright, the thought comforted Rosette. But she worried about Justa. Her cough was reminiscent to Vessie's in the latter days of her illness. *I'll bring her to Potter's Edge to my doctor for a second opinion. I can't lose my sisters now that I've found them again. Thank you, Jesus!*

Chapter 14

IT WAS SATURDAY. SYRIL DROPPED BY HIS OFFICE TO GET a head start on documents for Monday's meeting. Since his encounter with the gorgeous woman at the taxi station in New Jersey he found it difficult to concentrate on work. Never in his 31 years of life had he seen such a ravishing creature. *Marloe Vain.* From hair tumbling down her back in beautiful chestnut ringlets, to coal-black eyes dancing with the confidence of her stunning splendor, she had literally taken his breath away.

But in that same inhalation he perceived her to be arrogant. Her world was one that undoubtedly revolved around 'all things Marloe.' *No thank you, I've been down that road.* He had nearly married Olive Caster a few years earlier. Love had blinded him from her deeply ravenous nature. He was smitten not only by her beauty, but by a heart that he believed mirrored his own. The two met during his last year of law school and her first. After graduating he landed an internship at Fox & Moore, a distinguished law firm located in uptown Harlem.

He proposed to Olive six months into the relationship, but too late he realized like cotton candy, she tasted sweet, but had no substance. Olive wanted everything; and so vast was his love for her that he sought to provide the possessions that made her happy. She saturated her body in stylish clothing at the expense of his wallet. With adoring innocence, he financed her engagement gift, a brand new 1972 white Corvette. Olive's insatiable appetite for the high life soon put a drain on his bank account as well as his emotional stability. Yet, he was powerless to give her up.

The kick in the teeth came out of left field. Olive broke off the engagement leaving him with a mountain of debt. Shortly thereafter she married Larry Dulles, part owner of a celebrated law firm, Dulles & Banks.

In short, she ran with the highest investor, abandoning Syril when her "investment" with him no longer brought the monetary returns she desired. Her cold-blooded deception left him with a fractured heart that time had yet to fully heal. *Um, that Vain girl has the same high-class strut, definitely trouble.* He dismissed the notion that something magical happened when they met. *Enough of this, I better call Lawson and remind him about Monday morning.*

"Hey man, my car is in the shop. I'll be coming in on the train Monday morning on a tight schedule. We need to start the proceedings on time since I have to be back in Harlem by three o'clock. If we start at ten, we should be able to wrap up everything with the estate within a few hours. Please remind Ash."

"Ash is driving straight to the firm," Lawson advised Syril. "He's got some other business to take care of before our meeting. But we'll both be there on time. Hey, I can pick you up at the station. What time does your train get in?"

"Nine o'clock." Syril hesitated on the offer; his cousin Lawson was not known for dependability where time was concerned. *But it could save valuable time if he is on time.* Still, he oscillated. *The train could be late, or I might have to wait for a car at the taxi station.*

"Okay," against his better judgment he yielded to Lawson's suggestion. "But if you run into a problem call me before I leave home, that way, once I get into Potter's Edge, I can take a taxi to the firm."

"No, don't worry man. I'll be there on time; something I need to take care of in town that morning anyway. I can kill two birds with one stone."

"Alright, see you then." Syril hung up the phone, pushing away a twinge of misgiving for his decision. *It's better that way, best not to see her. I need to keep my mind clear of distractions, stay focused.* But even as he pondered the thought, he remembered how his blood raced with excitement as he looked into those vibrant midnight eyes.

A sudden cloud of grief settled on him. Images of his deceased aunt and uncle reeled in his mind. He sat down at his desk, placing his head in his hands. The cavernous void that the passing of his Aunt Dolly left filled him with unspeakable sorrow. She had been a tremendous force in his life; the only sibling of his mother, Alberta. Syril was just a baby when his father, Foster Barrett, perished in World War II. Stricken with double-pneumonia, Alberta succumbed to it in 1971.

Although Dolly too was encumbered with heartache, Syril credited her with helping him through the darkest period of his young life. Dolly was like a second mother, and now she too was gone. How incredibly lonely it felt without the two people he loved most in the world, never to feel their unconditional love again. *Why God? Aunt Dolly was so sweet and giving to a fault. All of the egregious behavior she endured from Uncle Jonas. She was like a saint.*

~ ~ ~ ~

Soon, Syril found himself lost in memories of the events that led to his ambivalent relationship with his Uncle Jonas and, the tense affiliation with his cousin Lawson. In Harlem, rumors of infidelity ran like wildfire about Jonas. The couple amassed a large network of friends and acquaintances as popular ballroom dancers. Nevertheless, Dolly had stiffened her back against the insidious gossip. She carried herself above the fray, determined to create the best life possible for her boys, Lawson, and Ashton.

After the couple retired from professional dancing they left Harlem for New Jersey, seeking a quieter lifestyle. Syril always suspected they moved to stifle the avalanche of tales about his uncle's questionable behavior. Being six years older than Lawson, Syril was well aware of the rampant grapevine. At age 16 he had a heated altercation with his uncle, a day he would never forget. During that period, the James family still lived in Harlem. Syril and Alberta took the subway from their apartment in East Harlem for a Sunday visit with Aunt Dolly and the family.

"'Get out Jonas!' he heard his aunt scream as they bounded the steps of the quaint brownstone owned by his aunt and uncle. "That girl got right in my face," Dolly continued. "Telling me you said you would leave me when the boys were older.'"

"'Aw, that's the biggest lie ever told Dolly. Those women just do that to get under your skin and you fall for it every time. I'm telling you the truth girl, and I'm not going anywhere. If anybody leaves this house, it will be you, and don't even think about taking my boys.'"

Alberta's feet froze on the steps, her face a massive jigsaw puzzle of confusion. Syril followed her cue, understanding her dilemma. To knock on the door would admit hearing the conversation, and to leave would suggest that she chose to look the other way.

A sudden gut-wrenching scream from the house pierced the air. So copious in nature was the sound that Syril felt he could reach out and touch his aunt's indescribable agony.

He stared at his mother, waiting for her to make the first move for the door.

"'Jonas, how can you do this to me?' Dolly shrieked. 'You say you love me...but I-I can't take it anymore. You've humiliated me for years. Does it even matter to you?'"

"'Dolly, haven't we had a good life? I've tried to give you and the boys everything you've asked for. But all you can do is nag me to death. There are plenty of women that would be happy to be in your shoes.'" His voice was loud and filled with self-righteousness.

Syril imagined his uncle behind the door, looming, threatening to his tiny built aunt. He had heard enough. He leaped up the last few steps with Alberta at his heels, pounding on the door. "'Open the door Aunt Dolly,' he shouted. 'It's me and Mommy.'"

He felt his mother at his back, her anxiety as close as the smoldering embers within him. The door swung open, and Jonas stood, tall and menacing. Syril peered beyond him to see Dolly sitting on the sofa sobbing. Ashton hovered by his mother; his face filled with bewilderment. Lawson stood beside Jonas at the door.

"'What are you banging on my door for like something crazy Syril? What's wrong with this boy, Bert?'" Jonas spewed his words at them.

Alberta ignored him, running to Dolly. It didn't matter that Jonas stood 6'4, and Syril was 5'9. He only knew that he wanted to wipe the haughty expression from his uncle's face with his fists. A torrent of pent-up bad feelings for the suffering of his aunt gave him courage to unleash his emotions.

"'We heard how you spoke to Aunt Dolly,' he shouted. 'You know she doesn't deserve that. She's never been anything but good to you.'"

"'Oh, you're trying to tell me how to run my marriage? You still got milk on your breath boy. What goes on in my house is my business Syril, you hear me?'"

"'Yes, I hear you,' but Syril didn't back down. Instead, he got as close as he could to Jonas, looking up, straight into his eyes. 'But if you make Aunt Dolly cry again and I hear about it, I swear, I'll make you pay'"

"'You'll do what?' Jonas's voice reeked of scathing pleasure. His long perverse laugh cut like a razor as he edged closer to Syril. 'Well, you've gotten a little too big for your britches son. I will wipe the floor with you. Matter of fact, Lawson could whip your skinny tail.'"

Apparently convinced that he had put Syril in his rightful place Jonas threw his head back, roaring with laughter. Syril glanced at Lawson in the same moment that a hint of smugness lit Lawson's face. It didn't surprise him. Lawson worshipped the ground Jonas walked on.

Jonas bent his head eye-level with Syril. "'Get out of my house Syril, and don't come back until you can show me some respect.'"

~ ~ ~ ~

Syril shook his head in an effort to rid himself of those ominous thoughts. Suddenly famished, he snapped his attaché case shut and closed up the office. It was three o'clock. As he walked the three blocks to Grace's Café, as much as he tried to allay thoughts of the past, they prevailed. He pondered their lives after that devastating encounter. His association with his uncle remained strained.

As for Lawson, the years proved that the apple did not fall far from the tree. He carried on his father's roving-eye legacy with attributes that put him ahead of the pack, being handsome, smart, and athletic. Ashton was clearly the lesser light of the two, borderline attractive; a bookworm standing in the shadow of his brother. Lawson had clearly stolen the family's gene pool of attractiveness, leaving Ashton the favor of inheriting Dolly's short slight frame.

Lawson's popularity with the opposite sex solidified itself early on. Syril stood in the wings; waiting for that ostentatious nature that he knew existed within Lawson to surface. He did not disappoint. Not long before his high school graduation, Lawson got himself in trouble with his high school sweetheart. It was the year Syril began law school at Syracuse University. Although they conversed about everything under the sun, Alberta was tight-lipped about that particular incident. Only when he pressed her did she reveal that Lawson had taken a hefty beating for some odious deed he committed against the girl.

Jonas sought to retaliate, but Dolly forbade it. The girl's family was well-connected, wealthy, and Dolly feared more harm might come to Lawson. So, the family physician came to the James' home and attended to wounds that had Lawson bedridden for weeks. Afterwards, he promptly left for Atlanta, Georgia to stay with close family friends until his first year of college at Morehouse began that September.

Following that incident, it appeared Lawson had learned his lesson. As far as Syril knew there were no flare-ups in college such as the one in high school. Still, whenever he saw his cousin during family get-togethers, Lawson never ceased to boast about his prowess with women. "I always get the girl," was his mantra.

~ ~ ~ ~

As for Syril, he was more introspective and intellectual with a heart bent towards the less fortunate. He understood scarcity which ultimately became his passion. He and Alberta came a long way since his childhood days of living in the Harlem River Houses. Alberta's "rent parties" were hugely popular and coupled with her in-home seamstress business, paid the rent. On Friday nights, Alberta and Dolly would transform Alberta's petite living room into a mini "Savoy Ballroom." They had survived the Great Depression, and for those who were financially pressed, the gatherings were a cheap escape from hard times. People from near and far came to "Bert's," hungry for the festive atmosphere, abundant soul food and drink.

As a young married couple in the 1940s, Jonas and Dolly frequented Harlem's Savoy Ballroom just about every Saturday night to swing dance. Their rhythm and grace on the dance floor caught the eye of a dance promoter. Soon they received an offer to join his dance ensemble and began touring the country. The monetary benefits were like a dream come true. Dolly gifted Alberta with start-up funds to open her own supper club, "Bert's at 125th". The large following built from her "rent party" years clamored to her new establishment along with many newcomers. It was a runaway success. New money flowed, Alberta and Syril moved to a swanky two-bedroom apartment near the business.

When Dolly's children came along, she and Jonas left touring and started their own local dance company, "James' Native Ensemble." This was their way of life for many years. Syril was sad when the James family moved to New Jersey upon their retirement. Although he did not miss his polarized relationship with Jonas, he sorely missed Dolly's presence in Harlem. She always looked out for his best interest and the feeling was mutual.

After beginning law school, on those rare occasions when he saw family, his conversation with Jonas was stilted. But his connection to Dolly never wavered. He called her faithfully every week. Lawson's first round draft pick to the NFL after graduating from Morehouse College, Cum Laude, was a time of great family elation. Ashton also attended Morehouse, graduating Summa Cum Laude. He settled in Meridian, Georgia to teach math.

~ ~ ~ ~

At Grace's Café Syril purchased his usual take out, an extra greasy cheese steak sub with fries. He then walked a few more blocks, boarding the train bound for his home in West Harlem. His conscience nagged him for allowing Lawson to pick him up on Monday. *That man will be late for his own funeral. But this is different. I can't imagine him not being on time for the estate settlement of his parents. Now Ashton, I can bet the farm he'll be on time.*

He shrugged his shoulders in an effort to think more positive thoughts. *We've been out of touch; perhaps Lawson's time-management is better these days.* He unlocked his apartment, vowing to catch up on deposition reviews, and to attain some much-needed sleep. Tomorrow was Sunday; church-day, a practice that Alberta and Dolly instilled in all of their children. No matter how much partying their parents did on the weekends, they were all in the "Lord's House" on Sunday morning.

Suddenly, the breathtaking aura of Marloe Vain's splendor flashed in his mind; the silky softness of her hand when they touched. He smiled within, remembering how flustered she became while attempting to remain professional. *A behavior in stark contrast to Olive's personality, nothing baffled her. Olive was like a lone shark in an ocean of guppies, consuming them all, one-by-one.*

He consoled himself that after settling Monday's business there would be no driving force to visit Potter's Edge. Hopefully, he would have his car back relatively soon. No reason to fret over the possibility of running into Marloe Vain again. His cousins no doubt would sell their family home. Upon his reading a copy of the Will, everything his aunt and uncle owned would be split down the middle between the two brothers. He devoured his food with a coke from the fridge and tried not to think about Monday because that led him to think of her.

~ ~ ~ ~

The train pulled into Potter's Edge station at eight-forty-five a.m. the following Monday morning. Syril breathed a sigh of relief. A seven-a.m. call that morning to Lawson assured him that he would be at the station to pick him up by nine. He strode off the train's platform and hurriedly made his way through the lobby to the designated area of the street for passenger pick-up and drop-off. It was sunny, but frigid, his coffee-colored cashmere coat and matching tam felt just right for the weather. Beneath his coat he sported a dark-blue double-breasted suit, complimented by Stacy Adams alligator loafers of the same color.

A quick glance at his watch advised it was nearing nine o'clock; a gnawing began in his gut. *Okay Lawson, where the heck are you?* Lawson would be driving Jonas' Cadillac. Dolly's crimson Mustang had been totaled in the deadly crash. Syril hastily walked the parameter of the area hoping to see Jonas' black Cadillac arrive with Lawson behind the wheel. But there was no sign of the car thus far.

If necessary, I can take a cab from Vain's and still make it there by ten. And that will have to be soon. He paced until 9:10, swearing under his breath. *Same old Lawson, when he said he had something to do in town I should have taken that as affirmation that he was singing the same old song.*

The last thing Syril wanted was to come off as irresponsible by arriving late at the law firm, word got around quickly in that world. He had taken great care in building a stellar reputation. As a result, he hoped to make partner that year with Fox & Moore. He pulled his hat down further from the glacial weather, enjoying the comfortable feel of his new shoes despite his irritation with Lawson. It had started years ago, his being keenly aware of his appearance whenever he and Lawson were together. He always felt he had to go the extra mile for anyone to notice he was "in the room." Lawson always appeared camera-ready no matter what he wore.

Checking his watch again Syril began a heated jog to the taxi station. When he arrived, he saw Jonas' shiny black Cadillac parked curbside. Anger sped his steps. *What the ...? Did I get it mixed up? Did we agree to meet at Vain's?* Even as he thought those words, he shook his head in denial. *That would be ridiculous, defeats the whole purpose. No, we specifically agreed that he would pick me up at the train station at nine.*

He entered the taxi station expecting to see Marloe at the center desk. He breathed a sigh of relief when another woman greeted him.

"Good morning, can I help you sir," she asked. "Do you need a car this morning?"

The sound of Lawson's laughter pulled his attention in that direction. He turned to see Lawson standing in the doorway of an office. He had his arm around Marloe's waist. Syril's fury was overridden by envy. It pulsed through his body like lightning as he observed the comfortable relationship the two apparently shared. Her eyes danced as Lawson leaned down, whispering in her ear. She threw her head back and laughed gaily. Both seemed oblivious to the world around them. Syril glanced at his watch. It was almost nine-thirty. They would never make it by ten. At that moment he despised Lawson for his carefree attitude.

The woman at the desk persisted. "Sir, would you like a car?"

"No thank you Ma'am." Swiftly, he walked towards his cousin. Lawson turned, when he saw Syril his smile quickly faded. His face became an enigma of apology.

"Hey Syril. Aw man, I'm so sorry. I started talking to Marloe and lost track of time. We can still make it on time. No worries, my man."

Not wanting to cause a scene, Syril managed to keep his emotions in check. Marloe stood to the side, beautifully attired in a red suit, her hair an elegant mass of cascading curls.

"Marloe Vain, meet my cousin, Syril Barrett. He's the uptight lawyer in the family."

She looked momentarily stunned, and then looked at Syril coolly. "Hello again, we met last week when Syril came in for a taxi. It's a small world, isn't it?" She sounded aloof. *Paying me back, I get it.*

"Good morning. Yes, so it is a small world. It's nice to see you again Miss Vain." He hoped to sound as indifferent as she.

He faced Lawson, still irritated enough to deck him. "Let's be on our way man." He could hardly wait to get in the car to give Lawson a piece of his mind. But even more so, he wished to abate the thrill that came over him when his eyes met Marloe's. Her gaze pierced straight to his soul, unearthing its vulnerability. *If only Lawson had stuck to the plan.*

"Have a good day Miss Vain," he said to Marloe.

"Please call me Marloe. You make me sound like a little old lady," she laughed. The sound of her laughter was lyrical, a melody of confidence and light-heartedness.

No faltering today, he thought. *Probably has something to do with Lawson's presence. If she wasn't one of Lawson's conquests, she was about to become one.*

"Sure, Marloe it is," he said. "Take care."

"Let's go man," Lawson playfully slapped Syril on the back. "We can make it there in twenty minutes cuz. You know how I drive. I'll call you later Mar." With that, he planted a light peck to her cheek. As Marloe escorted them to the door, Syril averted his eyes from her slender long-legged stride. He tried not to breathe in the intoxicating scent of her perfume.

~ ~ ~ ~

Her legs threatened to buckle as she bolted to her office and shut the door. Shaking like a wind-blown tree, Marloe sat down at her desk to gather her bearings. When her knees stopped knocking, she stood and circled the floor. *Lawson and Syril, cousins, how ironic.* While they slightly resembled, it was easy to see the striking differences in their personalities.

Lawson exuded a reckless self-confidence that complimented his athletic body and handsome face. However, as she discerned from her brief dialog with Syril, beyond his outward attractiveness was a strong, humble man. Despite the acidic tone of their first encounter he was clearly caring, smart, a lawyer.

Marloe shrugged her shoulders in an effort to disengage herself from vulnerable reflecting. She breathed deeply, once again sitting down at her desk. *Stop thinking weak. So, they're cousins. That's their problem. If Syril wants to come along for the ride, well...there's enough room in my treasure trunk for his recompense too.*

She pulled out her compact mirror to refresh her make-up. As her reflection stared back at her she calmed down, assured that she still had the goods for her next adventure. *It's all under my control.* Still, she felt uneasy, a foreboding of sorts. But she turned a deft ear to the Holy Spirit cautioning her that she was about to step into unfamiliar waters. She tucked the forewarning away as neatly as folding a hankie, placing it in her purse in favor of her all-consuming quest for revenge.

~ ~ ~ ~

Marloe picked at her salad with a fork at the restaurant. She didn't need food; she was full of all the things she needed to tell Jorene. Her friend sat across the table from her with wide-eyed anticipation, her cheeseburger, and fries uncommonly still intact.

"What in the world is going on Mar? You were so secretive on the phone. I know it's important since you called me for lunch on a weekday. And it must be about Lawson because girl you are glowing!"

Marloe waved one hand in the air in exasperation. It irritated her that Jorene remained infatuated with the idea that she and Lawson would once again become a couple. But their recent reunion had resolved any hope of that. Although there was a special place in her heart for him, love for him no longer lived there. She laid her fork down on the plate.

"Jorene, it really caught me by surprise. I-I mean, I always knew Lawson had relatives in New York, but never met them." A sweet little shiver ran up her spine as she thought of Syril with the dark scowl on his face that morning. *He looked so masculine.* This time his discontent had not been with her, but with Lawson.

"Rene, listen to me. Have you forgotten that Lawson ruined my life? Well, I blame myself too. But he made promises that he had no intentions of keeping. I know that now because he's still the same...I"

"Marloe," Jorene interrupted her. "Come on sweetie that was so long ago? You're not giving him a chance. He's obviously changed. With women chasing him all over the country, don't you think he could have married someone by now? He wants you Mar. He's waiting for you to realize you still love him."

"You're my best friend, but you don't understand do you Rene? You told me that there was power in my looks. Your words gave me confidence at a time when I had none. But one day my looks will fade, and so will my so-called 'power.'" She leaned in closer to Jorene. Her stomach slightly quivered. "I'm afraid of his cousin." There, she had said out loud the overpowering emotion hiding in her heart.

Jorene gave her a worried look. "Did something happen? You don't even know the man. Mar, has he threatened you in some way?"

Marloe quickly back peddled, needing to wipe the fear from her friend's eyes. "No sweetie, calm down, not a physical threat. It's just that I'm afraid of the way I feel when I see him. I somehow lose control in his presence. I've only seen this man twice and each time it's like my body turns to putty. I can barely breathe, and my heart goes crazy with some kind of mysterious pull. For eight years I've been able to handle any man I've dated and remained celibate. But when I see him all I can think of is how it would feel to be in his arms."

Jorene picked up her burger, hesitated on the first bite, and then sat it back on the dish. "It sounds like misplaced affection to me. You need a distraction from your true feelings for Lawson, so you're projecting them on to this person that you just met. It's called 'avoidance.'" She took a hefty bite of her sandwich, delicately eyeing Marloe.

Since the conversation was not in favor of Lawson, Jorene's assessment of the situation did not surprise Marloe. And although she loved Jorene like a sister, there was simply no way to make her understand her feelings.

"Chances are I may never see him again. He's come to town a few times to help Lawson and Ashton settle the family's estate. He's a lawyer in Harlem." She shrugged her shoulders, nibbling her suddenly tasteless salad.

"Be careful Mar. I couldn't bear to see you hurt again. You know you have to finish helping me raise them two little knuckleheads," Jorene laughed.

"Rene, no one will ever have the control to hurt me the way Lawson did. You know I don't let anyone get that close to me, never again. Don't worry. I was just a little caught off guard, but I can deal with it. I'll be fine Rene. I just needed to talk to you. Tell my babies I'll see them this weekend at church."

"Alright sweetie, love you," Jorene said.

"Love you too." They hugged as they parted. Marloe watched as Jorene boarded the local bus that would take her home. She had left the restaurant feeling somewhat melancholy, confused. *Perhaps Jorene is right. Maybe my old feelings for Lawson are hiding in there somewhere, and my mind is playing tricks. I've certainly learned to push things down.*

As she walked the four blocks back to her office the second glances and whistles began. Her spirits lifted; her stride became suddenly buoyant. To her, the attention she attracted was like a "Calling," a gift. After all, God had made her. The deeper issue was that she needed to get her feelings back in command. Somehow, the restraints that she had so carefully crafted around her heart seemed to be unraveling.

~ ~ ~ ~

During the heated ride to the firm that morning Lawson felt like a bird in a cage. Having to answer to people was not his forte. He glanced at Syril who sat stone-faced, angry, and spoke words that stung.

"This is something you asked me to do Lawson, and this is the thanks I get. You can't even pick me up on time? I thought you would have more respect for your parents; that you'd want to get this business taken care of as quickly as possible. If you had something to do that would throw you late, you should have said that man. I could have easily made my way like I always have."

Like I always have, here we go, Lawson thought. He was tired of Syril always playing the victim; that attitude had been a conscious idiom throughout their lives. Lawson and Ashton were perceived as being born with silver spoons in their mouths. Although Lawson received more of those expressions since he excelled academically and athletically. And while Ashton was a born scholar; sports was not his strong suit. Still, Jonas had ensured they kept level heads during their youth with assigned chores in and outside of the home. And he had not spared the rod.

Lawson was proud of his family's affluence; his parents had worked hard for everything they owned. They had even propped Aunt Bert up, helping her run her restaurant. Still, there was always an undercurrent of something that felt like resentment in Syril's attitude towards him. Syril was no shrinking violet when it came to intelligence. He received a full academic scholarship to college, earned a bachelor's degree in criminal justice and went on to complete law school.

Nevertheless, the backstory was the unspoken perception that Syril worked hard for everything he had, while Lawson played, and lived a life of luxury. To make matters more complicated, Jonas and Syril had a less than cordial relationship that, to Lawson's knowledge, never reconciled.

His parents' death was a living nightmare, no time to say goodbye, to tell them both how very much he loved them. As a child he believed his father rose and set the sun. Determined to emulate him, little did he know that his wish would come true. Unfortunately, the lust element that Jonas bequeathed to him, the sexual craving he was unable to rule, was his detriment. It was behemoth in its command of his father and caused his mother countless heartbreak. He adored Dolly, but his bond with Jonas caused him great parental conflict.

In the end, he gave up trying to understand his father since that would have required him to access his own less than admiral behavior in that respect. There were times when he longed to be more logical like Ashton or sensible like Syril, but the other component of his being was more powerful.

Sensible Syril, always on the up-and-up, trying to make everyone else the same way. Today he might have the right to be upset with me. I messed up, but what's the big deal about being a little late for the legal proceedings? So, we start a little late. It's no big deal. But that's Syril, always trying to be perfect, that's his problem.

"Syril, I had every intention of picking you up at nine, but I lost track of time, I apologize man. But hey, I think you're blowing this thing way out of proportion. They can't do a thing until we get there. They need us, remember?"

He laughed, and immediately regretted it when he saw the clench of his cousin's jaw. He would either blow up or shut down. The latter prevailed. Syril spoke not another word and the tension in the car was thick enough to actually make Lawson feel guilty. It settled around them like an ominous cloud about to dump buckets of rain on the world.

~ ~ ~ ~

The traffic leading to Baker Avenue was uncharacteristically slow. As they arrived at the entrance of the law firm, they were greeted by sirens from an ambulance pulling away from the curb. It was ten-thirty. Ashton stood near his car in the parking lot, his face filled with anxiety. The cousins bolted from the vehicle and rushed over to Ashton.

"Bad news," Ashton said, shaking his head. "Lamen Brown passed out in his office and was just rushed to the hospital."

Lawson glanced at Syril. He fought to contain his inward glee, not that he wished illness on anyone. But with all of Syril's irritation and attitude about being late, it appeared there would be no reading of the Will that day. He had even run a few red lights trying to make it as close to ten as possible. *I could have gotten a ticket. For what, now what have you got to say Attorney Barrett? Mr. Fix-everything, know-it-all, save-the-world, Syril.*

Syril looked stunned. "How terrible; when I saw him last Friday he looked well. Alright, clearly, we won't be conducting any business today. Let's go in and find out how we might work things out, set up a new date."

They entered the office and were greeted by Brown and Dunson's distraught, teary-eyed assistant. "Good morning. I'm sorry Mr. Barrett, but Mr. Brown was just rushed to the hospital. He may have had a heart attack. We'll need to reschedule the appointment. Mr. Dunson is in court today. I've checked his schedule for the rest of the week. It's possible he could meet with you on Thursday. I'm not positive though. I'll need to speak with him to confirm his schedule, especially in light of what's happened."

"I'm very sorry; I pray that all will go well," Syril said. He nodded in agreement with her assessment. "Well, since we don't know when Mr. Brown will return, if counselor Dunson is available on Thursday that might work. We'd still like to close this out as soon as possible."

"I understand sir."

Syril turned to Ashton. "Ash, I know you were planning to head back to Atlanta this evening. Can you stay in Jersey for a few more days?"

Ashton nodded in agreement. "Sure. I'll work it out."

"You okay with that Lawson?" Syril asked.

Lawson shrugged. "Yeah, sure, I'm going to be here indefinitely, so it's no problem."

Lawson couldn't wait to drop Syril off at the train station. Too much Syril in one day cramped his style. It wasn't that he did not have love for his cousin, they were blood; but they had never been on the same page about anything. Secretly, Lawson was glad for the miles that kept them apart while he lived in Atlanta. But for the immediate future the only thing separating them now was the Hudson River.

I know Mama loved me and Ashton, but her love for Syril was special. It was like she tried to make up for the father that Syril never knew. Pop never could form a close bond with Syril because there were issues that Syril just could not understand. I understood Pop well. But I refuse to go down that senseless road like him; controlled by lust. Marloe, if she was mine, I know I could control it. There is nobody finer than Marloe. If she hadn't come home early that summer, we would be married today. It's partly her fault, but she would never see it that way. I have to make her understand that she is the only one that can rescue me from myself.

~ ~ ~ ~

Syril would have known her lustrous stride anywhere although he had only laid eyes on her twice. Marloe Vain strutted confidently down the street headed in his direction, a vision of radiant beauty. He was walking towards the lobby area after Lawson dropped him off at the station, He had an hour to kill before the next train to the City. It was twelve-forty-five. In an effort to avoid Marloe he quickened his steps to turn at the next street. Too late, their eyes met. Hers unknowingly caused his heart to ache for the supple feel and touch of her. *I'll just speak and keep moving. No doubt she's rushing back to meet up with*

Lawson. He said he would stop by Vain's after letting me off. Yeah, he dropped me like I was the worst headache.

"Well, well, we meet again," Marloe cooed. She cupped her forehead from the intense sunshine, looking him dead in the eye.

"Hello Marloe. How are you?"

A hesitant smiled creased the corners of her mouth. "I'm fine; just finished lunch, heading back to work. You're already on your way back to New York? Lawson said the estate wrap-up would take a few hours. Looks like you all got done quite early."

I always get the girl, Lawson's infamous words echoed in Syril's head. *Well, nothing wrong with small talk, no harm, no foul.* Her curious gaze drew him in. "Yes, I'm on my way back to Harlem. Unfortunately, the attorney handling the estate became ill; our meeting is post-phoned. Did you have a nice lunch?"

As a criminal defense lawyer Syril worked grueling, draining cases, the source of his robust income. However, his pro bono work for tenants who fell below the poverty line was the occupation that brought him the greatest pleasure. Working with them he felt a sense of purpose.

On that day he had a four o'clock appointment with a few families who were in particular dire straits and needed his guidance to avoid eviction. Since he would now take the earlier train at one-forty-five there was no rush; he would make his meeting with plenty of time to spare.

Marloe's soot-colored lashes closed momentarily as she coyly looked down at the sidewalk. Syril's heart begged him to go out to play.

"Gee, I'm sorry to hear about the lawyer taking sick; I sure hope he's okay," she stated. "And yes, I had a very nice lunch with my best friend. We go way back, along with your cousin, Lawson. He was a year ahead of us in high school."

She looked uneasy. Syril recollected the high school incident that nearly cost Lawson his life. The lawyer in him wanted to interrogate, but he secured the urge as if he were at sidebar under the glaring eye of the judge. *Take it slow. It didn't have to be her.*

"So, you and Lawson have been friends for years, huh?" he remarked.

A whimsical smile crossed her face. "Oh, enough about me and my boring past, let's talk about you," she abruptly changed the subject. Where did you go to law school?"

"Syracuse University."

"Tough, wasn't it? I went to Rutgers, Douglass; straight through for a master's in finance."

"It was a rough road, but I expected that," Syril said. "Of course, the worst part was taking the bar exam. Hey lady, you weren't slacking either."

They laughed gaily as they walked.

"So, you went into the family business," Syril continued. "That's great. I've used Vain's services just a few times over the years. But most of the time I drive to Jersey, probably why we never met. Got some issues with my car lately, so I've been taking the train. I actually enjoy the ride because I can get work done during the ride in."

She smiled. "I wasn't sure if I would work in the family business. I briefly thought of nursing school, but I can't stand the sight of blood."

She threw her head back and laughed that delicious melodious sound that made his insides tingle. Olive was the barometer to which he now measured all women. She and Marloe had so much in common as far as looks and charm. Yet, he felt there was something deeply pure about Marloe that was void in Olive.

The car came out of nowhere. It sped through the street, clipping the sidewalk where Marloe and Syril walked. Instinctively, Syril reached out and pulled Marloe behind him, shielding her with his body. The caddy screeched to a halt a breath away from the curb. Lawson jumped out of the car, his face a mass of fury.

Syril stared at Lawson in disbelief. Anger overtaking him. His first thought was to clock Lawson in the mouth.

"What the hell is wrong with you Lawson, have you lost your mind?" he shouted.

"Don't you have a train to catch?" Lawson hurled salty words at Syril, staring him down.

And then it hit Syril. Lawson was jealous, foaming at the mouth with envy. *Isn't that a kick in the tail?* Indeed, something ominous was amiss. Syril never considered himself competition for Lawson when it came to women. But for Lawson to play a game with their lives because of unfounded resentment was totally bizarre.

"Since when do you question my whereabouts?" Syril yelled at Lawson.

"If that was your idea of a joke Lawson James, I am not laughing," Marloe screamed. Why would you do that? Are you crazy? You almost hit us!!

"Aww calm down, I was just playing, I had control," Lawson offered a sheepish grin, his anger subsided.

"The last thing I would do is try to hurt either of you. I had control all along. Mar baby, I stopped by your office, and they told me you went to lunch at the Atrium. I went there to surprise you; thought you would like a ride back. It's cold out here today."

"I like walking," she yelled, shaking her head. "If I wanted to drive, I would have done so."

Syril glanced at his watch. It was nearing twelve-thirty, time to go. His nostrils were still filled with the clean scent of Marloe's hair. His mind clouded with the cottony softness of her body when he pulled her out of harm's way.

"Well, time for me to catch my train. So long Marloe." He glanced at Lawson but said nothing.

"Thank you, Syril," she gave him a shaky smile. Her voice trembled and her beautiful bronze color had not yet fully returned.

"Are you okay?" he asked.

She nodded her head although her eyes did not agree. "Yes, I'm fine, thanks again. Take care Syril."

The irksome expression on Lawson's face told Syril he wanted him gone. He turned from them and walked the few feet to the stairwell that led to the trains. *Lawson has absolutely no common sense. He doesn't know how to treat women, especially a woman as special as Marloe.* She appeared to have the world by a string, intelligent, gorgeous, charming, but beneath her glorious laughter her eyes suggested a hint of private sorrow.

Initially, he regarded her as cocky, too many stark Olive features. But when her body touched his she felt as soft as silk. Someone that soft could not harbor a heart of ice. In contrast, Olive had not given herself time to be delicate, to soul-connect in their moments together. Later, he understood she had been busily mapping out plans to reach the lavish lifestyle she so desperately craved.

He settled back in the train seat and closed his eyes, seeking solace from the emotionally exhausting day. It seemed he might be back in Potter's Edge by the end of the week. His car would not be ready by then. He would need taxi service. Although he subliminally denied it, the best thing that came out of the day was talking to Marloe and the possibility of seeing her again.

Chapter 15

NOT AGAIN, MARLOE SIGHED. SHE SURVEYED THE newest vase of breathtaking beautiful red roses adorning her desk that morning. She didn't bother to look at the card, she knew who sent them. Since the near accident, fresh flowers arrived at her office each day from Lawson. Roses, carnations, tulips, gardenias, gorgeous arrangements aimed to melt her heart. But she would not take his calls, nor would she see him. She bent down to smell the sweet aroma of the luscious looking bouquet. Flowers from Lawson would have brought blissful tears many moons ago.

After Syril departed that day Lawson assured her that he had control of the car, telling her that his anger with Syril got the best of him. He wanted to shake Lawson up since they had words that morning. Ironically, it took years for Marloe to face her fear of seeing Lawson, and now that she had, she felt fearless.

Oh, I'll see him again, but in my own sweet time. He's not getting off that easy. In the short timeframe since they reconnected, she had begun to feel smothered. Lawson called frequently and started dropping in at the station unannounced. Oddly enough, his visits to her job seemed to always occur when her brothers were out. As much as she swore payback, Lawson's company was becoming excessive.

Working overtime, she closed the books for year-end. Once again confirming they were in the black. Through outstanding marketing and attentive customer service skills, the siblings grew the business into lucrative profit margins. Excelling in what Bailey envisioned for the company. For Marloe, their soaring success confirmed her value to the company.

Her six-figure salary afforded her the luxury of purchasing the finer things in life. Yet, there were times when carefree shopping sprees lost their appeal, becoming mundane, ordinary. Still, her desire for treasure in her trinket-trunk from suitors never waned. She wistfully examined the beautiful flowers that would shortly die. They overflowed atop the matching walnut-colored credenza and bookcase. She smiled ruefully. Who would remember or care that they once graced the room with such glorious splendor. No, trunk treasures were forever keepsakes, expensive trophies that would not fade away like morning dew.

~ ~ ~ ~

Words from the pastor's sermon of the previous Sunday echoed in her thoughts that evening during dinner with the family. "'Invest in others when trials come your way; you'll gain strength and forget your own troubles.'" Marloe had certainly become absorbed in her own personal turmoil of late. So much so that she had not given her mother's recent reunion with her sisters the attention it deserved. With supper over, she and Rosette washed up dishes and cleaned the kitchen. She studied her mother now as she moved through the kitchen straightening objects that were already in place. Bailey had retired to the bedroom to read his Bible as he did each evening.

"Mother, everything is spotless. Come. Sit down, relax. Let's talk."

She felt Rosette's curious gaze as she walked to the kitchen table where Marloe sat. This was the way she had longed to see her mother all of her life, vibrant, happy. And Rosette certainly appeared quite pleased with life these days. Even the perpetual worry lines creasing her forehead were visibly softer. She marveled at her mother's elegant appearance. Although Rosette always dressed gracefully, tonight she looked spectacular. Her attire mirrored the sophisticated style she weaved into every nook and cranny of the home. She wore a matching light-blue cashmere sweater and skirt with gold jewelry; a heart-shaped necklace with harmonizing gold earrings, bracelet, and watch.

"You've been busy working late just about every night Marloe. I thought maybe you just wanted to relax, and we could catch up another night."

Marloe noticed the dance in her mother's eyes, a definite rarity. In retrospect, they had always appeared permanently veiled in some unreachable pain. But now her big, beautiful eyes shined with pleasure. Marloe wanted to celebrate this newfound joy that seemed to radiate from Rosette's very soul. Her demeanor warm and inviting.

"I know mother, it's been hectic, but I'm not busy now. Besides, you know I'm never too busy to talk to you. Sit down sweetie. Tell me about my Aunties."

Rosette's face lit up like a Christmas tree, she sat down beside Marloe. "It's all still so amazing to me. That after all these years my sisters are back in my life. Oh, Marloe, I can't wait for you and your brothers to meet them." Her eyes moistened, and she blinked away tears.

"I know; it's wonderful mother." She touched Rosette's shoulder softly. "I'm excited to meet them too. I bet their beautiful just like you, classy."

Rosette smiled, taking Marloe's hand. "Thank you dear. Oh Marloe, me and my sisters have so much catching up to do. So many years lost." She shook her head sadly. "It's my fault. God forgive me for being so hard-hearted and unforgiving. Every day I ask Him to have mercy on me."

"Mother you can't keep blaming yourself. You were young and so were they. It's all in the past. Just try to think about everything that is ahead for all of you, for all of us."

"I know you're right Marloe. But every time I think of Justa and how ill she is I feel guilty. With my nursing background I could have been there to make sure she received the care she needed."

"Oh, my dear mother," Marloe reached out and hugged Rosette tightly. "You can't save the world. She had Jessie, and from what you told us they've done well financially. I'm sure Justa has good medical care."

"But with love Marloe, care with love? You can't ever have enough love, always remember that. There's no love like the love of family, blood, you know?"

"Yes, I know mother. At times I didn't appreciate it, but I cherish the love my family has shown me. I hope you know how much I love you mother, don't you?"

Rosette patted Marloe's hand with hers. It was reminiscent of Marloe's memories as a child, Rosette uncharacteristically soothing away some real or imaginary hurt.

"Yes, Marloe, I know you do, and I love you so very much. Listen to me, life goes by in the blink of an eye. Don't be afraid to love again. God doesn't mean for you to live your life alone. I want to see you happy before I die. I want grand kids." Her voice trailed off, as if she knew the instinctive response her words would bring from Marloe.

Mother knows I'm cursed. Why is she talking like this? "Now Mother, you know any grands will have to come from Eubie or Bailey. I can't marry, you know the story. How can you say such things?"

"Oh Marloe, you're not cursed. You're blessed. We live the consequences of our own sin, not somebody else's. I look at your situation as being God's mercy. You were all set to marry Lawson, but the Lord let you find out just what kind of man you would have married. You made a mistake Marloe. That's all you did, just like everyone does when their young.

"But I hope you are not foolish enough to take up with him again. Hum, we all know he's been trying to charm you since he came back to Potter's Edge. I heard all about the flowers at the shop. Now, you know those brothers of yours love you to death, and don't even mention Bailey...that's all I'll say."

Even after all these years, Lawson's deceit still had the unexpected ability to jab her in the heart like a knife. She wasn't afraid of her brothers harming Lawson again. *If they had wanted to rid the world of him, they could have done it that night.* She chose her words carefully.

"Mother, it's really just to help him through his grief. After all, he did just lose his parents." She had learned long ago to tell her parents the bare minimum concerning her social life. Although she enlightened Rosette of her many gifts from suitors, she did not share her vindictive desire for revenge.

The car incident definitely advised a zillion 'red flags' concerning Lawson's emotional stability, but Marloe's caring nature forbade her to totally abandon him. *It's a grievous time for him.* So, she took the high road, forgiving him for the vehicular incident. Still, it did not impede her craving for his recompense. *I'm gonna get that or die trying.*

Rosette stared at her as if looking for a sign that Marloe wasn't being truthful. "Well, as long as you have your relationship with him under control I won't worry. But Marloe, what I think you should do is to leave all that *curse talk* at the altar. If you're cursed, then I'm cursed; all the trouble I've seen in life. I could have easily said my mother's family was vexed by some evil deed because we were certainly outcasts. But I caused most of my troubles by lying. Just think about it Marloe, once you go to the altar, you can lay that burden down, give it to Jesus. I'm not talking about just mentally leaving it, but physically too.

"You're too tied to that jewelry; it's almost like you idolize it, and nothing should come before God. Take that trunk full of jewelry that you cherish so much to the altar and leave it there. Trust God, go on with your life just like anyone else, love, marriage, children."

Tears stung Marloe's eyes. She dropped her head and squeezed her eyes shut, willing herself to hold them back. *If only mother knew.* She had never divulged to anyone, not even Jorene, the many moments she imagined herself married. Sometimes drifting away in the idea of what it would be like to truly love and experience the love of another. Or even to bear children that would love her the way her god children loved Jorene with such innocence. But such daydreams always came to the same rude awakening; she could never experience such elation in her life.

Go to the altar, lay my burdens down? If only it were that easy mother. How can I give up my treasure trunk and leave it at the altar. It's part of me...all I will have in the end? God understands that.

The thought of relinquishing her trinkets paralyzed her with fear. How could she give up the very treasures that gave her so much comfort; the visual bounty from men whose hearts she destroyed? Dante, Calvin, Alex, Nathan, Arnold, Johnnie, Jasper, to name a few. The list was extensive. She consoled herself that the suffering she endured from Lawson gave her the right. The revelation of bringing them to their knees without compromising her body was all the more fulfilling. Swearing abstinence after

Lawson, she felt proud that she had not waivered. For her part, all of her relationships had been purely platonic.

She cold-heartedly broke off relationships when suitors fell deeply in love with her. Nevertheless, it had not all been a walk in the park. In fact, after giving Alex Cole the boot, he caused a shadow of fear to dog her for a time. Heartbroken that she would not reconsider, he begged, pleaded, and cried for her to stay with him. There were nonstop phone calls and impromptu visits to the station. But with a heart of stone, she steadfastly bid him farewell. When his despair suddenly turned into rage and menacing threats, it caught her off guard. He called her one night, demanding his gifts of jewelry back, $5,000 worth he threatened, or "'You won't live to wear it.'"

Ump, he doesn't know who he's dealing with, you can't antagonize me. She was near the point of enlisting her brothers to teach him a lesson. But before she could fabricate a plausible story, Alex banged out the headlights of her car. With that incident, her brothers knew something was awry. She told them half-truths, not wanting them to learn of her vindictive passion. In the end, she reluctantly returned jewelry to Alex, and thanked God that she never heard from him again.

Still, even that sinister threat to her physical well-being did not negate her ravenous desire for payback. She knew her behavior was reprehensible, but she also realized that someday the second glances would stop. And then her glittery treasures and remembrances of broken hearts might ease her loneliness.

Rosette eyed Marloe with concern, waiting for her response.

"I can't change my thinking Mother," Marloe stated. "Everyone ingrained it in me from a child, the family. I-I don't mean you mother, but just about everyone else in the family did. I don't know how to believe any other way. I'm afraid to live any other way."

Rosette was teary-eyed as she squeezed Marloe's hand.

"I know Marloe; I'm ashamed that I allowed it. I never believed that talk. But I was weak because I had my own battles with the family, and really no voice. But the choice is yours my dear. God is always a step ahead of evil plans.

"Oh, I know they said Juniper was cursed, but back in those days, they didn't have the medical knowledge they have today. From all accounts Juniper was a tiny woman; there were complications after she had her last child, that's how she hemorrhaged to death. Don't you see Marloe, it was all coincidence."

"And the first baby Mother?" Marloe stared at Rosette. "It was predicted that her first child would die, and it happened. That was also coincidence?"

"The baby didn't stand a chance; at birth she only weighed three pounds from what was said. Couldn't eat; she was sickly, that's why she only lived six months. Marloe, you can break all of that Vain curse ignorance according to what you do. There's no need for you to be tied to what happened to someone else in the past. This is your life. You're smart and beautiful; God didn't put you on this earth to fulfill what others view as a curse. He put you here to trust in Him and to live your life in love."

Live your life in love. Marloe reflected on her mother's words. Sudden elation filled her at the possibility but was quickly overridden by exceeding doubtfulness. The latter seized her and would not let go. *Love. What a horrible trick to give your heart and soul to someone only to find out eventually that you were nothing more than a conquest.*

"Mother let's not talk about it anymore tonight. But I promise I will think about what you said, okay?"

Rosette nodded her head. The dejected look in her eyes told Marloe that she did not believe her.

"Okay Marloe. I understand. It's alright."

"This conversation is supposed to be about you Mother, not me." She managed to smile despite the sadness that arose from the subject. The two continued to talk a while longer about Rosette's sisters and the arrival time of Annie Kate's permanent move to Potter's Edge. An hour later they hugged and bid each other good night.

~ ~ ~ ~

After cleansing her face of make-up followed by a hot shower, Marloe pulled back her pink satin bed covers. She picked up her Bible on the nightstand, intent on reading from the book of Esther as she slid between the soft sheets. Intrigued by the powerful story of Queen Esther, she never tired of reading it. She identified with Queen Esther as the queen who won a king over with her beauty. Thereby saving herself and the Jewish nation from extermination. *Yes, beauty is fleeting, but it definitely helped Queen Esther during the fight of her life.*

I have that power too. A ripple of excitement coursed through her body as she remembered how Syril shielded her with his strong arms and body the day Lawson went loco. She felt so protected as if she belonged right there forever. Those intimate moments felt incredibly right. In his grasp fear held no meaning; a remarkable instant that could only be relived in her mind for she knew the consequences of becoming too close.

Get a grip girl. She stiffened her resolve all the more. *Get your treasure trinkets from him when he bites and keep moving.* Even as she thought those words, the feel of him stayed with her like an overpowering shadow, threatening to dissolve the trustworthy walls she had solidified around her heart.

~ ~ ~ ~

On Thursday morning she swallowed her exuberance when Syril walked in the door. She had not yet made it to her office but stood chatting with Anna Jane at the dispatch desk.

"Good morning?" she was pleasant but determined to remain all business. *He's a client, nothing more.* Was it her imagination or did his eyes linger a moment too long on her face. She smiled; her thoughts momentarily muddled. He looked so clean, so strong and capable.

"Good morning, ladies." His smile was relaxed.

Oh, not so serious today, huh counselor?

"How are you, Marloe?"

"I'm well. Lawson told me you would be wrapping up his family's estate business today?"

There was an element of surprise in his eyes as he spoke. *Oh, he's surprised I'm talking to Lawson after what happened. That's none of your business counselor.*

"Yes, it shouldn't take more than a few hours as long as we start on time."

They both laughed because they knew Lawson. *No, Lawson was never a stickler for time,* she thought, *and apparently that had not changed. He still beats to his own drum.*

Syril cleared his throat. "In case you hadn't noticed, your friend Lawson and I are not on the best of terms. Well, I'll just say that Lawson and I don't see eye-to-eye on many things although we're family. Hopefully, one day it will work itself out."

My, he is in a pleasant mood today, talkative. She smiled as their eyes met. "Every family has relationship issues. Unfortunately, they don't always get resolved. But we could talk about that one all day long," she laughed. "You need a car I take it?"

"Yes please, round trip."

"This is Anna Jane. She'll be glad to help you."

"Thank you. I appreciate it."

She picked up her briefcase on the counter. "Have a good day, Syril." She turned and walked swiftly towards her office, but not before she caught the glimpse of longing in his eyes.

"You have a good day to Marloe."

Gotcha. Still, she knew he was not altogether meek and mild. After all he was a trial lawyer, used to playing hard ball. With him she needed to be on her emotional tiptoes.

"Excuse me, Marloe."

She turned. He walked towards her, and she tried to extinguish the flame that his gaze aroused. "Yes," she answered. "Is everything okay?"

He hesitated but then came closer. "Yes, everything is fine Marloe. Thank you. Would you have dinner with me this evening?"

She ran a suddenly trembling hand through her hair. Stunned out of her comfort zone she fought to find her voice. "Dinner, tonight?" The look on his face told her he was serious. *Isn't this what you wanted*; her thoughts played devil's advocate. *The opportunity to wield your command; to show him that he would just be another notch in the cleavage he would never embrace?* It was on the tip of her tongue to say no, to keep him hanging, but she couldn't say it. She actually wanted to know him better.

A smile crossed his lips. "If you have plans, I understand."

She played nervously with the gold cross around her neck, still attempting to control her shaky hands. "Yes, I'd like that." She hated that her voice quivered and wondered if he saw her anxiety.

He glanced at his watch. "I should finish up pretty early, but I can keep myself busy until you get off work."

His easy smile pulled at her conviction. *He is such a gentlemen, so virile and competent. Different. What am I doing? But I've already said yes.*

"How about four o'clock?" she smiled at Syril.

"That sounds good. You pick the place and I'll see you here at four."

"Sure, good restaurants on Main Street. So, I'll see you later."

"Okay, see you then Marloe, thanks. Have a great day."

"You, too."

~ ~ ~ ~

Arthur Brown finished reading the Will by 1:00 p.m. Dolly surprised them all with a separate codicil, leaving Syril her three-caret platinum wedding ring. He marveled at the revelation while riding in the limousine back to Potter's Edge. Taking the document out, he carefully read it once again.

"'My wedding ring I bequeath to my dearly beloved nephew, Syril Barrett. Ashton and Lawson, I know you two would argue over the ring, and I also know that Lawson would win. Therefore, to keep hard feelings out of it, I leave it to Syril. My dearest nephew, this means you have to marry someone worthy of your good heart, someone who will appreciate your deep capacity for love. I love you very much, always, Aunt Dolly.'"

He touched the inner pocket of his suit jacket where he had placed the ring. Warm remembrances of Dolly flooded his mind. She had not been fond of Olive from the outset, warning Syril that she found her bossy and arrogant. When their relationship came to its crushing conclusion, Aunt Dolly consoled him. She reassured him that Olive was undeserving of his affection; to wait on the Lord to send the woman of his dreams.

Although inconsolable at the time, he came to realize the tremendous favor Olive did for him when she tossed him aside like so much trash. After languishing in self-pity for a season, somehow, he began putting his shattered heart back together. It had been three years. Meeting Marloe disclosed just how much he missed the sweet persona of a woman.

He was just as surprised as Marloe when he asked her to dinner. Something about her eyes appeared troubled that morning, although she smiled brightly. In some strange way he felt the need to counteract the trauma Lawson had caused her earlier that week. He knew how much the incident had shaken them both.

As for Lawson that day throughout the proceedings he was withdrawn. Syril happily let him have his space. Neither he nor Ashton spoke when the lawyer read Dolly's last wishes regarding her wedding ring. *Really, why would they object? They both knew Dolly was my second mother. And she was right. Ashton could never win a fight with Lawson, been that way since they were kids.*

He turned his thoughts to what lay ahead, dinner with Marloe. If nothing else, perhaps they would strike up a friendship. There was no denying the powerful attraction he felt for her, even if the feeling wasn't mutual. He wondered if she knew how truly selfish Lawson was, or was she blinded by love as he once was by Olive.

I won't say anything. That would come off as sour grapes. But there's nothing wrong with making up for the bad impression I left the day we met. Pent-up frustration over losing Aunt Dolly; I let it get the best of me.

The limo dropped him off on Main Street in Potter's Edge; from there he walked to the local library. He would kill a few hours reviewing an upcoming brief for a client due in court the following week on an eviction hearing.

~ ~ ~ ~

During the 20-minute walk to the eatery Marloe chose, she felt deliciously special as she and Syril chatted. He strolled on the outer edge of the sidewalk closer to traffic, as if sensing her nervousness from Monday's experience. It was four-thirty when they walked into "Cove's Soul Food" restaurant. After helping Marloe remove her coat, he draped it on the back of her chair, pulling the chair out for her to sit down.

He then placed his briefcase on the floor by his chair, removed his jacket, and took his seat. *How utterly charming he is. He makes me feel so safe. I should not have a worry in the world when he is around.* She pushed the thought away. *He can't stay around. This will have to be quick and dirty.* Yet, her heart had never throbbed so intensely to know someone, not even Lawson.

The waiter came to their table with menus. "Would you like to start with drinks?"

"What will you have?" Syril asked Marloe. He smiled and his teeth gleamed perfectly white in the soft light of the restaurant.

She returned the smile. *This seems like a special occasion.* "I'll have a glass of white wine."

"We'll have two glasses of Chablis," he advised the waiter.

Her eyebrow arched, and a delightful glow permeated her body. *He certainly is a take-charge-kind-of-guy and knows good tasting wine. Ooh, I like that.*

They poured over the menu. "What do you suggest? But I must warn you it must be fried," Syril laughed.

Marloe's curly locks jiggled around her face as she threw her head back, laughing merrily. "Syril, Don't tell me you're a fried food junky?"

"Starting every morning with fried bacon and eggs," he laughed. "I mean I eat vegetables too, but something on my plate has to be greasy."

His rollicking laughter and easy sense of humor put Marloe at ease. She felt herself unwinding from the daily grind. "Well, if you insist on killing yourself the fried shrimp might be worth it," she joked.

Joviality came easily with Syril. It felt wonderful to get comfortable with someone who had not an inkling of the demons that daily tooled around in her head.

"Okay, shrimp it is. What will you have?"

"Oh, I'll just have a chef's salad. I'm not a big eater. Although I love shrimp, I have to have the taste for them, not tonight."

The waiter reappeared. "Ready to order?" he asked.

"Yes. A chef salad for the lady and the shrimp boat for me please. Thank you."

"It's been almost two years since my father's heart attack." Marloe found herself telling Syril about Bailey's illness seeing his love of fried food.

"He ate like you; fried food was an everyday thing. Oh, he enjoyed vegetables, but the bulk of his dinner plate consisted of fried fish or chicken, mashed potatoes heaping with butter and brown gravy, biscuits, or cornbread. And of course, a meal wasn't complete without dessert, a homemade piece of cake or apple pie, maybe two slices."

A look of concern crossed Syril's face. "How is he now?"

"It was rough at first, touch and go. But now he's doing well. He had to change his diet. My mother makes sure he eats right. The only time he's allowed to have fried food is during holidays or special occasions. It's been difficult for him, but he understands his life depends on it. The heart attack scared some sense into him."

"Thank God he's doing well. That's wonderful," Syril said.

The waiter came with their order. Syril's eyes lit like the sun as he observed his plate full of greasy delectable food., It brimmed with fried jumbo shrimp, Cole slaw, and the thick hand cut French fries that Cove's was known for. Marloe watched with curiosity as Syril drowned his potatoes in ketchup. She was famished, the day had busily slipped away, she dug into her salad having not eaten any lunch. As they dined and chatted, Marloe found herself becoming captivated with Syril's unpretentious charm.

She relished the attention that he lavished on her knowing their relationship must be brief. *With Lawson, it was all about him, he never really put me first. Even now he's still the same.* She remembered him not waiting for her in the restaurant foyer the night they met up. Instead, he stood at the bar, doing what he did best, socializing with the opposite sex. It was strange how she had been oblivious to that behavior when she was crazy in love with him.

Despite her determination to remain as cool as a cucumber during dinner with Syril, he drew her into his world as the evening went by. They conversed about many things, discovering they held mutual interest in certain areas of their lives.

Careful girl, your first meeting with him was shaky, remember? He's trying to fool you. Yet, she brushed the thought away. She knew genteel from brash, and Syril was definitely a gentleman. Time became the enemy, she found herself wishing the night did not have to end. It was eight-thirty when they departed the restaurant. Too soon they reached her car. She pulled her car keys from her purse.

Syril gently touched her arm. "Let me hold your keys."

She stared at him, puzzled.

"Just to open the door for you," he smiled at her, "to make sure you get home safe and sound."

Their hands touched briefly when she handed him the key. The delectable little tingle that she kept in check all evening ran through her body like fire. She tilted her head to the side, giving Syril a confused stare. "But I only live ten minutes away, I'll be fine. You have a train to catch."

He glanced at her as he opened the driver's side car door then waited for her to enter. "Yes, I know you'll be fine. I asked you out, it's my responsibility to see you to your door. Wait here while I get a taxi."

She sat behind the wheel, both amused and impressed. "You must be kidding. You're going to get a taxi, for what?"

"Just sit back and relax, alright?" He strode into Vain's while Marloe shook her head in wonderment. She waited in the car and soon Jab, one of their drivers, pulled up beside her car with Syril in the front passenger seat.

"We'll follow you," Jab yelled to Marloe after rolling down his window.

What? She pulled out of the parking lot with the taxi following close behind until they reached her home. Before she could release the car door to step out, Syril was there to open it. He took her hand as she lifted herself up and out of the car. Her hand seemed to shrink in the largeness of his. Hand-in-hand they walked to her door.

"Thanks for having dinner with me on such short notice Marloe. I really enjoyed your company."

She smiled as his eyes searched hers. "Sometimes unplanned events are the best. It was special. Thanks for asking Syril."

He leaned in and planted a soft kiss on her forehead. "Can I see you again?"

She stepped back, surely, he could hear the tumultuous beat of her heart. *Stay calm. You're in control. Don't let him think you're anxious. This is your game.* The two had exchanged telephone numbers at the restaurant. "Call me," she said. "Thanks again for a lovely evening." She smiled and turned from him to open the door to her suite.

"I'll call you real soon."

She stood in the doorway as Syril took his leave. He jumped in the taxi and Jab sped away. Her mind whirled in confusion, her body a crescendo of unanticipated desire. She quietly shut the door, leaning her back against it. *God help me. I think I'm falling in love.*

~ ~ ~ ~

Satan had led Lawson into his own private torment. He trailed the taxi as it escorted Marloe home. *So now I know.*

"Syril, that backstabbing, no good dog," his words pierced the night air in wrath. He had stayed a respectful distance behind the cab. "He stabbed me in the back even after I told him that Marloe was my girl. Well, we'll just see about that." His thoughts flashed back to the morning the three of them were at Vain's. Marloe had behaved differently. She smiled and was her usual sweet self, but when she looked at Syril there was a certain sparkle in her eyes. It reminded him of the way she once looked at him; mesmerized.

He groaned for the millionth time over losing her, the one true love of his life. Radiant, tantalizing Marloe Vain, whose bewitching locks had seduced his fingers along with his heart. Why could she not understand that without her he was a broken man, lost? She was the one woman who could make him a one-woman man.

The devil himself reminded him. *Liar, remember she wasn't the only one in high school? She was your girl then and it still didn't stop you. Face it, you're just like Jonas. It's in your blood. But you can get her back and have your cake on the side too.*

After the taxi had pulled into the train station, Lawson drove to the side street out of view cutting his lights. The devil hung on like a menacing passenger, attempting to persuade him to confront Syril as he walked to board the train.

Get out and tell him about himself before he gets on the train. He's trying to steal your girl. Look at him, all smug, feeling righteous. Go punch him out.

He fought the words of that demon off, only to encounter another. *If you do that you'll be playing into his hands. That's all Marloe would need to hear, especially after you scared her half-to-death. Call him up; get on his good side. He's got that soft heart; find out where he's coming from.*

Jorene was right; his foolish behavior had set the current situation in motion. He had called Jorene out of desperation. At first, she was reluctant to talk about anything concerning Marloe. But banking on her empathy for the past, when he and Marloe were joined at the hip, Lawson pressed her for information.

"'You frightened her Lawson, what did you expect? What got into you to do something as crazy as trying to run them off the sidewalk with your car? For that, you practically pushed her into your cousin's arms.'"

Her words had punched him in the gut with the brutal truth. Solidifying the reality that Marloe was again slipping from his grasp. *She's confused right now, but she loved me once with her whole heart and soul. I have to find a way to make her feel that love again. I have to beat Syril at his own game.* The relentless enemy temporarily pacified saw Lawson gun the motor for home.

~ ~ ~ ~

Syril stood in his office, dazed, the props knocked from under his feet once again. His hands shook and his heartbeat rapidly; he gripped the sides of the chair for support. Exhaling deeply, he sat down at his desk. At first, he thought it was a prank, but he had played the answering machine message more than a few times. There was no doubt in his mind that it was indeed Olive's voice.

It was a short message that filled him with the cutting reminder of her abrupt departure. He pressed the play button again. "'Syril, it's Olive, I'm in town on business. Call me at 555-4323.'" Her voice sounded weak, unlike the overly confident Olive he remembered. Following the shock of her call, he became infuriated.

I will not call her back. Still as self-centered as ever! She honestly thinks she can waltz back into my life like a summer-time strut. Never in a thousand years will I call her back. He wondered what drama was going on in her life that drove her to call him. *Maybe Olive didn't get what*

Olive wanted. The thought eased some of his initial panic. *I can handle this. Olive's got pride. If I don't call her, she'll just move on to someone else that she can get her superficial hooks into.*

He picked up the discovery folder on his desk and thumbed through it, he had less than two weeks to prepare for his next criminal court case. *I don't have time for Olive's games.* Yet, as much as he tried to concentrate on the file in front of him, it was hopeless. Exasperated, he laid the record down, stood up from the desk, and walked to the window. The view from his third-floor office overlooked a busy intersection on 125th Street. As he peered down at the hustle and bustle of people stirring about, he reflected on matters that transpired within the past few months.

He and Lawson came to a crossroads of sorts, some semblance of a truce. But he was not so naïve to believe that his cousin was fully trustworthy. Lawson called him a few weeks after the car incident and apologized for his 'poor lapse in judgment.' Syril had bristled as he listened to Lawson's lame excuse; quickly cutting the conversation short. But he had forgotten how persistent Lawson could be.

"'I just wanted to clear the air,'" Lawson assured him. Although laden with caution, Syril accepted his apology. During the call Syril made it clear that he and Marloe were friendly. He expected an angry retort from Lawson, but instead he was civil.

"'Hey man, it's a free country," Lawson responded. "But I need to tell you that I love her, and she loves me. We go way back to high school. She was my girl then and will always be my girl.'"

His words filled Syril with despair, believing Lawson was right; *he always got the girl.* Nevertheless, Syril concealed the hopelessness that came over him as the two talked of getting together to 'shoot the breeze.'

"'I'll come to Harlem,'" Lawson offered.

Syril found that gesture odd, since Lawson did not share the affectionate emotional tie with the place of his birth in the same way as he. Lawson had been a wildly popular athlete attending high school in Harlem. But he had also endured heckling from classmates where Jonas was concerned. Syril was away at college but learned from Alberta that on more than a few occasions Lawson was suspended from school for brawls having to do with disparaging remarks made about his Dad.

No, Lawson isn't particularly fond of Harlem, so why would he suddenly want to visit me. He's been to my place exactly one time, and that was about business when he signed with the NFL. He wants to get close to me so he can keep an eye on Marloe. The thought of her brought a smile to his lips. They had gotten together a number of times within the last few months, and each time they met proved more delightful than the last. He grew fond of the quaint restaurants of Potter's Edge where the two shared sumptuous dinners and lively conversation.

He found Marloe easy to talk to, witty, and opinionated. She was also a good listener, and soon he began sharing the ups and downs of his profession. And, how Alberta had lost her supper club to some underhanded financial sharks. At the time many restaurants and bars were opening in Harlem and Alberta went in debt to keep pace with the competition. She unwittingly took out loans with exorbitant interest rates, using the property as collateral. Business fell off.

Not wanting Syril to fret at college, too late he learned of his mother's financial woes. "Bert's at 125th" went into foreclosure, Alberta lost the establishment that she worked herself to the bone to make a success. His mother's broken heart was another gauntlet that propelled him into law. Perhaps he could save someone else from such unsuspecting deceit. He also painted a sketchy portrait of his ordeal with Olive to Marloe.

Never had he felt so in tune, so enraptured with a woman as he did with Marloe. While she assured him that she was not looking for a long-term relationship, her body language left him wondering. He had lost the ability to trust his own judgment. *After all, Olive used me like a roll of toilet paper, and I never saw it coming until it was too late.*

Yet, there was something special about Marloe that felt so right, an essence of purity, and a laugh that soothed the melancholy places in his heart like a soft caress. In spite of those feelings, the lesson of Olive haunted him even as his friendship with Marloe blossomed. Jaded, he anticipated the worse, but prayed for the best.

He glanced at the clock on the wall. It was ten-thirty. He sat down at his desk a bit calmer, rolled up his sleeves, determined to cease daydreaming and get to work. A cold shiver swept over him as Olive's voice pricked him from a grave dug long ago. *No, she wouldn't dare come here.* But even as the dreadful notion crossed his mind, he remembered how relentless she was for her needs. He could not shake the sense that Olive was near. So close that he could almost feel her presence; smell the scent of her heavy flowery perfume.

Chapter 16

THE DIAMOND NECKLACE WITH A GOLD HEART shimmered as if it invented the sun. Marloe savored the flawless sapphire blue stones and placed them around her neck to close the clasp. It was a gift from Syril. Never had she seen jewelry sparkle with such abandonment. The room gave off a soft glow as she gazed at her image in the full-length mirror. *I love it. I'll leave this one out and not place it in the trunk, not just yet.*

Thoughts of Syril rushed in as she pulled her hair back and placed the matching heart-shaped earrings on. He was certainly different from any man she had ever met, but then she knew that the moment she laid eyes on him. The raw magnetism between them was mystifying. Yet he remained guarded, careful. She vigilantly returned the favor. *This is not the way things are supposed to go. He should be chasing me with everything he has. We've been seeing each other for three months, and he's given me only one gift.*

"'A celebration of our friendship,'" he had said when he pressed the slim white box covered in gold gift wrap into her hand. *Well, he better make that celebration at least once a month since he doesn't have too many more to go.*

Each time they parted he either kissed her on the forehead or pecked her cheek, but he never touched her lips. Sudden panic gripped her. She turned quickly to the mirror. *Am I losing my strength, my looks?* She frantically pulled her massive curls up and tied her hair in a ponytail to better scrutinize her reflection. *It's my eyes. I do look a little tired today. Dealing with two men at the same time is making me crazy, been hanging out too much lately.*

It was Sunday morning. She would need to hurry if she were to make it to church on time. She smoothed one cheek with her hand and then the other. Her skin felt soft and supple, and her body looked long and lean in the light blue silk dress with matching jacket and navy pumps. *I'll need to get to the spa twice this week, that's all. I've been running myself ragged.*

Her mother's familiar rap on her door assured her that she needed to hurry. "Come in mother."

Rosette eased the door open, sticking her head in before entering the room. "You about ready for church dear?"

"Oh mother, I'm sorry. I forgot to tell you and father; I'm driving to church today. I'm meeting a friend for a bite to eat after service."

Rosette stared at her as though she wanted to say something but decided against it.

"That's a beautiful necklace set Marloe. You always manage to find the prettiest pieces. Where did you buy it?"

That was her mother's way of prying. *She knows darn well I didn't buy this jewelry.* "I didn't buy it Mother. It was a gift. Thank you, I love it too."

Rosette gave her a knowing look and turned towards the door. "Alright then, we'll see you at church."

"Yes, mother, I'll see you and father there." She felt relieved when Rosette shut the door. *Why tell her that I'm meeting Lawson for brunch. After all this game will be over shortly, no need to worry family.*

~ ~ ~ ~

During brunch at Cabaret's Lawson's faults jumped out at Marloe like grease in a hot frying pan. *No wonder he loves Cabaret's so much. He is just like the phony people that frequent it.* It was a high caliber restaurant where elitists seemed to bask in their celebrity and ostentatiously frown on the rest of the world. Lawson relieved her of her coat and pulled out her chair. Marloe couldn't shake feeling as if they were on stage. Lawson's actions did not seem to come from the heart but rather a display for his audience. The fixed smile he wore was transparent enough for Marloe to see straight through it. What she saw was his love of his big name and he played to the crowd's adoration. *He has not a humble bone in his body.*

Another couple joined them at the table, obviously friends of Lawson. After a cool hello to Marloe the woman cast her eyes on Lawson as though hypnotized. Marloe grew weary of what lay ahead for the next few hours when Lawson launched into what he deemed some of his 'greatest plays.' *This is where his true comfort lies, being in the limelight. Syril is just the opposite; always thinking of others and putting himself last. They're cut from the same cloth but are as different as night and day.*

Lawson eased the Cadillac into the driveway of the James' home. Marloe turned her car in behind his. A quick glance at her watch advised it was four o'clock. She was grateful to leave those pretentious people at the restaurant, but leery of what she was now doing. Lawson convinced her to take a ride to his home; he wanted to show her something special. She was nervous at first, but deep within her being she knew she needed to finally face her fears. *It's crazy that I drive five miles out of my way to avoid something that should have been put to rest a long time ago. Today is as good a day as any to resolve it.*

As they exited their vehicles, she began having second thoughts. *Why did I let him talk me into coming here? Why am I putting myself through this?* Her heart was in her throat as she looked up at the tree house. Strangely enough, neither the tree nor the tree house seemed as large as she remembered. The vibrant brown color of the house fading over time. She braced herself for the hurtful feelings that besieged her back then. Instead, the opposite happened. it was as if she shed a heavy coat weighing her down for years. Somewhere along the journey her phobia of this moment had been arrested, just as the deep love she once felt for Lawson had thankfully withered.

"I want to show you something Mar," Lawson interrupted her muse.

She cautiously followed him to the entrance of the home. "What is it Lawson? You've got me really curious."

"You'll see. Come on in." His eyes sparkled.

In spite of her resolve for revenge she felt sudden shame. *Poor Lawson, he really believes this is going somewhere. How stupid does he think I am? He tore my heart out without blinking. But I'm a Christian...Yes, and I'm a good one. Lord, you know my story, how I have suffered because of this man. I can never marry; never feel the warm tug of a first-born at my breast.*

With her heart sufficiently hardened she replied softly to Lawson. "Okay, after you."

A momentary taste of nostalgia came over her as she stepped into the foyer of the house. The years rolled back. Dolly smiled warmly at her while Jonas playfully slapped Lawson on the back. It was a regular father-son exchange, one she came to know as a sign that they understood each other. The James' home was the first place she and Lawson held hands as he introduced her to his parents, the venue of their first kiss, first-love admission, and ultimately...the regrettable nightmare.

Lawson took her hand, and she followed him; her daydream abruptly ending. "Come on in the living room Mar baby. Have a seat. Let me pour you a drink. Got some white wine?"

"Oh, no thank you. Remember, I told you I rarely drink, just special occasions. And I especially don't drink alcohol on Sunday."

She settled back on the white leather sofa, glad that she sounded calmer than she felt. Her stomach had begun to knot at the strangeness of the situation. She wanted Lawson to show her whatever it was that he had so she could leave. *Why didn't he bring it with him to the restaurant? He thinks he is so slick, trying to get me here so I could look back.*

Lawson hunched his shoulders, giving her a peculiar look. "You don't drink on Sunday, so what does that make you, a better Christian?" He tilted his head to the side as if he was in deep thought. "Alright, I won't drink either. I really don't like drinking alone," he laughed lightly.

"I don't know if it makes me a better Christian, but I give Sunday to God. I'm not a drinker, just a glass of wine every blue moon. Lawson, c'mon, what is it. What do you want to show me?" He had irritated her with his comments.

He sat down close to her, turning her face to him he spoke. "I need to tell you something first."

She tried to diminish the prickle of fear that came over her. He sounded so solemn. He leaned back with a deep sigh. "I have some kind of bone problem with my hip. I've seen a specialist, the tests he gave me show a lot of bone deterioration. They say I need surgery to repair it but, like I told you before, doc says my career is over. The surgery will restore it to a certain extent, but not enough for me to play again."

She stared at him, trying not to show that she did not fully believe him. *He's crafty. What the heck is he up to? Is this some ploy to make me feel sorry and win me back? You can forget about that.*

"Oh Lawson, I'm sorry. Maybe you should see another specialist? Get a second opinion just to be sure?"

He shook his head. "I saw the x-rays and the report, and truthfully, I feel it Mar. I'm 26, but some days I ache like an old man. But hey, listen to my idea. I'm thinking of reopening the supper club; making it a weekend kind of thing, upscale, you know. I have a huge network of friends, fans, a following, seems like it would work. What do you think?"

You don't want to know what I think. But she smiled and softly placed her hand over his. "Sounds like a good plan, a hefty challenge, but if you're talking about running it on weekends only that might work."

He squeezed her hand tightly. She attempted to ease it away. He loosened his grip but did not let go. "Marloe, I've never gotten over you, our love, the bond we shared. Don't you feel it? It's still there, just like always. Marry me Mar. Be my girl again, I love you, need you."

Gotcha.

"I have something for you," he released her hand and stood up. She watched, intrigued as he walked to the China cabinet in the dining room and opened it.

Oh, this is different. China? All of her gifts consisted of beautiful jewels and expensive perfumes. Lawson returned with a small gold box in his hand. Her heartbeat doubled as he lowered himself to sit beside her.

"Marry me, Marloe. We can do this thing together, run the club. Turn the world upside down, just the way we said we would, together, forever."

She didn't speak. He opened the box. The triple carat teardrop diamond winked at her with the resplendent beauty of a shooting star. A shiny band of gold held it tightly. As the chandelier above them bathed its light over the room, the ring beckoned to her earthly heart. She could almost feel the exquisite diamond on her finger.

How beautiful! I could never take it though, not a ring, too permanent. Satan's trying to throw me off course. She arched her back against the thought of how such a lavish gift would increase the monetary value of her already hefty bounty of treasures. Still, although the ring would never be hers, she could not resist her desire to taunt him, to move closer to vindication. Their eyes met as he placed the ring on her finger, a perfect fit.

"Oh Lawson, it's beautiful." She held her hand up for a closer look. "But I-I, you know I can't marry you, can't marry anyone." *I can do this. I have the power just like my heroine Esther of ancient times.*

Lawson looked dejected. "Don't tell me you still believe that curse nonsense Marloe." His voice was edgy.

"Because that's exactly what it is, silliness. You're too smart for that, the logic behind it is ridiculous and you're still letting it ruin your life. All that matters is that we love each other, and we should be together. I'm not letting you go this time. I refuse to lose you again. Mar baby, please say you'll marry me."

He pulled her up and drew her close. "Can you deny this, the way you feel in my arms?"

Romantic memories of their past began to play rancid little tricks in her mind. A soft trickle of affection released itself from her regal composure. She stepped back, pushing the conflicting reflections away.

Yes, I'll marry you alright, but only in your dreams. In control of her emotions, she played with his mind. "It's hard Lawson. You know, so much time has gone by. We're both different people, moving in different circles. I actually love my life, my job. I just don't know."

He cupped her chin and gently turned her face to look at him. "That's your only reason. We know each other girl. How could I ever forget anything about you? The way you used to whisper in my ear and hang on my arm as if your life depended on it. That was real love baby."

Marloe's face flamed. How dare he mock her feelings of being young and naive? She hit him back hard.

"Oh, Lawson, c'mon we both know that was puppy love, not the real thing."

He looked incredulous. "What, you really believe that? Well, I've never felt that way about anyone else, only you. But I-I, Marloe, listen…I." And then he abruptly stopped speaking.

He can't say I'm sorry, even in his letter he had not said, "I'm sorry." It stood between them like the parting of the Red Sea. She looked back as water rushed in, while he stood afar, his face a mound of confusion as the torrential waters threatened to wash him away.

"Don't count us out Marloe. Tell me you'll think about marrying me, please?"

Let him simmer in the pot. "Yes, I'll do that Lawson." *God forgive me for lying, but he deserves it.* She savored the rock on her finger one last time and quickly removed it.

~ ~ ~ ~

It was Saturday evening. Marloe hadn't felt this happy in years. Delightful little butterflies flitted every which way in her tummy. She and Syril planned to spend the day touring Harlem. While she was no stranger to Harlem, the opportunity to explore it with Syril was exciting. He picked her up early and they lunched at the Trolley House in uptown Harlem. He pointed out the night club Alberta once owned near west 125th street, and the bustling thoroughfare near the famed Apollo Theatre. Then it was off to his favorite jazz and entertainment club, the Wonder Lounge. Marloe wasn't unfamiliar with the supper club; Wesley had treated her and Jorene to an evening at the Wonder Lounge the year they turned 21. Feeling as captivated today as she was then, she vowed to remain coolly entertained. *After all, my desire is to come away with wonderful mementos to warm my heart in old age, and to break his heart. Stick to your purpose girl.*

Harlem became all the more fascinating with Syril at the helm. She loved everything about it, from its bluesy avant-garde culture to the pulsating soulful excursion wrought from artisans. Marloe found herself relaxing and enjoying the moment and, above all, loving the happiness she felt with Syril. But like a ship tossed about in a roaring sea, she fought to hold those feelings below deck.

~ ~ ~ ~

Syril smiled and Marloe was suddenly melancholy. *If only things were different perhaps this fairy tale could continue in truth.* They were back at Syril's apartment, winding down from what had been a spectacular day. He would soon take her home. She tried to shake it off, but sad feelings had somehow wormed their way into her heart. *Get a grip girl.*

"What are you thinking lovely Marloe?" They sat at his kitchen table eating chocolate ice cream. "You look a million miles away. I thought we were having a great time, huh?"

"Oh yes, I had wonderful time. I've really enjoyed our friendship; it's been great."

He laid his spoon down with a frown, studying her face. "Enjoyed? "It's been?" What's with all the past tenses? It almost sounds like you won't see me anymore. What's going on sweetheart?" Above wounded eyes, worry lines suddenly appeared.

The urge to comfort him came so easily it frightened her. *Oh, how I would love to cast this charade to the wind and yield to the night; to be free from this family prison.*

Suddenly, the taste for ice cream vanished. She stood up, intent on escaping the hurt in his eyes that she had caused. Syril rose from his chair. Their eyes locked, and it was as if he peered into the very depths of her being. She had to leave him, not just for the night, but forever.

"I've been thinking a lot about our relationship Syril. I don't want to become closer. Remember, I told you I'm celibate."

"Yes, you did, and I totally understand that. Have I disrespected you in some way Marloe? I care too much about you to go against your wishes. What have I done?"

"Nothing," she dropped her head. *You haven't done a thing except treat me like a queen.* "It's not you Syril. It's me. I'm not one for lasting relationships. It's too hard. You don't know what I've been through."

He pulled her close. "Marloe, I would never hurt you, ever."

He wrapped his arms tightly around her body. It felt perfect. *How can this be wrong?* He kissed her forehead and then tenderly kissed her cheek. When their lips touched all of her inhibitions melted away like the unfinished bowl of ice cream on the table. The world receded as she abandoned herself to their first kiss. Every part of her overflowed with tenderness, as she yielded to its ecstasy. Forever could not have done justice to the depth and breadth of the kiss.

"Bam, Bam!" someone pounded on Syril's front door. They broke away from each other as though they were thieves caught red-handed in the candy jar.

What are you doing silly girl? Don't you know he's trying to get inside your head? That's your first step at losing control. The strength of the kiss left her shaken. She hurried into the bathroom, intent on regaining her composure while Syril answered the door.

Wow, somebody really wants to talk to Syril from the sound of that loud knocking.

Sufficiently recovered, she opened the door to the loud voice of a woman. Curiosity got the best of her; she left it slightly ajar observing the stunned look on Syril's face. As she cracked the opening a bit further, she saw the woman standing in the doorway. She was tall and quite lovely. A sliver of envy pricked Marloe's heart; she strained closer to hear their conversation.

"Me and him split some time ago for good," the woman said. "It was off and on for a while, but then things got really bad. You never returned my call Syril. Why?"

Marloe leaned in a bit closer to hear his response. After what seemed an eternity, he spoke.

"You have one hell of a nerve coming here Olive. Did you honestly expect me to call you back? The fact that I didn't call you should have told you that I have no intention of speaking with you. Now, please leave my home. Your welcome mat was revoked when you walked away and left me with a boatload of bills."

The pretty lady smiled and tossed her head back. "Oh, that's how it is? Well, I don't believe you Syril. We had a good thing going. I messed up. I was wrong, I know that now. All I'm asking is that we start over as friends. We'll take it slow, no pressure."

Marloe had heard enough. *So, this was Olive. And he said he was done with her? Hum, this is the perfect out for me.* But instead of relief, she felt jealous. She entered the living room and picked her purse up from the couch. "I'll see myself home Syril. Sounds like you have unfinished business to take care of. Good night."

Syril blocked the door with his body, and then shut it. "Marloe, what are you doing? You know I'm not letting you go home alone. My unfinished business is with you. Please, wait one minute. Olive is leaving."

Olive smiled sweetly at Marloe. "Oh, you're a smart girl Missy," she said confidently. "Even if he won't admit it,

Syril and I have a lot to talk about. I don't know what he's told you, but we were engaged, madly in love."

Syril's eyes pleaded with Marloe for understanding.

Olive continued to speak. "I'm home Syril. So let Little Missy go."

Okay, that's the last time I'm going to be Little Missy? Who does this woman think she is? Oh, I will...! But I'm a Christian. This is a battle for the Lord. But then it's not really a battle because Olive has made leaving Syril easier. I'll settle for the one gift for three months of the best time of my life; I will treasure it forever.

Taking Olive firmly by the arm, Syril opened the door and escorted her out. "Goodbye Olive. Have a nice life."

"Syril, I need you," she pleaded. "I was a fool to leave you." She drew closer, reaching up and placing her arms around his neck. Tears spilled from her eyes. Syril forced her arms down and shut the door in her face.

~ ~ ~ ~

"Marloe, I'm sorry. Talk to me."

Syril's haggard countenance tugged at Marloe's heart. After much persuasion, she agreed to let him drive her back to Potter's Edge instead of taking the train. *Talk? There was nothing to talk about.* Olive's coming on the scene was divine intervention. It made parting ways all the more bona fide. *This is how it's supposed to be. He's hurting and I should be giddy with triumph.* But instead, she felt an overwhelming sense of loss.

She sat quietly in the passenger seat reflecting on how Olive's return was heaven sent. Yet for all of her quest for vengeance, she felt anything but victorious. She gazed at Syril momentarily and turned away.

He is so fine, so decent, Lord, help me. Unlike others, Syril had touched her in places of the heart that she regarded unreachable. The recompense she sought was replaced by a melancholy ache that refused to leave. *Time will heal that. I got too close to the flame.* Her heart was in jeopardy, making it all the more urgent to end what she now knew should never have begun.

"Syril, it's me. It has nothing to do with you. You deserve someone who can appreciate all that you have to give. My world is unique, and I can't risk making it worse than it is." *There, I'm telling the truth, being honest.* She glanced at him and then looked away. *He's crushed, just like he's supposed to be, why don't I feel happy about it?*

"You're not giving me a chance Marloe. I wish there was some way I could change your mind. Do you know what I think? I think you're running from your feelings. If you are truly honest with yourself, you can't deny there is something special between us. It's too strong to ignore, so you're running. Marloe, listen, every man is not like Lawson."

She caught her breath at the unexpected thrust to her heart. Tears welled; she quietly squeezed her eyes shut, determined to hold them back.

"You don't know anything about my relationship with Lawson," she struggled to calm her voice. "So please don't speak about something that is none of your business."

"Marloe, I know you were his girl in high school. I know how he hurt you. Ashton told me."

The realization that what happened between her, and Lawson was still fodder for gossip made for a slow burn. As Syril turned onto Spruce Street, she felt relieved.

This will be over in a few minutes. Better to say nothing; let him think whatever he wants. I won't be seeing him anymore. As if sensing she would bolt from the car when he stopped, Syril grabbed her arm, ruining her plan.

"Sweetheart don't do this to yourself; don't keep punishing yourself for mistakes in your past. I should know. I've been there many times."

She yanked her arm away. "Don't bother to get out Syril. I'll see myself to the door." *How dare he? That's my business, just like Olive is his business*. As she walked towards the door she did not look back. And for the first time since they met, Syril did not accompany her. *It's just as well. I have adorable trinkets for my trunk, that's all I need*. But her thoughts did not ring true to the bottomless ache in her heart.

What went wrong? She was the queen of switching feelings on and off like a lamp. *Pull yourself together. You're not "Little Mar" anymore*. She briefly thought to call Jorene, but quickly changed her mind. *I can't bear to hear her tell me again that I'm denying my love for Lawson. Oh God in heaven, I am so confused, please help me.*

She remembered her father's motto. "'At your lowest points in life, do something for somebody else and God will reward you every time.'" *How devastated Lawson must still be losing his parents and his career almost within the same breath. After all, I am a Christian; we're supposed to help one another. But a marriage proposal, we're barely reacquainted. He's still taking me for granted, even after all these years.*

While she craved retribution from him, she could not arrest the deeper pristine principle of her faith, helping others in time of need. After a hot shower, prayer, and 100 brush strokes to her hair, she slid between the silky white sheets on her bed.

Picking up her Bible on the nightstand she turned to her favorite book, Esther, imagining herself as queen. *What would Queen Esther do if Lawson held out the golden scepter, the ring?* She surmised that the Queen would handle the situation with royal dignity, come to his aid; help him with business aspirations, but clearly advise there would be no marriage. After all, just as the Jewish nation of old sought rescue in Esther, Marloe viewed herself as savior of her family name.

She could perhaps lessen the egregious damage to her lineage by relinquishing marriage, for marriage meant children. *My family would be spared further impact from the dreadful omen. That's the least I can do for them.* Conflicted and soul-weary, she laid the Bible down. *Jesus, you know the very number of the hairs on my head. Why should I worry? Give me sweet rest Lord.* And sleep slipped in like a thief in the night, carrying her away in dreams to a moonlit galaxy of rainbow-colored stars, and shimmering blue skies.

~ ~ ~ ~

"Get your joy back! Don't let the enemy steal what God gave you!" Syril cringed as the pastor's words hit him in the gut like a ton of bricks. Members of the congregation rose to their feet and responded to the message, joyously dancing, and clapping to the pastor's high-charged sermon. Syril looked on with a heavy heart. He had never been one to fake it, he stayed in his seat. He certainly did not feel exultant and, yes, he definitely had lost something precious, his friendship with Marloe.

Lord, what is it? Does Olive have some kind of pact with the devil to destroy my life? Soon, he was adrift in remembrances of last Saturday night. Olive had thundered back into his life unannounced and unwanted. And with her appearance his chances for a formidable relationship with Marloe went up like smoke. As if she had not done enough damage, Olive called the next morning, begging to see him. When he did not give her the response she desired, she cursed him like a mad woman.

"'I just needed to confirm the loser that you are,' Syril heard the disdain in her voice. 'Hump, you're still living in that same old apartment; same old boring Syril. I must have been crazy to think I could be with you again. I'd still be sitting right there with you, about to lose my mind like before.'"

Olive had always gone straight for the jugular. But news traveled swiftly in the world of black lawyers. That same week the true story of Olive's woes reached his desk like the morning newspaper. Her downward spiral began when she did not make partner at Dulles and Banks law firm and retaliated with insulting words of anger to Dulles. Adding insult to injury, the firm hired a young hot shot female attorney. Within a few years the new attorney not only made partner, but also stole Larry Dulles' heart from Olive.

Olive and rejection did not go well. She wanted the sun, moon, and stars wrapped around her. But when Syril once sought to provide her those things by working extra hours, Olive became sullen, disapproving. Advising he worked too much. Too late, he understood he could never satisfy her insatiable desire for power and wealth.

"'You really think that girl will stay with you?' Olive continued to hit him below the belt on the telephone that morning. 'As much as I hate to admit it, Little Missy is quite pretty, but you will eventually bore her to tears.'"

Her words stung with believability. After all, he had given Olive everything except the blood flowing through his veins and still she had left him. His confidence was at an all-time low.

In the dim light of his apartment that night he saw that Olive was still lovely, but she was pale and too thin. She had lost the shapely curves that she once flaunted with joyous conceit at the rest of the world. *Poor Olive, she ran with the highest bidder and suffered the consequences. Payback is wicked.* And yet, even after all of the unhappiness she caused he felt sympathy for her situation.

Perhaps there was some truth to Marloe's reasons for ending their friendship. There was no doubt in his mind that Olive's appearance at his door had not helped the circumstances. During the drive back to Potter's Edge that night he had tried to assure Marloe there was nothing between him and Olive. But she was silent for much of the ride. In an effort to understand her feelings he had said the wrong thing. A picture of the obstinate silent anger in her face that night haunted him.

Bringing up her past with Lawson was the worst thing I could have done. But I didn't do it to hurt her. I only wanted to assure her that I'm not like him. We're as different as night and day.

The rhythm and energy of their relationship, albeit brief, had awakened his soul.

"Saints, Jesus is the answer for your troubles. Give your burdens to him," the pastor's words aroused Syril from his daydream. He had missed the entire sermon.

"Are you hurting, heavy laden? Let Jesus fix it for you. The altar is open for prayer. Come to Jesus."

Slowly, Syril rose from the pew and pressed his way to the altar; something he had not done even when Olive deserted him. He had too much pride then, believing others might perceive his going to the altar as weakness. But this experience was too large for egotism. He knew this time in order to move on he needed Jesus. In three short months Marloe had worked her intoxicating aura into the very essence of his being. He was devastated.

~ ~ ~ ~

"Here they come! Marloe just pulled in the driveway. Be quiet," Bailey hushed the crowd assembled in the room, consisting of family and church friends. He was beside himself with needing this special night to go smoothly. Peeping out of the living room window, he watched Marloe park her car. She and Rosette exited the vehicle. It was dusk dark and the lights in the living room of the Vain home were turned off.

Although he knew Rosette disliked being the center of attention, this was her night. *She always put herself last; she deserves something special for her birthday.* As a guise, to get Rosette out of the house Marloe treated her to a shopping spree. Rosette had frowned on the invitation, stating she did not need another thing. It made Bailey chuckle. Rosette, who was exceedingly frugal because of childhood poverty now humbly advised that she had everything she desired, materially speaking. Bailey aimed to mend the emotional split between them. It had been a component of their lives far too long.

Shortly after Rosette and Marloe left the house that morning Bailey drove to Shomson to pick up Justa and Jessie. They had all secretly planned Rosette's surprise birthday party. The front door opened.

"Oh, my goodness, it's so dark in here," Rosette said. She fumbled for the light switch. "Why are the lights…"

"Surprise! Happy birthday!" Everyone yelled out.

The room suddenly flooded with light. Rosette dropped her armful of shopping bags; her hands flew to her face. Bailey came to her side, picking up the bags. Rosette shook her head, keeping her face covered until she could speak.

"Oh, my Lord; how did you all do this without me knowing?" And then she smiled. Her eyes gleamed bright with happiness.

Bailey breathed a sigh of relief. *She's happy. Thank you, Lord.*

Rosette playfully glared at Wesley and Eubie as they stood near Marloe. "And my boys even kept it a secret, my gracious."

"Yep, we had strict orders," Eubie said. Everyone roared with laughter.

"I know this had to be Marloe's idea," Rosette smiled knowingly at Marloe.

"No mother, not me. It was father's idea; him and the twins. The three of them nearly drove me nuts. "'Make sure you tell your mother early enough that you're taking her out for the day. You know how she likes to doodle around in the house, cleaning, and re-cleaning.'"

The house shook with gaiety. Everyone surrounded Rosette to sing happy birthday. Her eyes brimmed with tears. "T-Thank you all so much, this is so nice, so unexpected."

Bailey took both of her hands in his, holding them tightly as they sang.

"Baby girl, I thank God for you, happy birthday." *Lord, I have treated this wonderful woman so badly. Why should she forgive me? She still has that trunk full of money; maybe she's still thinking of leaving me. Rosette's a beautiful woman, inside and out, a prize for any man.*

"Alright ya'll two lovebirds, let's eat," Justa interrupted Bailey's momentary muse. "I'm hungry and we have all this food, c'mon everybody, dig in."

As everyone headed to the dining room Bailey smiled inwardly. He had grown fond of the twins. The marked improvement in Justa's health bordered on miraculous. The death-like cough that plagued her when they met was now arrested thanks to Rosette. She had taken Justa to a renowned pulmonary specialist who ran a series of tests. Diagnosed as a severe asthmatic they prescribed a host of medicines for Justa, and her illness was finally under control. As well, Rosette pumped Justa full of vitamin supplements and added beets to her sister's diet to build her blood up and strengthen her immune system.

As Bailey and Rosette entered the dining room hand-in-hand, he felt quite buoyant. Her sisters had turned the massive dining room table into a magnificently decorated, mouth-watering feast. Sweetnin' had arrived early to help the twins hang crepe paper and balloons.

Initially, Bailey was skeptical, unsure if the three women working together might prove a recipe for disaster. While life had tempered the twins, they were not so mellowed that they would not give Sweetnin' as good as she gave and more. They were not restrained like Rosette. Despite their financial prosperity they remained a bit rough around the edges.

Bailey had not minced words with Sweetnin' when they invited her family to the party. There could be no element of discord on Sweetnin's part concerning anything.

"'I'm done with that Bailey,' Sweetnin' assured him. 'Don't you see how Rosette and I get along now? I've grown to love that girl.'"

Perhaps this is something orchestrated by God, Bailey surmised. *It may be a way for Sweetnin' to make peace with the twins too. We're all family now.*

When Sweetnin' arrived, the twins had given her a chilly reception. However, soon, he observed his sister humbly ingratiate herself to them. She dragged her heavy body around, helping and following their lead. Bailey admitted Sweetnin' had come a long way from the uppity-talking, judgmental sister he once knew. He suspected that her own family troubles had brought her to this new day. Even so, she had not entirely abated curse talk; he surmised that only a work of God would liberate her from that albatross.

"Look how beautiful everything is," Rosette marveled as her eyes swept the table. "Oh, my goodness, all of this food; it's enough to feed an army."

The captain chairs of the huge dining table were dressed in cream-colored satin covers. Rosette's favorite color, a fuchsia silk table runner graced its center. Set in buffet style, the table was dressed in Fostoria "Navarre" china, tea glasses, with an assortment of gold silverware. Rows of fuchsia and beige crepe paper draped the sides of the Herculean dining room chandelier.

The sideboard held an assortment of mouth-watering dishes. Seafood; fried jumbo shrimp and scallops, oysters and clams on the half-shell, fried catfish, and whiting. Another section was devoted to chicken, baked, fried, and barbecued. Side dishes were snap peas, collard greens, rice, potato salad, macaroni and cheese, and sweet rolls.

Rosette gasped when she eyed the triple-layered chocolate chip cake. Her eyes welled with tears. "Aw, that's Mama's cake," she squealed in delight. "Mama always found a way to make me chocolate chip cake for my birthday no matter what. It's so beautiful. Jessie did you make it?"

Jessie nodded her head. "Yes Rosie, I made it just for you. I remember how you used to love that cake. It might not taste as good as Mama's, but I tried," she laughed softly.

"Thank you so much Jessie. I knew it had to be you because Justa burned anything she tried to bake." The sisters laughed loudly at the special memory.

"But you were a good cook Justa, just like Mama," Rosette hugged her sisters close.

"Yeah, me and baking didn't get along," Justa smiled wryly. "But cooking came naturally for me. I ain't bragging, but you both know Mama and me could put a hurtin' on food." They chuckled gaily, still embracing each other.

The house was alive with an atmosphere of joy as guests gathered around the table to enjoy the banquet before them. Bailey felt good. Everything had gone splendidly and, he hoped, the best was yet to come.

~ ~ ~ ~

The party was winding down when the black stretch limo pulled into the Vain driveway at seven o'clock. The doorbell rang and Marloe rushed to open the door. Sweetnin' and the twins had earlier banned Granny Kate and Rosette from the kitchen when those two began clearing dishes from the table. They now sat on the living room couch engrossed in quiet conversation. Bailey saw

Rosette look up, staring curiously at the chauffeur standing at the entrance. *Maybe I should call the whole thing off. It's been a big evening and, well she's probably tired.* He was losing his nerve.

"Father," Marloe beamed. "Jab wants to speak to you."

Marloe and the boys will be disappointed if I don't go through with it, and the twins. He braced himself and went to the door, all the while feeling Rosette's inquisitive gaze.

"Hey Jab, alright, I'll be with you in a few minutes."

"Take your time sir. I just wanted to let you know I'm ready and waiting in the car."

"Thank you."

Bailey broke out in a light sweat, fearful of Rosette's reaction. Her luminous eyes were now filled with curiosity as he walked towards the sofa where she sat with Annie Kate.

He bent down and pecked Kate on the cheek. "Excuse me mother, I need to talk to Rosette for a minute."

Turning to Rosette, he spoke. "Baby girl, the party's not over yet. I would love the pleasure of taking you to the City for the weekend for your birthday?" *If she turns me down, I'll just keep trying.*

The question mark on Rosette's face turned into confusion. "I'm sorry Bailey. What did you say? I couldn't quite hear with all the noise."

He leaned down close to her cheek. Annie Kate eyed Bailey and then looked at Rosette, apparently intrigued with their conversation. Justa and Jessie stood in the hallway with two large suitcases. Bailey had earlier asked them to pack some of Rosette's belongings for the trip. All eyes were on him, especially his children's and he knew he could not turn back.

He took Rosette's hand and gingerly pulled her to her feet. Again, he asked, "Rosette, would you be kind enough to spend the weekend with your husband in New York City?"

The stunned expression on her face told him she felt just as awkward as he. She seemed to calm down a bit when her children came close. "I-I, New York City, Bailey, are you sure?" Her voice was rift with uncertainty. "I mean, I've never been to New York, what will I wear? I'll need to pack."

"You don't have to do anything except grab your coat and pocketbook. Your sisters already packed your suitcase. The limo is waiting for us outside. You're going to have the best birthday you've ever had. Let's go, alright little girl?"

Rosette smiled at him, nodding yes. Not the guarded smile he was used to, but this time her face lit up, open and engaging. It aroused the memory of the many months it took to invoke such a smile from her during their courtship.

But like an idiot, I squashed her happiness, believing she didn't deserve any. I became her judge and jury. Lord, for whatever time I have left on earth, I'll make her smile every day.

In all the years they were married Bailey had never taken Rosette on vacation. *I'll make it up to her, I'll treat her like the queen she is.* His heart swelled with the brilliance of his love for her. *How could I have judged her so harshly; to allow all those years to go by with such unforgiveness in my heart?*

The twins entered the room with the luggage. With the suspense over, the party again became alive with merriment. Bailey opened the living room door to see Jab awaiting them in the car. Wesley and Eubie brought their suitcases to the limousine. As Bailey and Rosette parted the house to laughter and cheers of everyone, Bailey determined to bring the magic of yesteryear back to their marriage that weekend. They were off to the prestigious Harvin Hotel in New York City.

~ ~ ~ ~

As they cruised to New York in the limo, Rosette's feelings were all over the place like a livewire about to ignite. *Am I dreaming...if I am this is the best dream I've had in years. Has he truly forgiven me after all these years?*

Bailey took her hand and gently kissed it. She trembled from his tender caress. He pulled her close and she melted into his arms. She was afraid to speak for fear of ruining this sacred moment. He held her gently, as if she were as fragile as a China doll. Oh, how she had missed the security of his protective embrace. Of him wanting to hold her because he desired her, not just from physical need. She breathed in the smell and feel of him as if there would never be another chance. They held each other tightly. He buried his face in her bosom, and then he began to weep.

"Rosie, I'm sorry. Can you ever forgive me for all the hurt and pain I've caused you? Please forgive me baby. I promised God that I would make it up to you. Whatever your heart desires, just ask me for it. It's yours without question."

Bailey's weeping tore at her heartstrings, reminding her of that dreadful day in Calgon. But this time she felt he wept from a deep sense of relief.

"Oh, Bailey," she fought tears as well. "How can I not forgive you. I really brought it on myself for not being honest with you from the beginning, and I'm so sorry. The question is do you truly forgive me? My lies caused so many problems."

"Please believe me, I love you, Rosette. I've never stopped loving you, but pride, it blinded me. But God showed me during my illness how wrong I was to pass judgment on you. I prayed for him to deliver me from being unforgiving, asked him to teach me to say, "I'm sorry," and he answered my prayers. I'm so sorry sweetheart. I love you from the bottom of my heart. I cherish you."

Rosette's heart turned over with the endless love she had kept hidden from Bailey. *A lot of men in his shoes would have thrown me out and divorced me in a heartbeat.*

"I realized just how much I love you when you got sick. All I ever wanted was to make you happy Bailey, to be worthy of your love. That's all I want, all I ever needed."

Her tears flowed, and, in that moment, she felt the transgressions of the past wash away with their weeping.

God performed a soul-cleansing catharsis between them. She was 21 again and wantonly in love. But to truly participate in this second chance at love she knew she would need to follow the same counsel she had given to Marloe.

I think I can give up my trunk now, leave it at the altar with all those bad memories. The money can benefit the church. Dear Lord, please give me strength.

~ ~ ~ ~

"Hey man, did Marloe tell you we're getting married?" Lawson listened intently on the phone line waiting to hear Syril rise to his underhanded tease. Again, the enemy orchestrated the plot, with Lawson dancing to his never-ending tune.

"Oh, really?" Syril cleared his throat. A lengthy delay followed, long enough for Lawson to grasp that his words had stunned Syril into silence.

"No, she didn't tell me. Well, congratulations man. I wish you both the best."

Yeah, right. Sure, you do. He would have given his championship ring to witness Syril's riddled-with-shocked face at that moment. He initiated the phone call as a ruse to figure out if Syril was still spending time with Marloe.

In truth he knew Marloe would not accept his marriage proposal that soon. But he had dangled the ring before her like bait on a hook, laying the groundwork for the final catch. *Marloe loves fine things. And as beautiful as Mama's ring is, it doesn't hold a candle to the one I bought for Marloe.*

"Cuz, I acted like a real jerk the last time I saw you in Potter's Edge," Lawson continued his scheme. "And I'm very sorry about that, just had some things going on. Let's get together, talk some things out." He was itching to know how regularly Syril visited Potter's Edge.

"Lawson don't worry about it. It happened, you apologized. It's over. I'm keeping a low profile right now, but sure, we can get together some time soon."

"Yeah, we'll do that. I'll need you to draw up my Will, you know, look over my finances. I'd like to get everything in order before the wedding. Ash and I came to an agreement about the house. I'm buying him out. Oh, by the way, I'm thinking of opening up a weekend supper club; five-star, a lot bigger than Ma and Dad's." He eagerly waited for Syril's response.

"Sounds like big plans ahead for you. I'm sure it will be successful. One of our paralegals can handle drawing up your Will. We'll set up a date for us to meetup. I've gotta run Lawson; early court session tomorrow."

"Alright man, later," Lawson felt frustrated. He had given Syril something to chew on, but he didn't know if his cousin bit. *He's a master at hiding his true feelings, always was.*

"Later," Syril hung up.

Lawson pondered their conversation. He hadn't received the answer he was looking for during the call. *Dang, I wish I could have seen his face. He's a good lawyer, knows how to look you straight in the eye and get a person twisted. But if we were face-to-face, I would know what he was feeling. If only I can get Marloe to accept my proposal.*

It had been a long three months of nothing substantial with Marloe. There was one light as a feather kiss to the lips that only served to remind him of what he missed. *I broke her down once and I will do it again, but tonight I need....*

The intrinsic blood of his father surged through his veins, filling him with fleshly desire and brazen confidence. *Okay, so my sports career is over, but I'm financially stable. When Marloe and I hook up she'll put me on the map with investments. She was always a math whiz, not my strongest subject.*

He left his house and drove east away from Potter's Edge. Discreetness was the name of the game. Although it was early in the week there was always a willing creature for a one-night stand. Maybe it was the nostalgic background noise of Harlem during his phone conversation with Syril, the ingratiating liveliness. Whatever it was, it awakened memories of their families strolling uptown Harlem on free-spirited East 125th Street.

Suddenly, he felt an intense longing to be close to the essence of his father in Harlem. Jonas had lived and breathed the Harlem spirit, the unadulterated soulful culture. It was no secret that Jonas did not hold the same love of Potter's Edge that he held for Harlem. At Dolly's insistence, he had grudgingly obliged and moved the family to New Jersey. The reason was clear to Lawson, his father's wheeling and dealing reputation in Harlem was troublesome for the family. Although Potter's Edge placed Lawson on a pedestal as a local celebrity his roots were firmly planted in Harlem, regardless of his subliminal denial.

Harlem, I should take a ride there for old time's sake, but not to see Syril. He smirked inwardly. *I doubt if Syril wants to see me anytime soon.* Potter's Edge was becoming a bit stale. Already he had begun missing his celebrated platform in Atlanta. *I can bring that spotlight to Potter's Edge when I open the supper club. Maybe I'll check out Wonder Lounge tonight in Harlem; high-caliber, good music, and fine women. Get some tips for my own club.*

~ ~ ~ ~

He made his way to the bar at the Wonder Lounge, sat down, and ordered a beer. The woman sitting alone at the other end of the bar looked edgy. She tapped out a cigarette, and the bartender rushed to light it for her. Inhaling deeply with a lengthy exhale, she took a sip of her drink. Her eyes scoured the room and met Lawson's intriguing gaze. He waited. An hour went by and still she sat in solitaire. She was beautiful, but hard looking, with jet-black shoulder-length straight hair.

Forget Marloe tonight. The woman impetuously held up her empty glass to the bartender. No smile, no conversation, just a demanding gleam in her eyes. Tonight, he needed somebody like that; someone who did not care to know him, someone only desirous of a night of pleasure. He motioned to the bartender and sent her a cocktail on him.

Chapter 17

"I'M FINE," MARLOE SAID. SHE AND JORENE SAT conversing in Marloe's living room.

Jorene stared at her for a moment and shook her head. "No, you're not, Mar; you're pretending to be fine. You're talking to me, remember, no secrets between us. For the last few weeks, you've seemed so preoccupied. What is it, sweetie?"

Marloe bent her head. Jorene's words had struck a nerve. "Rene, I'm okay. Don't worry about me. It's just that sometimes I feel so lonely. People are all around me, but I'm lonesome. Look at you. How blessed you are with a good husband and beautiful children.

"I look at my future and it seems hopeless, depressing, nothing will ever change for me. Sometimes I wonder why I was born. And please don't remind me about the 'power' thing because I'm beginning to think that's the real 'curse' if you really want to know the truth."

Jorene looked confused, but Marloe was too miserable to defend her own words. If her 'power' was supposed to comfort her, lately it had been a nemesis. Why did her heart ache to see Syril if she had so much control over her emotions. It had been three weeks since they parted ways. After trampling on his heart, she did not feel the victorious rush that usually lifted her spirits. Instead, she felt wretched and depressed. In the interim she had spent time with Lawson, telling herself it was the Christian thing to do, to help him through his loss. Soon she would be done with him and have her victory. Nevertheless, Syril was never far from her thoughts.

"Marloe, listen to me," Jorene's voice filled with empathy. "Yes, Dugey is a good man and I love him and the girls with all my heart. But do you realize Dugey is on the road working more than he's home. Sure, his success as an owner operator allows me to stay home with my girls. But it also leaves me responsible for everything, dealing with the household and the kids.

"You don't know how I wish I was in your shoes sometimes. Talk about lonely. My girls are my life, but sometimes I miss 'grown-folk' conversation. And you're so busy with your job and social life that we don't see each other for weeks. The difference is that I'm lonely for my man because I have no choice, but you choose to be alone."

"But I…"

"Let me finish Marloe. You've let that whole curse thing take happiness away from you. Okay, so you made a mistake when you were 16. Do you really believe that God would continually punish you for it? God is good, he loves us. We listen to the pastor's sermons on Sundays, but are you truly taking his word in? Stop holding onto the past Mar, stop letting it control you. Ask God to help you, he wants you to live that abundant life that he promises to all who serve him."

Marloe felt the sting of hot tears. Truly Jorene was the best friend she would ever have. "Rene, I'm so afraid to trust my own judgment. I've listened to my family's guidance all my life. It's all I know. And when I did trust my own feelings, the consequences almost made me lose my mind."

"But you know God, you know Jesus."

"So do they," Marloe sadly blinked her tears away.

"But they can't know him for you. Oh, Mar, how I wish you could see things from my perspective. Lawson loves you so much. Remember how we said we would marry and live in the same neighborhood so our children could grow up together? We can still do those things Mar. Marry Lawson. Deep inside I know you still love him, but you're so wrapped up in the past that you can't see the bright future waiting for you. Let all that pay-back stuff go so you can walk into your future with confidence and love."

Marloe gazed at her friend. Jorene was correct in many of the things she said, but she confused Marloe's sympathy for Lawson with love. For that is all she felt for Lawson. She no longer felt the pressing need to hurt him for what he did to her. He had suffered enormously without her lifting a hand. Her dilemma was a simple one, yet painfully true. She had done the unthinkable, fallen head-over-hills in love with Syril Barrett.

"Thank you, Rene, sweetie, I feel better. You always give me strength. But every time I think of marriage, I'm frightened, you know? And I talk to God about everything. He just hasn't given me an answer yet."

She forfeited telling Jorene about her true feelings for Lawson; it would be fruitless. To rid herself of the many dismal thoughts in her head she changed the subject.

"So, let's talk about you girl, your birthday is next Friday. The big one, 25! You finally catch up to me. Will Dugey be home for your birthday?"

Jorene frowned and shook her head. "Heck no honey, he'll get in tomorrow and leave for Kentucky on Tuesday. He won't be back until next Sunday."

"Okay, it's settled then, I'm taking you out for your birthday on Friday. Where do you want to go? The sky is the limit."

Jorene's face beamed bright. "Oh girl, for real, anywhere?"

"Yes girl, we'll go wherever your little heart desires."

"Let's go to Harlem. We haven't been there together in years. Let's go to the Wonder Lounge. Remember how much fun we had when Wesley took us there when we turned 21?"

Marloe smiled at Jorene, but her stomach turned over with anxiety. For obvious reasons she had purposefully not told Jorene about her day in Harlem with Syril. *Darn, I forgot how much she loves that place too.* When they were youngsters, Jorene had ridden buckshot with her and Wesley a few times to take fares into Harlem. Marloe could practically drive that route with her eyes closed she had been there so many times with her brothers, tagging along in the taxi.

Seeing Jorene so happy she could not take that away from her. "I'll pick you up at eight o'clock next Friday. Remember you're married, so don't be dressing all fresh," Marloe teased, throwing her head back in laughter.

"Hump, I'm gonna find me the sexiest dress I can get my big hips into and have a ball. Dugey better recognize what he's got. Oh, goodness, New York, Harlem, I can't wait."

The mood between them was once again light as they laughed and chatted about Jorene's big day. *Syril's favorite spot, the Wonder Lounge.* Marloe sighed and did her best to alleviate the uneasiness that came over her as she smiled brightly at Jorene.

~ ~ ~ ~

It had been three weeks since Syril spoke to Marloe and each day proved gloomier than the previous. Out of desperation he had called her a few times at her work only to be told that she was out of the office. How he missed her beautiful smile and the sweet thrill of her laughter. Yearning to hear her voice he dialed her home number a few times but there was no answer.

"Your order is ready Mr. Barrett."

Food, that would help him through the evening, but come three o'clock in the morning his heart would turn over with despair, rendering another restless night. *Why did I ever make that first move towards her, ask her to dinner? Lord, help me get through this with my mind still intact.*

"Thanks Rollie. Keep the change." He walked out of the greasy spoon. Desperate to abate images of Marloe from his mind, he kept long hours at the firm and fervently dug into his pro bono cases. Yet, nothing helped, not the heavy-duty soul food that he loved, nor the rewarding feeling of helping someone who could not afford attorney fees. He worked, he ate, then tossed and turned many nights as sleep eluded him.

I knew her story with Lawson almost from the beginning. First love, what was I thinking to throw that in her face? Ashton had confirmed that Lawson was indeed the victim of an unmerciful beating from Marloe's brothers. He had not spared the gory details. Even so, Syril was hard pressed to believe his cousin's skirt chasing days had waned. Still, it appeared he had convinced Marloe otherwise, so much so that she would actually marry him.

Was my vibe with Marloe so off that I alone felt that breathtaking connection when we were together? How could she marry Lawson when the force between them was so pristine, almost tangible in its existence.

He understood that Lawson had called him to gloat, to thrust the knife in and turn it as deeply as it could go. He had won. *But I need to hear it from her.* He glanced at his watch. It was six-thirty in the evening, she should be off work. He apprehensively dialed her home number. After four rings he was about to hang up when someone answered.

"Hello," the elderly voice on the line was not Marloe's. "Who's calling?" the woman asked.

"I'm sorry Ma'am; I must have misdialed," he stated.

She doesn't want to talk to you. That's why she had someone else answer her phone. He quietly placed the receiver back in its cradle. His pride fallen to a new low.

"Lord, strengthen me to accept Marloe as Lawson's wife. If that is your Will, your Will be done." Drained in mind, body, and spirit; he laid across the bed, drifting into a blessed overdue slumber.

~ ~ ~ ~

"I let that curse talk continue for too long Rosie," Bailey lowered his head sadly. "Although I didn't believe in it, I never refuted it to the family. So, they took my silence for belief, I'm just as guilty. I shouldn't have allowed anyone to place such a burden on Marloe; I should have had more backbone."

He sat at the kitchen table berating himself for the many ways he believed he had failed his daughter. Rosette quietly poured him a cup of coffee and then sat down beside him. She shook her head in disagreement.

"No Bailey, I think you did the best you could in the situation. This thing has been entrenched in your family for generations. It wouldn't have made any difference to them if you disagreed. But you still have time to remedy it, to let Marloe know how you really feel. It's not too late to turn things around, to try to make her understand that God wants her to live her life like any other young woman."

It had been a few weeks since their weekend in New York. Bailey was still floating on a cloud, comforted that he and Rosette were as one again after so many wasted years. Their love gloriously renewed, and the passion of their early days rekindled like the strength of a blazing fire.

God has given me a second chance. He smiled inwardly as he reflected on how New York peeled away Rosette's reserved nature. She was enamored with the city, the bright lights and, without a doubt, the Harvin Hotel. After a room service candlelit dinner that Friday night they renewed their love in every sense of the word. As she slept in his arms, he wondered how he had breathed without the great passion that came with fully loving her.

That Saturday night Jab escorted them to the upscale "Corner Restaurant" in uptown Harlem. It was truly a marvelous, clandestine weekend. But the harm he believed he was responsible for towards his daughter marred his ability to truly bask in the renewal of their love.

He felt the softness of Rosette's hand as she placed it over his. "Bailey did you hear me? You can turn this around. Talk to her, she always took your word like gospel."

He shook his head in disagreement. "All I ever wanted was the best for my family. I wanted to make everybody happy, but I failed Rosie. Do you really believe Marloe will understand after all this time? I mean I let mama and the other women in the family shape her to their thinking."

"What are you two lovebirds doing?" Marloe asked gaily, bustling into the room. She bent down to kiss her mother and then pecked Bailey on the cheek.

"Hey baby girl," Bailey prayed she had not overheard their conversation. He felt anxious, but Rosette gave him a look of confidence and squeezed his hand tightly.

"Hello dear, you're home early this evening. Is everything alright?" Rosette asked.

Marloe plopped down in the chair next to Bailey. "Yes mother, everything is fine. I had some business to take care of at the bank, so I left work early today. Where's Granny Kate?"

Bailey cleared his throat. "She was a little tired after dinner and went to bed early."

"What? It's only five o'clock. Let me go check on her."

"She's fine Marloe. I helped her prepare for bed," Rosette assured her. "She fell asleep before her head hit the pillow. Stop worrying so much. Are you hungry? I made meatloaf, your favorite. Let me fix you a plate."

"Thanks mother, but I'm not hungry. I had lunch with Jorene today, still full."

Rosette frowned. "I don't see where you put it. You're just as thin as can be."

~ ~ ~ ~

It was Friday, Jorene's birthday. Marloe was excited about their upcoming outing at Wonder Lounge. But even with the delightful expectations of the night, anxiety filtered its way into her thoughts. Memories of her evening with Syril at the Wonder Lounge haunted her. They were vivid, intoxicating. The way he held her hand with such firmness, as if he would never let it go. His eyes reflected a vibrant energy in sync with hers. The profound spiritual and sensual connection that she felt for him caused an emotional storm in her soul.

She tossed her head back trying to rid herself of the sweet recollections that carried her away to her own private world of painful ecstasy. *This is Jorene's night, forget about me.*

Her emerald green, silk party dress lay on the bed. She picked it up, unzipped the back and quickly slipped it on. She loved the velvet bodice and the plunging rear neckline, replete with elbow-length sleeves. *I'll leave the plunging front necklines to Jorene.*

She anxiously opened the new jewelry set she had earlier placed on top of the armoire. Luscious diamonds in green winked at her from every direction. She picked up the teardrop choker gleaming in its splendor with matching earrings and bracelet. After carefully adorning herself in the jewelry, she slipped her feet into black round-toed stilettos. Taking hold of her ever-ready Alberto VO5 hair spray, she squirted generously. One last look in the mirror assured her that she could make even the most moral minded man fodder for her desires. Grabbing her purse, she strutted out of the door.

It was six in the evening when she pulled into Jorene's driveway. A sudden wave of melancholy enveloped her as she vacated her car and walked towards the front door of the home. The house was a small red brick ranch replete with a white picket fence. In the balmy April weather evidence of Jorene's green thumb ran rampant as lush evergreen hedges favored the inside areas of the fence. Picturesque scarlet rose bushes adjacent to the front porch welcomed guests. Jorene lived the life that was once Marloe's dream. She had married the love of her life; bore his children and seemed destined to live happily ever after. Marloe sighed ruefully, putting on a happy face, she rang the doorbell. *I'm happy for her. Stop looking back.*

"Hey Mar," Jorene squealed with delight after opening the door. The two women embraced.

"Look at you, you look gorgeous. I love your jewelry," Jorene exclaimed.

"Thank you, sweetie. Talk about me, look at you! Oh, my goodness. I love your dress." Jorene was decked out in a red knee-length satin shift dress with short sleeves and a pleated front. To Marloe's surprise the neckline of the dress was round and appeared to have no plunge in the back. "Turn around girl, let me see the back."

"I'm married girl. My cleavage belongs to my husband," Jorene laughed. She turned around so Marloe could see the back of the dress.

"Ok girl, I love it," Marloe said.

She pulled a gift for Jorene out of her pocketbook and handed it to her. "Happy birthday Rene."

"Oh Marloe, you shouldn't have."

"But I did," Marloe laughed lightly. "So, open it, hurry up so we can get this party going girl."

"Oh Marloe, it's lovely!" Jorene held up the shimmering

red jewels, a necklace and earring set. "I love it. Thank you so much."

"You're welcome. When you told me you would wear red, I couldn't resist buying that set when I saw it. I got it the same day I bought the one I'm wearing. Here, let me help you put it on."

The necklace of red rubies gleamed between the brilliance of marquise diamonds along with accompanying earrings and bracelet. Jorene fingered the jewelry as she observed her reflection in the hallway mirror.

"Marloe, this must have cost a fortune. You shouldn't have spent so much money on me. You're always buying stuff for the kids, and you never let me pick up the tab for anything. I-I…"

"What else have I got to spend my money on?" Marloe interrupted her. She rolled her eyes toward the sky in exasperation. "Rene, you're the sister I never had, and you know I love those babies like they were mine."

"Thank you so much Marloe. I love you girl."

"Love you too."

As they hugged, Marloe felt that somber ache again; the feeling that life was passing her by and she had no real future to look to, just material things and loneliness. *Shake it off, stop thinking about yourself. God give me peace. Help me make my friend happy on her special birthday.*

"Let's go Rene."

"Mar, remember how we used to stop traffic when we were teenagers? Well get ready for double action tonight. Harlem will never be the same!"

Marloe smiled, fighting to overcome the gloomy reality of her life. *And I'll never be the same after Syril.*

~ ~ ~ ~

If they were given a quarter for second glances received walking from the parking lot to the entrance of the Wonder

Lounge the cover charge would have been free. Jorene was like a schoolgirl at recess. She wore her hair in a French twist, leaving her neck to highlight the sparkling jewels surrounding it.

She looks lovely, Marloe thought, observing the joy on her friend's face. *She deserves to have some fun on her 25th birthday.*

As for herself, she trembled from the troublesome reality of growing tired of her '*calling.*' Lately, the idea that men desired her for beauty alone had taken on a negative truth begging her to face it. It was all so superficial, so hollow. *They don't even know the real me, yet they buy things for me thinking they can own me.*

Satan stepped in, whispering in her ear. *Don't be foolish, that's all you have. Enjoy it while you can. Remember, you'll have all those fine jewels to hold close to your heart years from now when the second glances end.* And like a slave to one's master, she arched her back, smiled, and put on her best strut.

After paying the entrance fee they were escorted to the fine dining area in the ballroom to seats near the front of the stage. As the 'Wonder Band,' played softly, they nibbled on hors d'oeuvres served butler style.

"This is so cool Mar. We get to see Mom Casey too. She's hilarious," Jorene said. Mom Casey was a famous comedian who frequented the trendy clubs in Harlem.

"Yes, it looks like we picked a good night. The band sounds great," Marloe attempted to be in the moment with Jorene. Yet shades of Syril haunted her at every turn. She felt him in the pulsating music, in the familiar smell of the soul food that he savored, and in the calming mellow atmosphere. Determined to brandish ghosts of the past, she picked up her glass of 'special-occasion' champagne.

"Happy birthday Rene." They toasted with a clink of their glasses.

Suddenly, Marloe's hand froze in mid-air. She did a

double take as she stared at the man entering the bar.

Lawson? What was he doing here? He had long ago shared with her that although he was born in Harlem it was not his favorite place, he basically avoided it. And true to his word, during their courtship they had never once visited Harlem.

Um, perhaps he's had a change of heart, getting bored with Potter's Edge. Maybe this is where he hangs out when he's not pestering me.

"Rene, Rene, quick, turn around. Look at the bar entrance."

Jorene did a whiplash turn. "T-That's Lawson. Mar, did you tell him we were coming here tonight?"

"Heck no I didn't tell him. I was going to ask you the same thing. Did you tell him Rene? This is your birthday night, just us girls, that was our plan."

Jorene shook her head profusely. "Marloe, I swear, I didn't tell him a thing."

"It's alright, really. I wouldn't be surprised if he came here to pick up tips on running a nightclub. He's thinking about opening one in Potter's Edge, 'five-star,' his words."

"Yeah, you told me. But honestly Mar, I haven't spoken to Lawson in months. I only hear what you tell me." She stared at Marloe and then leaned in closer to her. "You know you might as well get it over with, the curiosity is killing you."

Marloe nonchalantly waved her hand in the air, shrugging her shoulders. "What do you mean curiosity? I really don't care why Lawson is here if that's what you mean." But something about the situation was a bit bizarre. She was intrigued. Jorene could never lie and keep a straight face, so she knew she hadn't told Lawson about their outing.

"You're flicking your nails, Marloe. You know; that little thing you do when you're anxious."

"No, it felt like I cracked a nail. I'm just checking."

Jorene stood up, placing her hands on her hips. "I refuse to let Lawson James ruin my birthday. C'mon, let's go find him and put your mind at ease. Then we can have our dinner and enjoy the show in peace."

Not wanting to appear overly interested, Marloe took a sip of champagne and slowly rose from her chair.

"Lawson is free to do whatever he likes. I just find it odd that he's here. He was never crazy about Harlem. Okay, let's go check him out, but we'll make it clear that he can't join us. He bugs me to death as it is. C'mon, we need to hurry back before they bring our dinner. Take your shawl sweetie." She handed Jorene her black silk scarf. "It might disappear."

They stepped into the bar where stools were full, but there was no sign of Lawson. They walked through the area checking out the booths. Soon, Marloe spotted him. He sat in a small booth in the corner of the room. "Rene, there he is. C'mon."

Lawson did not see them until they stood before him. A woman sat across from him in the small cubicle. Since her back was to them only her hands were seen along with smoke-filled ringlets she blew in the air.

"Well, hello Lawson, fancy meeting you here," Marloe laughed lightly. Lawson gazed at her like a deer in headlights. Words were unnecessary. It was all there in his eyes, surprise, fear, but most of all guilt. His face held an old expression; it was just a new day. The woman at the table stubbed her cigarette in the ashtray and turned in their direction. *What!* Marloe was stunned. She stared directly into the hollow eyes of Olive Caster.

"Let's go Mar," she felt the tug of Jorene's hand on her arm.

"No, it's fine Rene." Marloe faced Lawson. "So, you've changed, huh? You see how God reveals things. This confirms what I knew in my heart all along; I just wondered when the true Lawson James would show up.

Marry you? I never gave it a second thought. Please go straight to hell."

Lawson jumped to his feet, a vision of anger and bewilderment. He got in Marloe's face. "What the hell do you expect, 'Miss Goody-Girl Marloe.' All these years I've waited for you to get that curse mess out of your head. But you're just an educated fool, won't marry; won't have sex, all because of some junk that happened in your family decades ago."

Marloe's temper flared. "Well, I bet this fool is educated enough to know that you're crazy. Like I once told you, I'm dead to you Lawson. And that's for real. We are not friends or enemies; we are nothing to each other."

Jorene stepped between the two, glaring at Lawson. "Don't you ever call me again about Marloe. In fact, don't call Dugey either. And you better be glad I know Jesus, or I would really tell you what I really think of you. Just remember this, 'you reap what you sow.'"

"Marloe is everything alright?" Syril's voice came unexpectedly like soothing salve to what threatened to spiral out of control. She turned in disbelief. *Syril? Syril is here.* It was pure serendipity that during this sudden near chaotic moment, he had once again swooped in to rescue her. The irony rendered her speechless. Before she could get her tongue out of lockdown, Olive bolted from her seat. She ran to Syril with outstretched arms.

"Syril, I knew you would show up one of these nights. I've been waiting for you baby. I knew you would come here eventually. The Wonder Lounge was your work week shake off, your spot to unwind. I didn't forget baby."

Syril looked shock. Olive stood before him, tears streaming down her face.

Marloe clutched her purse tightly to her side in an effort to conceal her shaky hands. *I don't know if he's more stunned by her words or the fact that she's with Lawson. Just remember the last time you saw him, and he threw*

Lawson up in your face, walk away. Yet, at the sound of his voice her heart filled with joy. As much as she tried to tell herself that their connection was folly of the mind, the undeniable love she felt for him gnawed at her very being.

"I-I'm fine," Marloe's tongue blessedly came unglued. She quickly turned away from the scene in front of her, unwilling to witness Syril's reaction to Olive.

"C'mon Rene, let's go."

"Yes, Little Missy, and make sure it's for good this time. Syril doesn't want you; he loves me, and he always will."

Marloe's cheeks flamed in indignation. She momentarily slipped into unsaved status as she approached Olive.

"Well, 'Miss Know-It-All!'" she screamed loudly at Olive. "Why isn't he with you tonight? And why is it every time I see you, you're putting on a freak show? You're pathetic."

Syril stepped in. "I'm not going through this with you again Olive," he said, shaking his head. "All the drama, you know there is absolutely nothing between us."

Olive shrieked like a cat pouncing on a rat for dinner as she lunged for Syril. He caught her arms, holding them tightly as she fruitlessly thrashed her skinny body about, attempting to break free. Finally, silently, she gave up the battle, slowly backing away from Syril. The crocodile tears were all dried up, her face defeated, worn. Like a robot needing a rewind she returned to her seat. Lawson sat wild-eyed, nursing a drink. *They deserve each other,* Marloe thought, *two back-stabbers.*

Syril turned to Marloe. His eyes mirrored the wanton melancholy she endured since their departure. "It's really good to see you again Marloe."

"It's nice to see you too."

Jorene gave Marloe a curious look.

"Oh, I'm sorry. Jorene this is Syril Barrett. Syril, meet my best friend, Jorene Scott. We're celebrating her birthday tonight."

"Nice to meet you," Jorene gushed as she and Syril shook hands.

"And you as well, happy birthday."

"Thank you."

Marloe was desperate to keep her pounding heart in control. *I have to leave before I make a fool of myself.* "Take care Syril."

"Yes, and you do the same Marloe." He took a step closer to her, his eyes entreating her for understanding.

"Can I call you sometime…friends?" he quickly added.

It was so tempting to give in; such a wonderful dream to again be with him. *But there is no way we can just be friends. Doesn't he remember that kiss that sent us both to nirvana?* She looked at Jorene for support.

"Mar, I'll wait for you in the ballroom," Jorene stated.

Marloe could not believe Jorene would leave her to sink or swim. "No, wait Rene. I'm coming with you." She hurriedly turned to Syril. "Call me tomorrow if you have time. It will be good to talk." The sudden spark of light in his eyes made her weak in the knees.

"Okay, I'll call you tomorrow. I'm here for take-out, and then I'll be on my way. Enjoy the rest of your night ladies."

Marloe and Jorene hurried back to their table in the ballroom. "Marloe, please listen to me," Jorene's eyes sparkled. "It's my night, but it's yours too. It's obvious that man is crazy for you, and you feel the same way about him. I'm sorry Mar, I was wrong about Lawson, that no-good chameleon. Whatever I thought I saw from the past between you two was all in my head. But what you and Syril have cannot be denied. It's beautiful Mar, stop fighting it. Sweetie, can't you see real love is staring you in the face?"

Marloe's mind reeled with indecision. Flashbacks of her time with Syril played in her head like a wonderful movie that she could watch again and again. "Oh Rene, it's so hard." She shook her head in despair. "I think I fell in love with Syril the day I met him. It's so intense it scares me; consumes me, makes me vulnerable, weak. When I'm with him I lose all sense of power. I feel like putty in his hands. What am I going to do? I can't go through it again, you know, I can't love again."

"Yes, you can Marloe. Love makes us all vulnerable. That's the chance we take, but it's worth it. Look, I know I share some of the blame for your dilemma. I told you to use your looks to your advantage, and I'm so sorry for that. But at the time you needed something to bring you back. And I tried with everything in me to help my best friend. I felt lost without you Mar."

"Aw, Rene sweetie, you did help me. Your encouragement helped me return from the lowest point in my life. I know you meant it for good. Don't feel bad about it, promise?"

"Okay, I promise." Jorene scrunched her nose, giving Marloe an under-eyed stare. "You've been holding out on me though. Who the heck was that nut case with Lawson? Wow, she is something else, hanging out with the devil in sheep's clothing, but going after Syril."

Marloe smiled. "It's a long story Rene. I'll tell you about it some time when I have the strength. But not tonight, we came here to celebrate your birthday and that's what we're going to do. No more talk about anyone but you, alright? They probably brought our food while we were gone. Let's get the waiter."

"Yeah, right, all this commotion worked up my appetite," she laughed. "Marloe, I know you hon, don't be stubborn. Please talk to Syril when he calls you tomorrow, promise me?"

"Rene, he may not call. I refused his calls at work and sometimes I didn't answer my home phone for fear it was him."

"Promise me."

"Alright, alright, I promise." *Lord, please help me if he does call.*

Chapter 18

KNOCK, KNOCK. "BREAKFAST IS READY DEAR."
Marloe moaned and sank deeper into the bed. She pulled the covers over her head as her mother spoke through the closed bedroom door.

"Are you up Marloe? Granny Kate's asking for you."

It was Saturday morning and Saturday breakfast at the Vain home was a ritual as customary as Sunday dinner after church service. The three siblings rotated weekends at the station, and this was Marloe's weekend off. It was Wesley's Sunday to work and Eubie had some issues to deal with at the fish market. Neither would make breakfast. Marloe reluctantly pushed her body to a sit up position. She couldn't disappoint Granny Kate and not go to breakfast.

"Okay mother," she spoke loudly towards the door. "I'll be there shortly."

She jumped up, hastily pulling leisure clothes from her closet, Levi jeans and a red cardigan sweater. Thoughts of the previous evening rose to the surface like a cool wind whipping at her back. Jorene's milestone birthday outing was riff with uncanny surprises beginning with her choosing the Wonder Lounge to celebrate. *Lawson, Olive, a pair? My, my, I don't even want to know the story behind that one.* While it was shocking that they were together, from a romantic aspect her heart was null and void. The incident only served to substantiate the duplicity that dwelled in the essence of Lawson. A deceit so well hidden in the shadows of her youth it had ultimately caused her to live her life in the minor key. She had again caught him hands down in his indelible game of choice. How coincidental that Olive was the object of his deception. She shrugged her shoulders; he had done her a favor. *I got what I wanted from him.*

For his own narcissistic needs Lawson had showered her with lavish jewels over the past few months. She had come away with her heart in tow and her trunk heavier. Obviously, Olive had used Lawson like a pastime to twitter her nights away at the Wonder Lounge, all the while waiting for Syril to appear. *What a maniac she is, Lawson got the right one this time.* She smiled within, remembering her mother's words of caution, 'you get what you put out.'

A light smile played on her lips as she recalled the abounding laughter echoing throughout the ballroom of the Wonder Lounge when Mom Casey delivered her brand of comedy. She had desperately tried to turn her thoughts away from Syril for Jorene's sake, determined that her friend's birthday would be a night of happy memories. However, it was difficult to repress the remembrance of her heart melting like hot wax when she laid eyes on Syril. She realized how deeply she missed his presence in her life. *If he does call, what will I say? Perhaps he won't call.* The latter thought left her cold.

R-I-N-G! R-I-N-G! The blare of the telephone startled her back to reality. She stared at it as if it were a time bomb about to blast. Her heart pounded. She glanced at the clock. It was eight-thirty in the morning. *He wouldn't call this early.* With a shaky hand she picked up the receiver.

"Hello. Good morning father," she breathed a sigh of relief. "I'll be right over. Yes, yes, I'm sorry. I know you're hungry, me too. Be there in a jiffy. Love you."

During the commotion of the previous night, she had lost her appetite, but now her growling stomach reminded her of how fiercely hungry she was. She hung the phone up, thankful that it wasn't Syril, yet fearful that he might not call. Her heart was at a dangerous juncture; her feelings strewn about from last evening. She shut the door to her suite and scurried down the hallway to the kitchen entrance.

~ ~ ~ ~

"Pile your plate up with food baby girl," Granny Kate chuckled from her seat at the dining room table. "You could use some more weight on you."

Marloe smiled lovingly at Kate while spooning food from the silver chafing dishes sitting on the buffet counter.

"Don't worry Granny, I'm starving." She finished a plate and placed it in front of Granny Kate, kissing her on the cheek. She then put two biscuits on another plate with grits and eggs. Too frail to cook now, Granny Kate had handed down her biscuit recipe to Rosette. Marloe swore to learn it one day. *But it's not like I'll have children to pass it on to so there's really no hurry?*

The table looked elegant, white china on gold chargers with accompanying silverware. Whether entertaining large or small gatherings, Rosette always used her fine china. She also loved to prepare everyone's plate. *Not this morning mother, that's the least I can do.* Marloe picked up another dish, intending to serve her father when Rosette whisked into the dining room.

"Oh, aren't you the little smart one this morning," Rosette laughed playfully, noticing the prepared plates. She sat a jar of strawberry preserves on the table next to Bailey.

"No syrup on biscuits for you Bailey. I've gotten to the point where I enjoy the preserves better than the syrup myself," Rosette laughed.

Bailey chuckled. "That syrup sure looks good, but I like

living."

He and Rosette exchanged a secret smile. Bailey said grace and Saturday breakfast at the Vain household began. There was always lots of talk and family catch-up time.

"Did you and Jorene have a good time last night?" Rosette asked Marloe. She stood, scooping food in a plate for Bailey.

Marloe flinched. She did not want to talk about the prior evening. "Yes mother, we had a wonderful time. Jorene and I haven't been to Harlem together in years. She was incredibly happy."

Her mother looked at her curiously, as if waiting for her to say something more.

"What about you, are you happy baby?" Granny Kate asked softly.

Her words caught Marloe by surprise. "Granny Kate, I have a good life. Of course, I'm happy." She spread butter on her bread and took a bite, desperately needing to change the subject. "Um, this is so good Mother. Granny, I'm so glad you taught Mother your biscuit recipe."

Sudden tears welled in her eyes. Lately it did not take much to bring on the waterworks. She was thankful when Bailey spoke.

"I remember a time when I would eat five or six biscuits for breakfast," he chimed in. "Now I eat one and…"

"And sometimes you try to sneak in two," Rosette teased him. "If you think I'm not looking."

Marloe forced a laugh. She felt Bailey's concerned gaze. She sometimes felt he read her mind.

"Marloe, what's wrong? You smile, but you look like something is bothering you. Is everything alright?" he asked.

The tears she battled to hold back had their way. They trickled down her face like soft rain, and then it started to pour. She sobbed uncontrollably. Even the alarmed expressions on their faces did not decrease her salty tears.

Bailey leaned over and gently placed his arm around her shoulder. Marloe buried her head in his chest and cried all the more. Granny Kate squeezed Marloe's hand tightly while Rosette kneeled beside her and held her other hand, tenderly rubbing it with hers.

Marloe's emotions were tap dancing in her head. "I'm scared," she cried between bouts of tears. "God is paying me back for all the evil things I've done."

"Aw....no..." Bailey shushed her. "You don't have an evil bone in your body."

She shook her head. "Yes, I do father. You don't know. I've been playing a 'payback' game with men for years, since Lawson. They fall for me; I take their gifts, and then walk away just to hurt them. All because I felt justified that God would understand, because I'm a condemned woman."

"Condemned? No Marloe." Bailey hung his head and then quietly lifted his eyes to look at her. "That's not true. I blame myself for the way you feel. I let the family lay that curse burden on you all of your life. I should have stood up to them. I knew it wasn't right."

Marloe was thankful for the tissue Rosette pressed in her hand. She focused on what Bailey said while wiping her eyes and blowing her nose.

"You are not cursed any more than the next person. God's word is clear," Bailey continued. "The son will not bear punishment for the father's sin, nor will the father bear punishment for a son's transgression." It's the consequences of sin that can make life difficult for generations that follow. I'm so sorry Marloe. Please forgive me my sweet baby girl."

Granny Kate cleared her raspy throat. "Marloe, listen to me. Yes, Grandma Juniper did sin by getting pregnant so young and not being married. Her sin caused her children and family on down the line to suffer ridicule and disgrace from others. But nothing beats prayer. Prayer is what brought us through everything, God's mercy. One thing I'm sure of, we are all born blessed by God and he is the righteous judge. It took me years to understand that, but it's true. You're blessed, my sweet granddaughter, you are so blessed."

"Marloe," Rosette's eyes filled with tears. "I know it's hard to understand when something's been hammered into your head all of your life. But Jesus gave us freedom from any curse by dying for our sins. So, if someone says the family is cursed, it's a lie. Like Bailey said, we, you, are no more cursed than the next person. We are a praying family, and God has answered our prayers. Be free dear heart, you're free to live your life like anyone else, love, marriage, children, happiness."

"I'm so confused," Marloe's voice broke. "I've met someone, but I don't know how to react to him. Oh mother," she squeezed Rosette's hand tightly, "he's kind and humble, but strong and secure at the same time. He's a good man, but I pushed him away because of my fears. My heart says we belong together, but what if it's a trick of the devil and he turns out to be like Lawson?" She bowed her head, still shame-tinged from that dreadful episode in her life. "It's safe to be alone."

"Safe yes, but not happy baby," Granny Kate's eyes moistened as she looked at Marloe. "We all made mistakes when we were young Marloe, that's what life is about. You learn from mistakes and try to get it right the next time."

"Call your friend Marloe," Rosette pleaded. "Talk to him. As a matter of fact, why don't you invite him for Sunday dinner tomorrow?"

"Oh mother, I couldn't. We aren't on that level." She didn't care to tell them of the ambiguous nature of their relationship. "He said he would call me today."

Her mother gave her a knowing look. "You've never shared much of anything about any of the young men you've dated. So, I know there must be something special about this one."

"What's his name?" Bailey asked.

"Syril, Syril Barrett." She didn't tell them that he was Lawson's cousin. *I better ease into that one if and when it's necessary.*

"You should have given him our number too," Rosette added. "Just in case he calls while you're not at your place."

Marloe shrugged her shoulders as she stood, her tears gone. She began clearing breakfast dishes from the table.

"Well then, he'll just have to call back if he really wants to speak to me." She was surprised that her voice sounded stronger than she felt.

~ ~ ~ ~

That won't do. Marloe charged through her gargantuan closet in search of something suitable to wear. Nerves had her tummy vacillating between the "rope-a-dope" and a merry-go-round ride. Syril had called and he would come to Potter's Edge later that day. The hostility she felt the night they parted dissolved like sugar in hot coffee when she saw him at the Wonder Lounge. *Absence indeed makes the heart grow fonder.*

In honesty, her anger had stemmed from the truth of Syril's words that night. She knew she ran away from him because of Lawson. After her gut-wrenching confession at breakfast and the outpouring of loving support from family, there came a release, the dawning of a new perspective. Her soul was suddenly ignited with new reasoning, her heart ablaze with new hopes and possibilities.

A colorful cotton twist-knot dress with the Bamberger tag still on it jumped out at her from the rack of neatly hung dresses. The dress sparkled in chartreuse, blue, and bright red colors, and seemed to match the incredible carefree attitude that overtook her. *Lord, thank you. Please guide my steps in this journey. I promise to follow your lead.*

A sudden stream of brilliant sunlight bathed through the bedroom window, drawing her to it like a magnet. She gingerly pulled the drapes back, silently basking in the warm glow of the sun's radiance. God had reached out and touched her with his presence, giving her a peace that passed all understanding.

~ ~ ~ ~

"You're still eating that bad food, huh?" Marloe laughed as she playfully eyed Syril. They were at the Cove. He had ordered cheese steak and fries to go. *How marvelous to be with him again, how effortless, and natural. But didn't you feel that way about Lawson at first? Don't let him fool you, that old mindset fought to return. All men are the same. You better get that treasure for your trunk while you can.*

"Well, you weren't around to try stopping me, so what can I say. That little salad you ordered is about enough food to feed a bird," Syril teased her back.

She had had enough of Satan's innuendos. She fought to retain her newborn freedom, throwing caution to the wind.

"I'll have an order of fries," she said to the waitress at the counter.

Syril gazed at her in astonishment. "You have got to be kidding, not Marloe, the health food junkie."

"At least I'm not a fried food junkie" she shot back, laughing.

The waitress brought their order and they playfully bantered back and forth about their meals as they walked to Syril's car and returned to Marloe's place. *He's keeping things light because of the way we parted.* She now wanted to move beneath the surface, to emerge from the loveless cocoon she had painstakingly spun around herself. Yet, she didn't know how to break out of it.

"Tell me what you're thinking," she asked.

He looked at her curiously. "You really want to know?"

"Yes, and don't tell me you're hungry."

The sun had begun setting as they entered her suite and sat down at the kitchen table. They reached for the bag at the same moment, their hands touched. A delicious thrill traveled down Marloe's spine.

"Oh, but you can say you're hungry, huh?" he laughingly prodded her.

"Yes, I'm starving. Don't change the subject. What's on your mind?" She picked up a fry, bit into it, gazing at him, waiting for his answer.

"Okay, okay, beautiful, I'm thinking how good it is to be back in your company. I don't ever want us to stop being…friends."

"Never," she confirmed. Her heart fluttered; he was so fine, so enjoyable to be around. Dressed in brown khakis and a beige leisure shirt he looked irresistibly handsome.

"These are so good," she stated, ravenously downing more fries. "I do understand how people get hooked on unhealthy food. I really believe I have my father's genes when it comes to that. That's why I rarely buy it."

"See, that's one reason I need you around to keep me in check," Syril laughed, biting into his sandwich. After a few mouthfuls he put it down and took Marloe's hand. His expression suddenly became serious. "What are we doing Marloe? What is going on in that sweet little head of yours? I'm mad about you girl. Honestly, I don't think the way I feel about you can be contained to friendship."

He was again delving into her soul, extracting the raw truth; she burned with the desire to be close to him. *Oh God, how can I resist this man? He is so adorable and lovable, but is it real? How can I be sure?* She averted her eyes from his.

"Look at me, sweetheart," he touched her face gently and turned her head towards him.

She stood up quickly, her skin on fire from his touch. "I, Syril, it's complicated. If you knew how confusing it was, you would probably run like the wind."

He stood and gathered her in his arms. "Try me, just try me, Marloe."

Momentary panic seized her as she pondered sharing her family's innermost secret. It was like giving her heart away. She had divulged it that other time when she thought she was in love, and it came back to haunt her. The uncertainty was unsettling, but deep within she felt Syril's heart. It was soft and gentle, trustworthy.

She could tell her family liked Syril when they met him that day, even Wesley and Eubie. The men had gotten into a conversation about sports and Marloe could hardly get in a word. Annie Kate's body language and quiet smile conveyed that she had equally warmed to Syril. *I trust him.* Falteringly, she shared her family's oracle, and the loathsome incident involving Lawson. Syril grasped her hands in his as they sat on the sofa, squeezing them gently.

"And so," she advised him. "You will now understand why I can't have a long-term romantic relationship. Why I can't marry, or have children," she broke off sadly.

"Yes, you can Marloe. You can have whatever God has for you. He wants the best for you, for everyone. I too was in an unbelievably bad place when Olive left me. Back then I confused lust for love, while she confused money for love. It would never have worked because wealth is not my life's objective, helping those in need, that's my reward. That's my passion as a lawyer, I'm not in it to get rich."

"But the curse," Marloe persisted.

He frowned at her. "Marloe, it's only a curse if you believe it is. I know it's hard to deny something that's been instilled all of your life, but Jesus died for our sins. You don't have to sacrifice your life for something that's already done."

She pondered his words that paralleled the conversation of that morning with her family. Being a slave to that paradox for so long she could not imagine living out of its shadow. *Perhaps Lawson was correct when he called me an 'educated fool.'* Fatigued from the emotional combat within, she leaned her head on Syril's shoulder. He reached up and caressed the hair in her ponytail.

"Your hair is so soft and beautiful, just like you." He undid the clasp and a tidal wave of curly tresses spilled past her shoulders and down her back.

The scene felt reminiscent of the way Lawson once played in her hair, begging her to let it hang long and flowing when they were alone. Syril gave her the same adoring gaze as he stroked her hair.

"What if I didn't have this hair, would you be attracted to me?"

"It's not only your hair; it's everything about you Marloe. If you were bald, I would feel the same way about you. I would still love you."

Her heart turned over in wonderment. *He loves me.* Oh yes, she had heard that countless times from past suitors, but now the implications of her own feelings were in the mix. She could either carry the relationship through or go back to the safety of her dismal fantasy world.

As she looked into his eyes her heart ached with an overpowering love, the latter thought was no longer an option. She was hopelessly in love. It hurt too much to think of being away from him. Still, she had to know if his love was real if he loved her for her heart and soul alone.

"Syril are you free to spend the day with me tomorrow, church, then Sunday dinner with my family?"

His eyes lit with happiness. "Sure, I would love that. What time should I be here?"

"Service starts at eleven in the morning, so if you can make it here by ten-thirty that would be great. The church is only a ten-minute drive away."

"No problem. I'll be here."

He kissed her on her forehead and then softly, ever so gently, kissed her lips. The flame lit and this time she would not let the embers die. Placing her arms around his neck as they stood, she yielded to the sweet authenticity of their first kiss. He held her tightly, sending her to paradise. The kiss left her breathless and yearning for more.

He buried his head in her hair, whispering in her ear. "Marloe come with me sweetheart. Stay the night with me. No strings, you can have the guest bedroom. I just want your company, to be near you. I've missed you so much. You can pack a bag and we'll come back in the morning in time for church."

Like a sinister shadow, temptation was all over her. She yearned for the passion that lay beneath the heat of their embrace. But she was older now, wise enough not to make the same mistake twice. Marloe had a plan and was determined to follow it through. She reluctantly pulled away.

"Syril, no I'm sorry, I can't. I have something that I need to do tonight. It's really important. But I do look forward to seeing you tomorrow morning, okay?"

He traced her face gently with his finger. "Alright darling, I'll see you in the morning."

Chapter 19

"**O**H MY GOD, MARLOE, WHAT HAVE YOU done!?" Rosette's eyes resembled headlights as she stared at her daughter's bald head.

"Mother, mother, please calm down. I had to do it." She gripped Rosette's hands and quickly pulled her to the lounge chair in her bedroom. "Sit down, mother. It's okay. Please, just listen to me."

Clearly dumbfounded, with her eyes glued to Marloe's head, Rosette slowly took a seat. Marloe squeezed her mother's hands and then quietly released them. Rosette's hands flew to her mouth, her eyes still wide with disbelief.

"Breathe, mother. It's okay. It's only hair. I know what I'm doing."

With trembling hands and lips Rosette silently reached up and touched Marloe's head as if feeling it might somehow make it believable. A look of devastation seemed to hold her in a trance, her voice quivered.

"What in the world could ever make you shave off all of your beautiful hair, Marloe, why? It's crazy, I don't understand," her voice was filled with anguish.

Marloe sighed as she looked at Rosette, but she remained resolute to her purpose. "For that very reason, mother, beauty, hair, it's all superficial. I'm so confused, and I need to know the truth. Does this man who says he loves me want me for what he sees, which is going to fade with time, or does he truly desire me for the person that I am within? Is his love authentic mother? I must know because I care deeply for him. If his feelings are not genuine, I will walk away now with strength and dignity."

Rosette nodded her head as if she tried to understand Marloe's actions, but her eyes remained fixated on Marloe's bare head.

"Oh, my goodness, Marloe, it's so drastic," Rosette's eyes suddenly filled with tears. "But I-I can't say I don't understand your reasoning. I knew it was wrong, the way they shaped you. But Bailey's family was impossible. I was so wrapped up in my own misery, I failed to help you. I'm so sorry, sweetheart. The Lord knows I want you to be happy." She touched Marloe's face lightly with her hand.

"If it makes your burden lighter, I'm behind you all the way. You are still my gorgeous baby girl with or without hair. Look at you, not a lick of make-up, hairless, and you're still just lovely. Your skin feels as smooth as butter."

"You're biased, mother," Marloe smiled wryly at Rosette. "Mother," she paused and gave Rosette a lingering stare. "I'm giving up my trunk like you suggested. How about you, are you going to take your own advice and leave your trunk at the altar?"

"What?"

"C'mon, mother. We all know about your trunk, even father. It's time for both of us to let the past go. The trinkets in my trunk are such a part of me; they've given me a sense of peace. Something to look forward to in the future that are mine for life. But I realize jewelry, gifts, is not enough to fill the empty places within me. Only God can fill them. I'm going to give it all away mother, so I can live in the love that God wants for me; the love that you all say I deserve."

She kneeled down in front of Rosette and took her hands in hers. She knew how vulnerable her mother must have felt at the idea.

"Let's fast and pray tomorrow morning mother for strength, no breakfast before church. We can walk to the altar together during altar call. Please mother, I need you. Walk with me."

Leaning in, she hugged Rosette close. They embraced, mother and daughter, each trapped in their own private quagmire. "I can't do it without you mother."

"And I can't do it without you dear Marloe. Thank you. I love you."

"I love you too mother."

~ ~ ~ ~

"I pray that you find someone who appreciates your kind heart," Syril sat in the chair by his bedside, again reading aloud the letter from Aunt Dolly. How he missed her wisdom. Surely, she would have loved Marloe's sweet nature just as he did. Ecstatic that he would see Marloe the following morning, he pondered the circumstances that mysteriously brought them back together. Prior to that night, he had purposely avoided the Wonder Lounge, acutely aware that Marloe's shadow would painfully hound him there.

Her infectious laugh: the way she tilted her head back and let the gaiety of the moment overtake her. The brevity of their time together, three short months, did not negate the reality of the most cherished time of his life. He rested in the assurance that it was the will of God that they again found themselves in the company of one another at the Wonder Lounge. And now perhaps he would have the opportunity to make matters right between them again.

Lawson and Olive! While he was amazed by that disclosure, his surprise turned into a chuckle of sentiment for his cousin. Olive appeared as delusional as ever, proclaiming her love for him while in Lawson's company. *What a relentless blow to Lawson's ego.* "'I always get the girl.'"

As far as Syril was concerned Lawson had hit the jackpot with Olive and all of her love for drama. He further understood that her recent fixation with him was all about the chase, and for her comfort. Had he allowed it, she would have eased back into his life. Only to abandon him like a child grown weary of a newfound toy when a better plaything came along.

Thankfully, he had not heard from her after seeing her at the Wonder Lounge. He was cautiously optimistic that she had finally conceded; and he would not hear from her again. Pulling out the little black box that held Aunt Dolly's wedding ring, he opened it and imagined how perfect it would look on Marloe's ring finger. *If only. I would be the happiest man on earth. Not too fast. You'll run her away again.*

From conversation at the Wonder Lounge, it was clear that Lawson lied about being engaged to Marloe. *He wanted to use her, trample on her heart again... cold-blooded loser.*

He mindlessly slipped the tiny box into the vest pocket of his black double-breasted suit. Picking up his Bible, he thumbed through to Proverbs 18:22, "He who findeth a wife, findeth a good thing." To wake each morning to Marloe's earthy laughter and tender spirit would be heaven on earth. She was a praying woman, a virtuous woman who needed someone to show her the crowning jewel that she was.

He kneeled down by the bed and placed his hands on the Bible. "Father, help me to be the man of Marloe's dreams, to ease the pain in her heart. Show her that any 'curse' was null and void when Jesus died for our sins. I pray that you will make Marloe "bone of my bones, flesh of my flesh," and I will cleave to her all the days of my life."

~ ~ ~ ~

Marloe's heart pounded in anticipation as she sat in a church pew between Syril and her mother. Annie Kate and Bailey were seated alongside Rosette. After swearing her to secrecy last night, Marloe borrowed her mother's pink and coral bucket hat. It fit snuggly to her head, hiding her bald-headed secret. Although filled with anxiety over what she was about to do, when she glanced at Syril, his rock-steady countenance calmed her. Her heart stirred with an amazing love. Clean-shaven, and dressed in a charcoal suit, he looked as if he stepped off the cover of Jet Magazine.

They had arrived early to church and at Rosette's request Bailey spoke to the pastor who allowed them to place the trunks in the alcove near the altar of the sanctuary. Marloe tucked her head, remembering the curious stares of parishioners as Bailey and Syril wheeled the two suitcases inside the church. Thankfully, Syril asked her no questions.

Marloe had called her brothers last night, asking them to attend a special Sunday church service involving the family. They assured her they would be there. Well-oiled machines, the station and the fish market could certainly run for a few hours with their staff.

Although Marloe had discreetly managed her jewelry hoarding, her brothers became respectfully inquisitive. *I can thank Alex Cole for that one.* While Eubie and Wesley were as close as peanut butter and jelly, Marloe was the bread that held the siblings together. Their concern for her wellbeing trumped all, as did her loyalty to them. *Today will be a new day for all of us, a new beginning for our family. If I release my fears, so will they.*

Jorene and her girls entered the church. As they made their way to a pew, Jorene pointed to Marloe's hat with an inquisitive stare. Marloe smiled and blew them a kiss. Her appearance was uncharacteristic since she never wore hats to church. Although she advised Jorene that Syril would be coming to church with her, she purposely did not share her plans of last night's date with Bailey's hair clippers.

She looked over her shoulder in time to witness Eubie and Wesley entering the church. The fearlessness that overtook her the night before surged through her body at breakneck speed as the pastor's poignant sermon on shattering generational curses aroused the crowd. She jotted down his scripture of focus, Proverbs 26:2, "Like a fluttering sparrow or a darting swallow, an undeserved curse does not come to rest."

The message added credence to her chosen path. *An undeserved curse can't come to pass. Dear God, I've asked for forgiveness through Jesus Christ for all of my sins over and again. I'm not cursed, I'm blessed because you have forgiven me, thank you Father.*

"The altar is open for prayer," the pastor's closing remarks were like soothing balm to her soul. "Bring the burdens you have carried for so long to the altar this morning. Give them to Jesus. Let those things go that rob you of the joy the Lord meant for you, trust Jesus."

Marloe eagerly glanced at a poised-looking Rosette. However, when they locked eyes, she could tell her mother was a bundle of nerves. She took Rosette's hand and the two women stood to their feet. With arms linked, they walked to the alcove and pulled their trunks to the center of the altar amid other parishioners making their way there too.

An amazing liberation enveloped Marloe as she transported her chest to the center of that sacred abode, filling her with tranquility. Rosette's eyes welled with tears; Marloe prayed for their strength. She would not cry, not today. Instead, she would be joyous. *Help us Jesus.*

Bailey stayed in the pew, his face a myriad of concern. Marloe glanced at her brothers who appeared equally confused. Granny Kate rocked slowly in her seat, whispering in prayer. Syril sat silently, a nebulous gaze on his face. Presently, she would see if he ran like a Cheetah when she revealed her new look. Bailey suddenly eased himself up and walked to the altar. *Father you can't fix this,* she knew Bailey thought he could. She and her mother must handle this single-handedly, for each had stockpiled their bounty in willful solitude.

Reaching down, Marloe opened the latch to her case, exposing the vast treasure of sparkling jewels inside. As much as she tried to resist, jubilant tears overflowed. She placed her arm around Rosette's waist as she too opened her trunk filled to the brim with cash, a barrage of dead presidents. They were neatly rubber banded in abundant rows of 100s. A collective gasp went up from the congregation, followed by stunned silence as everyone stared at the enormous endowments on the altar.

Feeling unshakable, Marloe stepped forward. Someone pressed a microphone into her hand. "Pastor, I thank you for giving us the opportunity to speak. God has changed my life for the better today. I ask God for forgiveness for 'laying up treasure on earth where thieves break in and steal,' when I should have been laying up treasure for His Kingdom. I bestow the jewels that you see before you today to the church."

Rosette lifted her head, and, despite her anxiety, her words sprang forth with boldness. "'So is the man who stores up treasure for himself and is not rich toward God.' I bequeath the $55,000 in my trunk to Eternal Baptist Church today for the church building fund."

"The jewels in my chest were appraised at $150,000.00," Marloe stated. The rush of altruism that God laid on her heart gave her courage. "I too donate each piece to the church for the uplifting of God's Kingdom. To be sold and the proceeds given to the needy.

"And from this day forward," she continued, "the threat of a curse on the Vain family is over. Today we are set free from everything not like Jesus. I don't need to seek retribution for past hurts, for God is the righteous judge. Thank you, Jesus!"

Suddenly, it seemed everything that had breath within the sanctuary happily rocked the church. Saints holy danced amid shouts of "hallelujah," and "praise the Lord." There was running, clapping, and unrestrained joyful weeping. Bailey embraced both women in a bear hug.

Shortly, her brothers walked up, aiding Annie Kate on her cane. Suddenly, Syril stood beside her. As he hugged her close, she sighed in elated wonderment. This was a defining moment, a time of purging her heart and soul from seeking retaliation. The chains of a non-existent curse that held her captive all of her life fell away.

"I'm free," she cried as Syril held her close. "I'm finally free."

Syril gently whispered in her ear. "Marry me, Marloe. Let me show you how true my love is for you. I'll take care of you forever. Give in to our love Marloe. We've waited so long for true love, baby don't you see? We are the ones our love has been waiting for."

Although surrounded by others at the altar, to Marloe it was as if she and Syril were the only two people on earth in that moment. Filled with empowering confidence, she eased her hat from her head, revealing her search for the ultimate test of his love. She held her breath as she witnessed the varying degrees of surprise in his eyes. He appeared stunned, confused, in search of answers to the sudden naked-headed anomaly standing before him. Their eyes met; time suspended as she waited for the verdict.

He'll surely walk away from me now. As agonizing as that thought was, she had to bare her soul.

"This is me Syril, no hair, no make-up. Do you like what you see now, am I still the one your love has been waiting for? What if I stay bald, would you still love me? I mean really genuinely love me for what is inside me, my mind, my heart, my soul?"

She grabbed Annie Kate's hand and turned to Syril again. "See my beautiful grandmother, who I love with all my heart. Should God bless me to live as long, I'll be her Syril. Where will your love be then?"

Searching her eyes, Syril reached into his jacket, emerging with the tiny box that held Aunt Dolly's ring. He turned towards Bailey and Rosette, seeking their approval for what he was about to do. They smiled in consent. Bending down on one knee, Syril held Marloe's hand.

"Marloe, I love you for your heart, soul, and spirit, not for your hair, or for how very lovely you are. I can't say that I wasn't attracted to you because of your outward beauty, but your heart makes you the most precious woman in the world to me. My love for you is ageless; endless. Marry me, Marloe. God is on our side; how can we lose?"

Standing to his feet, he held the ring out to her. It was King Xerxes extending the golden scepter to Queen Esther. The only exception was that Marloe stood in Queen Esther's royal shoes and Syril had stepped back in time as King Xerxes. How she longed to reach out and accept the gift, to revel in his promises. Tears of joy trickled down her cheeks as the last tremor of fear took its leave from every facet of her being.

'If I perish, I perish,' Syril truly loves me, and I love him. And Jesus loves us both. "Yes, yes, I'll marry you," she cried in jubilance. "I'll marry you. I love you, Syril. I love you."

A tear trickled from Syril's eye as he placed the ring on her finger. Marloe tenderly dabbed it away with her tissue. He gathered her in his arms and their tears of joy mingled in a kiss. Marloe was confident that whatever the future might hold, today she had freed herself and her family from the 'curse' through faith in Christ Jesus.

About the Author

Cindy Williams Newsome is a history and inspirational writer. She is the award-winning author of *Hobbstown: The Forgotten Legacy of a Unique African American Community*, and author of the popular inspirational novel, *The Vain Girl*. Her second award winning book, *Chasing Baseball for Life and Other Adventures: Dedicated to Nearo Williams Jr.* is a memoir begun by her late brother Nearo and completed by the author in his honor. Her love of God is first, followed by family and friends. At her church, she is ministry leader of Pastoral Care and Children's Church.

The author graduated from Caldwell University with a B.A. in English Literature.

Contact Cindy at: cinspiration9@gmail.com
https://sites.google.com/view/cinspirations/home
FB: Cindy Williams Newsome
FB: Cinspirations – Cindy Williams Newsome

2006 winner of Somerset County Historic Preservation & History Award from Somerset County Cultural & Heritage Commission for "*Hobbstown: The Forgotten Legacy of a Unique African American Community*"

2022 winner of Somerset County Historic Preservation & History Award from Somerset County Cultural & Heritage Commission for "*Chasing Baseball for Life & other Adventures: Dedicated to Nearo Williams Jr.*"